A Leprechaun's Lament

Wayne Zurl

Published by
Melange Books, LLC
White Bear Lake, MN 55110
www.melange-books.com

For Bazzie.
Of all the driveways in all the towns in the world,
I had to walk into yours.

I think about the little guy often. Murray McGuire looked like a leprechaun. He played darts like a pub champion and drank stout like a soccer star. If you worked for the city of Prospect and had problems with a piece of office equipment, 'Typewriter Murray' worked tirelessly to remedy your troubles.

However, after I interviewed him for thirty minutes, I could have cheerfully strangled the little bastard. Thanks to him, I dream of a redhead I wish I'd never met. I can't see a turkey buzzard without remembering a tragedy, and I'll always look over my shoulder with a modicum of trepidation.

For days, Murray was a man who didn't exist.

Chapter One

I dialed a number at the William R. Snodgrass Tennessee Tower on 8th Avenue in Nashville and reached the local Office of Homeland Security. After a brief shuffle, the operator connected me to a woman with information on how local government agencies could obtain grants to pay for enhanced security—one of the "bennies" of our Patriot Act.

"Do you foresee a problem in Prospect, Chief Jenkins?" she asked.

"Not specifically. I just thought your idea of conducting background investigations on civilian employees who work with a police department was a good one."

"Oh, we've said that?"

"Yes, ma'am, and I like your thinking. I also believe there's grant money available to finance these investigations. With a small police department like mine, there'll no doubt be a necessity for overtime."

"Oh. You're looking for financial assistance, not personnel to conduct the investigations."

"Correct. If you've got the cash, I've got the cops."

Wendy Clabro chuckled. "You make it sound like you're leading a band of mercenaries."

She had a nice voice. I wondered if she looked as good as she sounded.

"I'm willing to work for nothing," I said. "To protect and serve is enough reward for me, but I like to take care of my officers as best I can."

"Should I really believe that?"

Oh, yeah, great voice.

"I'm a cop…would I lie to you?"

"Chief, you sound like an All-American hero. I'd enjoy meeting you some day."

I was looking for grant money, not a personal relationship.

"Call me Sam. Everyone does. I'm here Monday to Friday, nine to five or by appointment. There's always fresh coffee, and my desk officer tells me I have a nice smile."

Sometimes I have difficulty controlling myself.

"Your desk officer?"

"She's a shameless flirt."

She laughed again. "I hear it's beautiful in the Smokies this time of year. Maybe I'll stop by one day—just to see where the grant money goes, of course. Right now though, I'll bet you want me to send you the format for making a grant proposal. I really don't see a problem getting you an approval."

"Just what I wanted to hear, Ms. Clabro. Thank you."

"Please, Sam, call me Wendy."

I gave her my email address and thanked Ms. Clabro for her help and encouragement. We chatted for a few more minutes, and I ended by telling her she was doing a fine job keeping Tennessee and all of America safe for democracy. I dropped my telephone back onto the console feeling confident I could still schmooze my way around the bureaucratic system and glad I sounded younger than I often felt.

But the simple job I thought would be a walk in the park became a nightmare I never saw coming.

Chapter Two

I entered Prospect PD that morning by the back door, the way we brought in prisoners. My old Scottish terrier, Bitsey, came with me. I took her to work on the days my wife spent out of the house.

Bitsey made a straight line for Bettye Lambert, our regular desk officer.

"Hello, Bitsey, darlin'," Bettye said, as the little dog gyrated next to the reception desk.

Bettye turned to me, flashed a good morning smile, and wiggled her fingers as a greeting while she scratched Bitsey on the chin with her other hand. After the dog received most of the attention, Bettye said, "The mayor," pointing toward the lobby of the municipal building.

"The mayor? The mayor what?" I feigned an attitude.

"The mayor wants to see you, Sammy. He's in early, and he's already called down." Bettye's accent could turn Rhett Butler into a lovesick 200-pound lump of Silly Putty. Being a beautiful forty-two-year old blonde worked wonders on me, too. After years of living in Tennessee, I'd become a sucker for southern girls.

"All you say is, 'The mayor?' No explanation? No good morning, boss? You point and expect me to trot upstairs without another word? What happened to all that respect and adoration you showed three months ago when I got here?" I behaved like a sulking little boy.

"Oh, Sammy darlin', you know I love you. All the girls do. Once they get to know you, they can't help themselves. Now go upstairs and see our fearless leader...please."

3

"All right, I'm outta here. Keep an eye on the mutt for me." I turned and passed through the two glass doors separating us from the rest of the first floor.

"Morning, Ms. Connor. You two are in early today," I said to the mayor's secretary. "You think Ronnie's wife will get jealous?"

"Mr. Jenkins! What do y'all mean?" Trudy Connor was in her mid-fifties and looked like a proper lady—a stereotypical librarian or old-fashioned schoolteacher.

"Just kidding. I'm non-judgmental." That was a lie. "You guys can do whatever you want. No business of mine. He wants to see me?"

"Yes, sir. Go right in," she said, with a shake of her head and a look...the kind women reserve for guys who say embarrassing things or plant whoopee cushions. I opened the shiny oak door to the mayor's office and stepped in.

"Hey, boss, what can I do for you?" I asked Mayor Ronnie Shields.

"Sam, you doin' aw right today? Sit down. I've got things to see you about," he said, all smiles.

Ronnie always tries his politician's act on me. I suppose he figures if it gets by a cynical ex-New York cop, it'll fly anywhere.

I sat in one of the green chairs near his desk and thought all the pleated leather furniture in his room must have cost the taxpayers a small fortune. After taking office, he re-decorated the mayor's command center in an eclectic blend of cabin-craft and American sportsman motif. Wildlife prints, stuffed dead things, fly rods and a hand-painted canoe paddle were among the interesting trinkets hanging around the room.

"Yes, sir," I said. "'It's your dime."

Ronnie looked like he could be a southern politician, a televangelist or a used car salesman. At forty-five, he appeared overly well groomed with a fifty-dollar haircut and a Joseph A. Bank suit. He oozed friendliness at every opportunity.

"First, Sam, I want to say we all think you're doin' a fine job these last three months. A fine job."

"Thanks." I tried to look humble and embarrassed.

"Wednesday night we'll vote a yea for the record on the promotions for your two sergeants. It'll be effective next pay period. Who's the lucky pair?"

Whenever a politician offers me something, the term *quid pro quo* comes to mind.

"Bettye Lambert and Stanley Rose. Bettye will stay on the desk—day shift, and Stanley will do all four-to-twelves. He'll be the night supervisor. We'll make a rotating chart, to get the squeals, if someone needs supervision during the midnight tour."

"Squeals?" He looked as if I said a dirty word.

"Sorry. Old New York police term. Means the calls."

He smiled and sat there nodding. It all seemed too easy.

"Oh, by the way," he said, "we got us a quick approval for the subsidies from Homeland Security. Now you can do the background investigations on the civilian employees who work with the PD."

Good old Ms. Clabro.

"That means complete investigations on all future hirees and also for those already on board," he said. "Trudy will give you the personnel files when you're ready."

"Okay, I'll get some people on those right away. And just so I can tell the new sergeants when they get promoted, when does the next pay period start? I want them to have their stripes sewn on."

"What's today? Tuesday the 10th?" He looked at his desk calendar. "Two weeks from yesterday."

"Great. I'll tell them it's official. Everyone in the department is happy for Stan and Bettye. Life is tranquil in our little banana republic."

"Real fine, Sam. Jest real fine. I keep tellin' the council y'all are the finest department in the city."

"Ronnie, you sure know how to lay on the schmaltz."

"Do what?"

I began to think I should give Yiddish classes for Prospect's employees.

* * * *

"Officer Lambert, let me be the first to congratulate you," I said. "In less than two weeks, you will officially be Sergeant Lambert.

"Oh, Sammy," she said. "Are you serious? It's really gonna happen?"

I nodded.

"I never would have gotten this if it wasn't for you. I could just kiss you."

Not an unpleasant thought, but even I have professional standards. And a wife.

"Steady, Blondie, if a shoofly sees us smooching, we'll be in hot water. I could end up walking a foot post around the town square on the midnight tour."

Bitsey, who acted as Bettye's guard dog, stood up and seemed to feel excitement in the wind. I saw a tear on Bettye's cheek.

"Oh, Lord have mercy, Sam. I think I'm gonna cry."

Why do the women in my life do things like that?

Bitsey, now up on her hind legs with her front paws on Bettye's thigh, looked at me, wondering what I said to make her partner cry. Bettye hugged the dog. A few more tears rolled down her cheeks.

"Oh, Bitsey, your father is such a good guy."

"Hey, don't let that get around. I have a reputation to uphold," I said. "But you earned the promotion. I didn't get it for you. I only shook up those yahoos on the council."

"Thank you, Sam...so much."

"You're welcome. Now go fix your eye make-up. I only want beautiful women working here."

She smiled between the tears. "I take everything back. You're a proper beast."

"Thank you. It's good to be best at something."

Before she retreated to the lady's room, Bettye insisted, "Now before you do anything else, please call Old Town Police Supply in Knoxville. They called...again and need you to pick up your uniforms, the ones that were ready more than a month ago."

"See why I didn't give them my home number?"

* * * *

Thursday, October 12th

When a citizen complains about a civil servant, they most often say, "Hey, I pay their salary." They're right. If the populace pays our freight, why not give them the best employees we can find? Background investigations help us do that. With the assistance of my new friend, Wendy Clabro, my request for grant money went through the system as slick as grease on a flat rock in August. My cops could begin the investigations and collect a little OT in the process.

Ms. Connor sent down the personnel files for the nine current employees: four ladies from the typing pool who document all our reports for posterity as well as Earl Biggins, the city auto mechanic and his assistant, Logan Mapes, who work on the police cars. Plus old George Files, the municipal building custodian and his helper, Spurgie Dent, two guys who could be found in and around the police offices all the time. And the guy everyone called Typewriter Murray—Murray McGuire, the guy in charge of office machine maintenance and a fixture at the center of Prospect city government for twenty-eight years.

Back when administrative offices relied on typewriters and calculators to keep ticking, Murray serviced all of Prospect's machinery. After personal computers and all the bells and whistles attached to them became the necessities in a modern office, Murray learned how to provide our workers with limited day-to-day service. He changed ink cartridges, updated all the little things that needed updating and transported ailing computers to the real experts for serious repair. All the clerical ladies loved little redheaded Murray.

The nine workers sat casually scattered around the PD squad room. I planned to tell everyone all they needed to know about how we'd learn their innermost secrets.

Getting the logistical chores out of the way quickly would allow the cops to begin their police work. I'd save time and some of Wendy Clabro's hard-earned cash.

I began by explaining the necessity for our investigations as part of the post-9/11 world and progressed to handing out the paperwork.

An hour later, Officer Bobby John Crockett walked into the squad room and stood off to the side as my party broke up.

George Files, the ancient custodian who reminded me of Walter Brennan, mumbled something about my investigations being nothing but 'derned foolishness'."

Eight of the employees filed out of the squad room. Murray McGuire stopped next to the desk where I sat dangling my legs over the edge.

"Hello, Chief," he said.

"Hi, Murray." I intended to get up and leave, but he continued the conversation.

"Need anything?" he asked. "Miss Bettye need anything? Nice for her to get promoted, ain't it? She's a good woman. I like Stan Rose, too."

"I think we're in good shape. Thanks," I said. "I'll tell Bettye and Stan you were asking for them."

"Okay, you need anything, just gimme a whistle. Want a new calculator? I know you like them better than using your computer."

"The one I've got works just fine, but thanks again."

"Yes, sir. Remember, you need somethin', you just call me. I'll fix you right up...Yes, sir." With that said, Murray left.

Bobby walked over with a big grin. "Man, I never knew Murray had such a brown nose."

"Maybe he's got blue coat syndrome. Some people get nervous when they deal with a cop."

"An' mebbe he's got him some reason fer suckin' up ta ya."

"Well, find out. I'll let you do his case. Maybe he'll offer to clean your laptop."

Investigating eight of the city's employees provided no challenge.

Murray McGuire ended up being a completely different ball of wax.

* * * *

Friday, October 13th

At eleven o'clock, I called a Knoxville number. A young-sounding female answered the phone at WNXX-TV.

"Hi," I said. "I'm sure she's not in this early, but can I leave a message for Rachel Williamson?"

"Yes, you may, but I saw her not long ago at a meeting. I'll connect you to her line. Perhaps she's at her desk now." The operator spoke with a Midwest accent.

"Thank you." I waited. The voice mail kicked in.

"This is Rachel. I'm not at my desk right now, but at the tone please leave a message, and I'll return your call." Beep.

"Hey, Rachel, this is Sam Jenkins. Remember me, the Dirty Harry of Prospect? I investigate murders and stolen overalls," I said. "I'm inviting you and the Polish cameraman out here for the next big news. Call me if you're up for another road trip. Bye."

There was a pause, and then I heard, "Sam? I'm on the line. Don't hang up. Hello."

"Hi, I'm here."

I thought about the last time I saw her. Rachel has dark eyes and a cute little dimple on her chin.

"It's good to hear from you," she said, all bubbly. "What's the big news?"

"Well, perhaps I exaggerated a little. But since you guys give air time to high school ball games and Cub Scout car washes, I thought you'd be interested in two officers at Prospect PD being promoted to Sergeant."

Silence.

"Hmm. What's special about police promotions?" she asked.

"Well, they're the first we've ever had at Prospect. One officer is a nice lady, a mother of three. The other is a very large black man. He looks like a cross between Sasquatch and a pro-linebacker. These are not your average police promotions in East Tennessee."

She laughed. The last time we spoke, she laughed at something I said, and it sounded great. If I wasn't old enough to be her father—she's forty—I'd do anything she wanted just to hear her laugh again.

"Sam, I don't know if that's something we could fit into the six or eleven o'clock news, but I'll talk to the producer of Five O'clock Magazine. I'm sure I can get you a spot there. You want the ceremony taped and shown on air?"

"That's great. Our mayor loves to get on camera. You arrange that, and he'll buy you a glass of sweet tea."

"Sweet tea, yuck," she said.

"Okay, pass on the tea, and stick around for lunch. I'll buy you a glass of chardonnay and John Whatshisnameski a beer."

"It's John Leckmanski, and I'm not sure I can get out there for an interview on someone else's show. John can do the camera work though. Will that work?"

"It will. I'd like to see you do this, but I'll settle for second best. I appreciate your help and owe you something."

"Okay, I'll remember. And someone from Five O'clock Magazine will call you."

Arranging for a Federal grant was my first good deed that month. This was my second. At least one of them went unpunished.

Chapter Three

At 3:30, just before the shift change, I sat in my office, sports jacket hanging behind the door with my feet up on my desk, while I read over some of the paperwork that makes a small police department go around. Stanley Rose stuck his head in the doorway and rapped his knuckles on the jamb.

"Hey, boss, I just wanted to say thanks for arranging a promotion ceremony. My wife and kids are excited about being on TV."

"My pleasure. Come on in."

Supervising the three police officers assigned to do the background investigations was Stanley's first job as a soon-to-be sergeant. At six-four and 235 pounds, the ex-LAPD street-crime cop took up a large portion of the guest chair in front of my desk.

"We've got a problem," he said. "Bobby's having a hard time with the work on Typewriter Murray."

"What could go wrong with Murray? He's lived up the street for almost thirty years."

"In a word...everything. Big problems with this guy. Bobby got faxes back on most of the inquiries he sent. The high school Murray listed never heard of him. He gave us a bad driver's license number. He's got no mortgage. No credit cards. The credit bureaus say he's never applied for a card, a loan or life insurance. The most Bobby could find is a local checking account with about a hundred bucks in it. Nobody knows him but us and the Army. There's no trace of him before 1975. He's a phantom."

"Let me see your paperwork," I said.

The top pages were his application and a brief personal history. I thumbed through and saw that he listed a six-digit driver's license number. Tennessee licenses have eight.

"Did you run him through Department of Safety? Maybe he just put down the wrong numbers?"

Stanley shook his head. "No license. Never had one. Never applied. Never registered a car. Just like everyone else we've checked with, they never heard of him."

"He's got some balls driving a city car without a license. Have you or Bobby spoken with him yet?"

"Bobby's been talking with him, but Murray's got no answers. What do you want to do?"

"Crockett's going off duty now, so tell him to stop in tomorrow morning. What's in Murray's Army records?"

He handed me a few additional sheets of paper.

"Let's see if he has an honorable discharge," I said.

"Yeah, he got an honorable after three years, 1975 to '78. Then a couple short-term mechanic's jobs, a nighttime business school in Knoxville and finally his job here. We've got nothing but his word about what he did before that. And he's got none of the usual stuff everyone else on the planet has."

"Whose bright idea was it to do these investigations anyway?" I asked.

"Yours, boss."

"Nobody likes a smart sergeant, Stanley."

* * * *

Thursday, October 19

Bobby John Crockett stood in my office looking at the shadow box containing my Army medals and badges when I walked in at 8:45. Bobby, a six-year veteran of the department, was twenty-nine years old. He claimed to be a descendant of the famous David Crockett's younger brother, Wilson. Bettye says Bobby looks like a younger version of me. When I started work at Prospect PD, I borrowed his uniform shirts when

I needed to look like a cop.

"Sam, this guy Murray's makin' me crazy." Bobby sat in one of the guest chairs in front of my desk and stretched out his legs. "I never heard of someone without a damn credit card."

"A lot of people made me crazy over the years, kid. 'That's why I feel ten years older than I am. You have a pad?"

He nodded.

"Ready to take notes?"

He nodded again.

"I want him to talk about the driver's license business. That's an outright lie and could get him fired. We've got to keep him from driving a city vehicle. Now, what do we know about his school? We may as well start there."

"Says he attended Huey Long High School in Baton Rouge, Loosiana, 1969 to 1973. They say they never heard of him—got no records

"Either he's lying or they have faulty records," I said. "You have a number for them? Let's give them a call."

I dialed a number in south Louisiana and, after a brief conversation with the operator, got connected to the chief clerk in their records section.

The phone rang three times.

"Good mornin', records, Mrs. Thibideaux speakin'."

"Good morning, ma'am. My name's Jenkins. I work for the police department in Prospect, Tennessee. Would you have a minute to help me out?"

We started a conversation about the weather, how I loved Cajun food, the state of New Orleans since Hurricane Katrina and how the world in general was going to hell in a hand basket. Mrs. Althea Thibideaux spoke with the best Cajun accent since 'Old Boudreaux'. We finally got around to the reason for my call.

"One of the investigators here sent you folks an official inquiry several days ago asking for information about a Murray McGuire. Would you know anything about that?" I asked.

"Yes, sir, I surely do. I handled that myse'f."

"And you have no record of him attending any school in your

parish?"

"No, sir, nuthin' in our records, and we do handle the records for all the schools."

"I wonder why he listed Huey Long High School if he never attended. That's easy to verify. Would you run the name Murray Neil McGuire forward, backward and any combination of inside-out you can think of to see if someone remotely like our man attended any of your schools between 1965 and 1975?"

She said she'd call back.

Loving the idea of delegating work, I handed Bobby a list of things to check with the Tennessee Bureau of Investigation, Blount County, our own records sections and the Fed's Automated Fingerprint Identification System and National Crime Information Center. I'd call a friend at the FBI myself.

"Get his fingerprints for AFIS and TBI then check with NCIC," I said. "Take a couple mug shots, too. Ask Bettye about the going price for the Feds and TBI to do a full-blown search on him and then ask Finance for the appropriate checks. When you're finished, bring him into my room of truth."

"Room of truth?" Bobby grinned.

I shrugged.

"You got it, boss."

At 10:30, Mrs. Thibideaux called back. Bettye answered. She asked for Detective Jenkins. Bettye said we had a Chief Jenkins, bless her heart. Mrs. Thibideaux said I'd do and was connected to my line.

"Mr. Jenkins, I ran this name ever' way possible, all the way back to 1946 when we started centrally recordin' these t'ings. There is no record of this man goin' to any one of our schools, I guar-on-tee."

"Is it possible someone, before your time, didn't record this man's information?" I asked.

"Honey, I *have* been here since 1946! I started jest after I lef' high-skoo, me. If he was here, I'd know about it." Her accent had gotten a little thicker.

I did some quick math and hoped I'd be that sharp at seventy-eight.

I thanked her for the help, wished her a good day and told her to think of me the next time she ate crawdads or shrimp etouffee'.

A few minutes after I hung up, Bobby wandered back into my office with Murray in tow.

The little guy sat in one of the chairs across from me. Bobby stood leaning against the closed door to my office. I've noticed policemen everywhere love to lean against something. Stand a cop on a foot post in the Mohave Desert and he'll find something to lean on.

"Murray," I said, "we're having a problem getting information on you."

"Really? That's strange. I'll help if I can." Murray spoke with neither a Tennessee nor Louisiana accent. He wore a wrinkled white shirt, brown polyester pants and a cheap striped tie.

I could tell that Bobby didn't like Murray's answer. He probably heard the same story too many times before and rolled his eyes, shook his head and ran a hand through his dark hair.

"First thing," I said, "you can't drive a city vehicle any more. You gave us a bogus driver's license number. What's the story?"

"I know, Chief. I'm sorry. I never got around to gettin' a license. I never needed a car of my own, but I did drive for the city when I had to. When I was hired, the old chief, the man before Buck Webbster—Peanut Crowder, said he'd take me for a learner's permit. But I never got around to it. If you want me to get a license, I will. I'm really sorry."

Buck? Peanut? Damn, I need a nickname.

"Next thing," I said, "is your high school records. Baton Rouge says you never graduated—never even attended school there."

"Can't understand that, Chief. Can't understand that at all. I graduated from Huey Long in '73."

"You didn't give us copies of your birth certificate or high school diploma. You have them lying around the house somewhere?"

"No, sorry, sure don't. I lost those years ago."

I took a moment to stare at our problem child. Murray was so Irish looking he could have had Guinness for blood. He stood about five-and-a-half-feet tall, with a slight build. His curly red hair was streaked with gray and combed straight back. I wanted to hear a classic Irish accent, but heard nothing that told me he came from any particular part of the country.

"How about telling me your life story?"

He nodded.

"Start with your parents, and when you were born. Take it from the beginning."

"Sure, Chief. My father was born in Ireland. My mother's from Louisiana."

I interrupted. "What's your father's name?"

"Kenneth Murray McGuire."

"How about your mother's maiden name?"

"Mary Margaret McNeil."

I jotted down the appropriate notes.

"They have any siblings?" The word didn't immediately register with him. "You have any aunts or uncles?"

"Nope."

"Are your parents still alive?

"No, they both died in Montana."

Bettye walked past my windows and looked inside. Bobby shifted position and folded his arms across his chest.

"Montana? When?"

"Dad died first. He had a heart attack, maybe 1974 or early '75. Mom died when I was in the Army. 1976, I think."

"Where did you live in Baton Rouge?" He hadn't listed an address for that period of his life.

"The address?" he asked.

I nodded.

"Sure don't remember."

Bobby looked like every answer annoyed him a little more. When he heard an obvious lie, he rolled his eyes. I watched the muscles in his jaw knot up and relax.

I listened for ten more minutes, asking questions along the way. *Vague* seemed to be the theme of the day.

"Okay, you graduated in 1973. You were eighteen. What happened next?"

"We moved to Montana. Bozeman, Montana."

"You wanted to be a cowboy?"

He smiled and shook his head. My patience had disappeared quickly. I wanted to wring his neck, the lying little weasel.

"My father got a construction job up there, working on the highways. I worked in a gas station. I learned about fixing cars."

"You're an only child?"

"Yes."

"Your Mom work?"

"No."

"Dad get to be a citizen?"

"Maybe not. He never said."

"What do you remember about the gas station? Its name? The owner?"

"It was a Texaco station."

"That's it?"

"Yeah, sorry."

"You don't remember the owner's name?"

"It was a long time ago." He shrugged, the little creep.

Crockett, who's six feet tall and looks like he spends a couple days a week in the gym, flexed his shoulders, gearing up to rip off Murray's head.

"You have to sign a release addressed to the Social Security Administration so we can get a print-out of all your wages since you started working," I said.

Without a criminal investigation pending, Social Security records were closed to us. Someday before I retire again, we might get those documents back. The Feds are notoriously slow.

"Sure," he said, "Anything you want. But, Chief, I worked off the books as a kid."

"More than a year off the books?"

"Yeah, the station owner saved money that way."

Murray was getting closer to strangulation every moment.

"Your Social Security number starts with 553. Is that from Louisiana or Montana?" I already knew the answer.

"Montana."

"Okay, you're pumping Texaco gas and tuning up Chevy pick-ups. What happens next?"

"I joined the Army in February of '75."

"You have a copy of your DD-214?"

"No, sorry."

I remember hearing a saying once, 'Nothing is as it seems.' I wondered what Murray wanted to hide.

"I've got some paperwork from the Army here," I said. "You need to tell me a little about your time in the service, and the places you were—fill in some blanks for me."

He smiled again and nodded, brushing some lint from his tie.

"Okay, you were twenty in January of 1975?"

"Yes."

I continued to read from the Army document. "You went to basic training at Ft. Ord, California, then diesel mechanic's school. You must have done well there because they sent you to advanced automotive repair school."

"I liked working on engines."

I shifted in my chair, feeling the frustration generated by the little man.

"Your first permanent assignment was at Headquarters, 24th Division at Fort Stewart, Georgia. Where'd you work there?"

"Headquarters and Headquarters Company, motor pool," he said.

"What big town is near Fort Stewart?"

"Savannah."

"What else did you do in Georgia?"

"Got married to a girl from Hinesville."

"What was your wife's name?"

"Missy Joan Townsend."

"Her date of birth?"

"You're gonna hate me, Chief... Oh, May 30th, don't know the year."

Bobby scowled and stuck his hands in his pockets. My jaw tightened. Cops hate liars.

"How old was she when you two got married? Did she do it on her own, or did her parents have to sign permission?"

"No, she was of age. Eighteen, I guess. Yeah, I was twenty-one. She was eighteen."

More quick math. "If she was eighteen in 1976, she was born in 1958."

He nodded and then shrugged, always happy to agree. I didn't share his glee.

"What month were you married in? Don't say you can't remember. Any wife would kill you if you forgot your anniversary."

"We were married in June. June 16th."

"Thanks. I don't suppose you still have your marriage license?"

"Nope."

Bobby sniffed, looked like his blood pressure elevated a few notches and folded his arms over his chest again.

"Where is your wife now?"

"She died. Cancer and a heart attack, in '99, at St. Mary's in Knoxville."

"I'm sorry. She was very young."

"Yes."

That sounded like natural causes, but who knows? Did I have a reason to wonder?

"What county were you married in down there?"

"Liberty. Maybe. I'm not sure."

"Did you have a civilian job there, too?"

"A part-time thing at a gas station."

"Off the books again?"

"Afraid so."

"What's the info on that station?"

"A Gulf station. Owner's name was Buford. I heard he's out of business now."

"Why am I not surprised?"

Murray shrugged.

"Did you have a driver's license in Georgia?"

"No, just an Army license. They made me get one."

"Why no state driver's license? Young guys always like to drive. You were a motor head. You worked on all sorts of vehicles. How did you drive the cars you worked on?"

He shrugged again.

"How did you get to and from work? Drive to get beer? Drive to meet girls? Drive to get off post? Why no license?"

"I drove a little, other guys' cars sometimes, Army vehicles mostly.

The other guys never asked if I had a license. I didn't have the money for a car. I got rides a lot, hitching. The station was less than a mile from the house. I could walk. I never really wanted a license."

"No kidding? Everyone wants a license. Why not you?"

"Don't know. Just didn't."

I took a turn shaking my head. It wasn't even lunchtime, and I wanted a drink. I looked at Crockett. He shrugged. I took a few seconds to regroup.

"Okay, Murray, you get orders for Korea. You go to the 19th General Support Group. Where's that?"

"Seoul."

"What did you do there?"

"Motor pool again, Headquarters, 19th GSG. I worked on Jeeps mostly, some three-quarter and five-quarter ton trucks. Some staff cars, too."

For the first time he showed signs of getting tired of my questions. Another ten minutes covered his time overseas.

I wanted to chase him out, put my feet up and take a nap. But I sat upright, acted like a professional, and continued.

"Okay, you get back to the States, what do you do next?"

"I got out of the Army at Fort Lewis and flew to Georgia."

"And?" I drew the word out.

He wiggled in his chair and brushed at the non-existent lint on his tie.

"We lived in a rented single-wide again. I got a job at a gas station for a couple months, fixin' cars. Georgia was too hot for me. I didn't want to live there."

"How'd you get to Tennessee?"

"Missy's family used to come up to Gatlinburg in the summers. She liked the mountains."

"So, you move to Knoxville, you get a job at a garage and go to school and learn how to fix typewriters. If you liked working on engines, why switch to typewriters?"

"I thought it would be better paying. It was a cleaner job. Missy didn't like my hands always being dirty."

If nothing else, his answers sounded unique.

"And then, right out of business school, Prospect hires you?"

"Yes."

"For twenty-eight years you've lived just up the road, walking distance from town?"

"Yes."

"After Missy died, did you go out with anyone?"

"No, I figured I was too old. I really didn't feel like dating."

"Do you go anywhere in town? To eat, for a drink, anywhere?"

"I go to Howell's Pub sometimes. I can walk there or take my bicycle. I like to play darts. They have a league. I also like the Guinness they have on tap. It must be an Irish thing. You know, I got it from my father."

"Yeah, sure. I like Guinness too—good stuff."

I fancy myself a pretty good interrogator, but I'd gotten nowhere.

"Bobby, you have anything to ask?" I said.

"No, sir. I'll just get that release for Social Security and do some more work on this."

"Okay, Murray, thanks for stopping in." I watched him get up to leave, but before he reached the doorway, I added, "Hey, Murray, why can't we find anyone who knows you? I'm convinced you joined the Army—our Army, but why no other records? Are you really who you say you are? You're not a spy or a space alien or something like that, are you?"

He smiled. "I don't know what to tell you, Chief. I've been here almost thirty years. I just don't know what to tell you."

"Yeah, thanks again."

He opened my door and left.

Bobby and I stared at each other with confused looks. Murray could have been the poster boy for the passive-aggressive society. By invoking "the power of the weak," he'd have us wasting time and energy chasing down every obscure lead and possibility. Outwardly he cooperated, acquiesced to our every wish, showed up on time or early for appointments, but he also took great advantage of his right of memory loss.

Why was he lying or omitting the actual facts? I wondered if his image showed up in a mirror. Maybe I should check the immigration records from Transylvania.

"We didn't get a lot there, did we?" I asked Bobby.

He shook his head. "No, sir, we sure didn't."

"Call the Montana State Police, Bozeman PD and the sheriff of whatever the hell county Bozeman is in. See if they know anything. Call the Provost Marshal and criminal investigators at Fort Stewart. Maybe they keep records that far back. Ask one of the agents to check with the PMO and CID at Yongsan in Seoul to see what they know. Then call the Georgia state cops and look around at the PDs surrounding Fort Stewart for anything they may have. If he's not in the criminal records system anywhere, maybe someone has informal records like field interrogation cards where he may show up. Shit, try anything else you can think of that we haven't already tried."

Bobby added notes to the list of things to do I handed him earlier.

"Then there's the garage in Knoxville and the business school," I said. "I don't know what you can learn there, but call them anyway. Maybe one of them has an old application with some clue or inconsistency on it.

"When you try the Knox County offices," I added, "see what the death certificate says for Missy McGuire. See what Montana says about his dead parents." I continued thinking out loud, tossing out any possibility I could come up with.

"Okay, boss, I'm on it."

When Bobby left, Bettye walked into my office.

I looked at her and said, "Grrrrr!"

"What's wrong, darlin', you havin' a tough day?"

"If they find Murray's body in the parking lot, don't tell anyone you think I killed him."

"Oh, my poor Sammy. Don't worry, you'll figure out what to do. You always do."

I needed Bettye's confidence, but I came to wish I never mentioned killing Murray.

Chapter Four

I put a homemade sheepskin slipcover over the passenger's seat in my silver blue '67 Austin-Healey. The cover not only offered comfort for my dog, but also insured that her grungy claws wouldn't scar up the Connelly hides used to make my custom leather upholstery. I opened the right side door, whistled through my teeth, and Bitsey came running like a shaggy fullback. Paying little attention to me, she hopped into the Healy and sat on her backside looking out the windscreen. I had already looped her leash around the seat back and then hooked the snap to a D-ring at the back of her harness giving her the security of a canine seat belt.

With the convertible top down and hidden under its fitted cover, I slipped on my Ray-ban shades, tapped the shifter into neutral, switched on the ignition and pressed the starter. The big three-liter engine started instantly, and the exhaust pipes emitted a sexy gurgle as I goosed the accelerator to get a few extra revs out of the engine.

"Off we go, Bits." I pushed the shift lever into first, let out the clutch and listened to the tires crunch over the gravel of my long driveway.

The morning was overcast, cool and crisp, the sky as bright as tarnished pewter. We drove a short distance over a tree-lined country lane and turned right onto US 321 heading east. The low clouds over Chillhowee Mountain gave the landscape a look much like the Cairngorms of central Scotland.

Our summer drought left the foliage in Walland Gap looking more like an ancient, weathered tartan than the vibrant reds and yellows and oranges of years past. So far, everything about the day felt subdued.

It was Saturday, and I was off duty. Even in the city of Prospect, Tennessee with its police department of thirteen officers, the chief gets the weekend off, unless something monumental happens requiring the ultimate supervisor. That day, they needed me about as much as Donald Trump needed a cash advance on his credit card.

Bitsey and I motored along, heading for a used bookstore on South Main Street, an old building just below the Prospect town square. We made a detour, stopped at the Post Office and then turned north over the Little River Bridge and west on Old Walland Highway, intending to invade Prospect from the southeast.

A few more miles and I pulled into a parking lot next to the bookshop, taking an open spot alongside the owner's old Jaguar XJS. Bitsey, a well-known customer, didn't need a leash during her visits. The owners, Derek and Eleanor Foxwell, loved to see her. Eleanor especially fussed over Bitsey, covertly giving her pieces of the digestive biscuits she kept on hand to serve with the tea she offered her favorite visitors.

The Foxwells originally came to the US from Lichfield in Staffordshire, England. But like my wife Kate and me, they moved to Tennessee from New York when Derek retired from a famous auction house in Manhattan.

They called their shop The Fox and Quill Used and Antique Books. The sign hanging over the sidewalk looked more appropriate for an English pub, a lanky fox dressed in a scarlet hunting coat, the name written on a piece of parchment with a white goose quill.

I swung my legs out of the cockpit of the Healey, stood up and straightened my Polar Fleece vest. After unsnapping Bitsey, she jumped out of the car, ran up the three steps to the front door and waited impatiently. Her backside swayed from side to side, and her hind legs fidgeted. I didn't move quickly enough to open the door, so she tried two throaty woofs to express her displeasure.

Before I could turn the knob, Eleanor swung the door open and with a big smile said, "Oh, Bitsey. My good friend, Bitsey. Do come in, dear, come in."

Bitsey scrambled into the shop and wiggled enthusiastically, her tail moving at almost a thousand RPM. Then she sat at attention and waited for Eleanor to scratch her chin and make some sort of goggling baby noise.

Derek came from behind the register counter. "Hello, Sam. Lovely day, isn't it?" Then he began giving the mutt his own form of greeting.

As Derek took over the preponderance of affection, Eleanor diverted her attention momentarily and placed a comforting hand on my forearm. "Hello, Sam. Good to see you, too."

Neither Derek nor Eleanor would ever see sixty-five again. Ellie was short and a few pounds overweight. Her long gray hair was deviously wrapped around her head in a style somewhere between that of a Gibson Girl and Mrs. Katzenjammer. She wore a long denim dress, wool cardigan and shoes that looked like surplus from the Prince Of Wales Division.

Derek was tall and thin, perhaps no more than 140 pounds. He wore his gray hair in that slightly too long, casual style often seen on British academics.

His outfit of corduroy pants, Tattersall shirt and striped tie looked dreadfully English. They acted like surrogate grandparents to my terrier who turned her allegiance at the drop of a biscuit.

Derek, ever the proper gentleman, took up a position on the floor and made attempts to kiss Bitsey on the nose. While such conduct may perhaps lack a bit of sophistication, it was just nuts to the dog that played along and uttered a friendly "Boof!" with each feint made in her direction. After the playmates had gotten a little noisy, a new employee came from the back of the store to investigate noises sounding vaguely like those one might hear at a circus.

She emerged from the stacks, tilted her head and smiled as she watched Derek acting like a bull from Pamplona.

She looked like one of those beautiful women from a 1940s movie. Her red hair, parted on the left and combed to the side, fell partially over her right eye—Veronica Lake-style.

"Looks like you're having quite a workout for yourself, Derek." She spoke with a lilting Irish accent, looked at me and smiled. "Hello. I think you must be the owner of Derek's playmate."

"I am. Hello."

Eleanor broke in, "Oh, where are my manners? Sam, this is Bridget

Dwyer. Bridget started working for us since you've last been in." Ellie spoke with a Midlands accent. "Bridget, this is Sam Jenkins, Bitsey's father."

"Ellie," I said. "I thought you were going to tell me this was Grace Kelly—no—Maureen O'Sullivan. She looks like an Irish movie star."

It was difficult for me to believe, but my compliment altered Bridget's expression. It lasted only a moment, but in the middle of my flirting, she changed her beaming smile to a dark, almost brooding look, but then replaced it with another smile, giving her a look that rivaled Helen of Troy.

Finally, Derek decided to come up for air and left Bitsey alone on the floor. Having paid no attention to anything more than Derek's impersonation of a raging bull, Bitsey was taken by surprise when she saw Bridget standing nearby. Flexing her terrier spirit, she looked at the girl and started barking.

"Bitsey, no!" I said, and slapped my left leg. Bitsey, the wonder-dog, shuffled over to my left side.

"What a grand little dog," Bridget said. "Are you Welsh or Scottish, Mr. Jenkins?"

Obviously, she knew my family name was common in either place.

I can be quite personable when I want to. Well, for fifteen or twenty minutes anyway, so I turned on the charm. "My family is Scottish on both sides. But please, call me Sam. Anything more formal makes me feel older than I'll admit to."

"Oh, go away with you," she said, familiar with oozing a little charm herself. "You can't be much over thirty-nine now, can you?"

"Yes, I can. Just a little. But I'm younger than Jack Benny."

She laughed. I was surprised someone in their thirties knew Jack Benny.

"After a line like that," I said, "I'll guess you've been a lot closer to the Blarney Stone than most of the people around here."

"You've a good ear for accents, Sam Jenkins," she said, making me feel like one of her favorite boyos. "I'm from Killarney, not too far from Blarney Castle at all."

"I know there are lots of Dwyers and O'Dwyers down in that southwest corner of Ireland. But you're right. I do have a good ear for accents, and I'd have thought you were from the opposite corner of the country."

"No, sorry, Sam, I've never been north of Connemara. Do you go to Ireland often then?"

"I've been there several times, but I'm a highland lad and spend most of my holidays in bonnie Scotland." I used a wee bit of an accent to make my claim sound authentic. "But I've traveled all over, even to Derek and Ellie's hometown once or twice. I stopped there to visit Dr. Johnson's house."

"Well now, I see you're a world traveler, and at such a young age."

"Too much blarney for one day, young lady," I said. "I don't want to keep you from your work and get you in trouble with your bosses. So, I'd better give them my attention and ask about a book I need. It's been nice meeting you. I hope to see you again."

"Yes, sir, it was for me too. And you shall." She smiled again and returned to the stacks.

Derek and Ellie waited for me to explain my presence.

"I've come for a fairly uncommon book, *March to Quebec* by Kenneth Roberts. Do you have one or can you find one for me?"

"You'll need a fat bank account for that book, Sam. It will cost you a few bob," Derek said.

"I know. It's probably the most expensive Roberts' book there is, except for that two-volume, edition of *Northwest Passage*. Can you look around for me? A first edition's not necessary, just not ex-library. And with a dust jacket if possible."

"Why don't you look on the Internet, Sam?" Eleanor asked.

"I'm not much of a computer guy, Ellie. I tried that once, but I never believe the descriptions people use. I'd rather you find a nice book. That's your business. I wouldn't expect you to catch all the criminals in East Tennessee, so you can't expect me to find all the good books."

"Right, Sam," Derek said. "I'll start me search on Monday. I'll let you know as soon as I find one that meets your requirements." He spoke in a characteristic "black country" accent.

"Okay, folks. I'm going to take my hound and go."

"Oh, good-bye, Bitsey," Eleanor said. "Come and see us again. Good-bye, Sam."

"Bye, Ellie. Bye, Derek. Nice seeing you. Have a good weekend."

Derek gave me a wave, and Bridget stepped from behind a bookcase.

"Good-bye, Sam," she said. "So nice to meet you. Good-bye, Bitsey." She waved.

Bitsey seemed less impressed than me.

"Bye, Bridget."

I made an about face and snapped my fingers. Bitsey fell into step as we left the store.

Bitsey was often on a leash. Someone should have introduced me to one and added a choke collar.

Chapter Five

On the morning of the promotion ceremony, I stood in front of the kitchen sink looking out the window. Occasionally a female hummingbird would come to the feeder attached to the casement sash and stick her needle-like beak into a flower-shaped port and take a drink of the sweet sugar water Kate brewed up for those little buggers. It wouldn't be much longer, and they'd begin their winter trek to Mexico. The ruby-throated males already started off on their scouting flight more than a week earlier. The girls remained, on borrowed time.

Drink up some more sugar water, girls, I thought. *Pack on a few more calories for the long flight.* The tiny birds amazed me. *Good luck, ladies. Have a safe trip. See you in the spring.*

I rinsed out my coffee cup and placed it in the sliding rack of the dishwasher.

At Bettye's prodding, I went to Knoxville and retrieved the police uniforms Old Town had waiting for me. I'm overly lax when it comes to how chief-like I look at work. Three months ago, I started out wearing polo shirts and jeans, sport shirts and khakis or a borrowed uniform shirt and blue jeans. More often than not, I wore plain clothes.

I spent most of my New York police career as a detective. I wasn't used to wearing a uniform and had never been too fond of doing so. But that day felt different. I dressed up in full pack and only carried a small five-shot, .38 caliber revolver that wouldn't make an unsightly bulge under my newly tailored, charcoal-green dress tunic.

At 8:15, I began getting impatient. I wanted to be in the office by nine. The ceremony was scheduled to kick off at ten o'clock.

I put on my uniform coat, walked into the downstairs bathroom and looked in the mirror. Above my oval silver and gold badge, I wore the medals I received back on Long Island. A gold distinguished expert firearms badge and seven enameled bars with various color schemes of blue, white, and red. They represented the nineteen commendations I received at the PD from where I retired years ago.

From the image in the mirror, I could tell I was ready to march. Nothing left but to round up my vicious twenty-eight-pound terrier, kiss my pretty wife good-bye and hit the road.

"Hey, soldier, you look pretty nifty," Kate said as I stepped back into the kitchen.

"Thank you, ma'am. I'm glad you good-looking females take notice of us All-American heroes."

"I've never seen you in this new uniform. It looks more like your Army greens than your police blues. I'm surprised you're not wearing spit-shined Cochran boots."

"I planned on wearing a pair of Converse All-Stars so I'd look like Mork from Ork," I said.

"Surely, Samuel, even you would maintain some dignity and decorum at such a solemn occasion." Kate can put on a pretty fair British accent herself.

"Yes, of course, surely even me. Hey, you look pretty snazzy. Where are you going today?"

"Athens," she said.

"Greece? You'll be home for dinner?"

"Don't be silly. Athens, just south of here. People from a few library groups are meeting at the regional offices to see what I can tell them about membership drives for their FOL groups."

"I should talk to them. Tell them to recruit the toughest husbands to hang out at the library entrance and grab some of the patrons after they check out books. If they refuse to join the Friends of the Library, throw them up against the wall and threaten to break their thumbs. That would work in Italian neighborhoods. Can't see why it wouldn't do here."

"You're incorrigible," she said.

"Thank you. I try to be innovative."

Katherine wore a gray tweed pantsuit with a short double-breasted jacket. The front closed low enough so, with her sexy push-up bra, I saw plenty of cleavage.

"By the way," I said, "snazzy isn't an adequate description. You really look damn good."

"Aren't you sweet?" she observed.

"Yeah, you're pretty cute for an old bat."

"Oy, what a smoothie."

"That's me, very smooth with the ladies."

I kissed her and whistled for Bitsey. The dog came thundering in from the living room where she'd been resting up after her night's sleep.

"See ya later, Katzy. Be careful on the interstate."

"Bye, Sambo. I love you."

* * * *

At quarter to ten, it looked like our ceremony would start late—thanks to the mayor. I've convinced him it's better to be five minutes early, but he operates on 'Tennessee time'.

I stood out back near the rear door to PD headquarters. Bitsey roamed around on the end of her leash, sniffing the grass and the trunks of the decorative redbud trees. A white mini-van with WNXX news logos pulled into the lot and took a spot marked for police vehicles only. Under the circumstances, I curbed my obsessive-compulsive desire to tighten up the driver.

Cameraman John Leckmanski got out of the driver's side. He waved, circled around the back of the van, and started extracting his camera, battery pack and some other gadgets from the cargo area. The passenger door opened, and a pretty girl with long dark hair stepped out. She straightened the jacket of her sage green pantsuit, picked up a clipboard and microphone and walked toward Bitsey and me. I wore a police uniform so I couldn't masquerade as the hired dog walker. Leckmanski followed closely behind her.

When she smiled, her face lit up. It looked like a genuine smile and not the canned expression some media types use while they're on duty.

"Is that a police dog?" she asked.

"She's a policeman's dog. That's a little different. She's trained to sniff out pork chops and scalloped potatoes. But she's not too good at finding drugs or explosives."

Few women can resist my wit. She smiled again, and her red lips parted slightly for me to see perfect white teeth.

"Hi, I'm Tess Haley from 5 O'clock Magazine."

"I know. I'm Sam Jenkins. Thanks for coming."

We shook hands, and I resisted the temptation to kiss the back of her fingers as Hercule Poirot might have done.

"Does your station hire anyone who's not beautiful?" I asked.

"Oh, thanks. That was so nice."

I nodded and smiled again.

"Whattaya say, John?"

"How's it going, Chiefski?" John's a Polish smart-ass.

Tess took a step closer to me. My guard dog kept sniffing, ignoring the possible threat to my person.

"What are these colored bars for?" She pointed at the commendations above my badge.

Starting at the top and working down the row, I pointed at a few and explained, "That's for bravery. This is for valor. The one here's for heroism. And this is for modesty." Then I showed her my shy boyish grin.

"Why do I think this isn't the first time you've said that?" she asked, still standing very close.

I could smell her perfume. The sun made her almost black eyes shine. *Yikes.*

"Well, maybe not the very first time," I said, with a self-deprecating expression as I looked down at her.

Even wearing high heels, she couldn't have been more than five-three. The women at that station are not only good-looking and sexy, they're all very short. Maybe the general manager is a dwarf with a personal image problem.

"Why don't my partner and I show you two inside?" I said. "You can use my office to get set up, and I'll find out when the mayor might be ready to kick off this thing."

I thought of locking Bitsey in one of the D cells, but knew as soon as I closed the door she'd start to howl. I went into my top drawer, took out a king-sized Milk Bone and threw it onto the plaid doggie-bed sitting in the corner of my office.

"Stay here, you obstinate little beast," I told her.

Bitsey walked over to the bed and picked up the bone. She juggled it for a few seconds, made two circles on the cushion and dropped down like a duffle bag falling from the tailgate of an Army "deuce-and-a-half." *Good dog.* Glad she behaved herself in front of company.

"She is so sweet," Tess said.

I smiled like a proud father and nodded.

"I have fresh coffee made," I said. "John knows where the cups are. Help yourselves. I'll be right back." I pointed at Bitsey and held up my palm, hoping she'd stay put. She did.

In our reception area, Stanley Rose, his wife, son and daughter all stood with Bettye and Donnie Lambert. Their three children were in school.

The mayor had ordered a dais and a dozen folding chairs for the lobby. Ms. Connor scurried around making sure everything looked presentable. She adjusted the state flagstaff. It and the U.S. flag now stood equidistant from the podium. People began to mill around looking at their watches, the mayor still nowhere in sight.

"Trudy," I said to Ms. Connor, "It's five after ten. Did Ronnie get hit by a garbage truck or something?"

"Oh, Chief, he'll be along directly," she said.

In Tennessee, you never know if *directly* means in five minutes, forty-eight hours or sometime during the next planting season.

"Perhaps if you tell him the photographers are here and want to take his picture, we'd get results," I suggested.

"I'll go up and see what's keepin' him. Y'all be patient now, and don't you worry."

I growled to myself again.

Back in our reception area, Tess and Leckmanski had made themselves at home. John's camera cranked away while she spoke with Bettye and her husband. I kept my mouth shut until she said, "This is Tess Haley at the Prospect Police Department. Now back to you, Russell."

Tess thanked Stanley, Bettye and their families. She could give lessons on how to get the public to love you. John Leckmanski lowered the heavy camera and set it on Bettye's desk. His Atlanta Braves cap sat backwards on his head.

Tess turned to me, waiting for a progress report.

"I'm told the mayor will be down...directly," I shrugged and hoped to convey the unspoken message, *So hang in there and enjoy our company just a little longer.*

Fortunately, *directly* came quicker than I thought. I glanced into the lobby and watched Ronnie Shields descend the main staircase with the charm and posture of a dictator from a third world republic. As usual, his dirty-blond lacquered hair looked glued in place, and he looked like an animated mannequin in his expensive gray suit. He waved to the crowd, pointed his finger at a few people and grinned like a benevolent despot. Ms. Connor followed closely on El Presidente's heels. She could have graced the cover of the National Secretaries Association newsletter. Too bad her boss was never on time.

"Folks," I said to the small crowd, "I think it's show time."

Thankfully, Ronnie's program didn't last long. After a short speech, the two honorees were called to the dais and their spouses followed. Ronnie stepped to a spot in front of them and administered a short oath of office. He shook their hands, thanked them for their past services and wished them good luck as supervisors.

I stepped forward. Donnie Lambert joined me on Bettye's left, and I handed him a new sergeant's badge. He slid the long pin through the little metal holder on Bettye's Ike jacket and fastened the clasp. He finished with a kiss on her cheek and a handshake for me. Donnie, an electrical contractor, was forty-five-years-old. About the same height as Bettye, he had short dark hair, broad shoulders and the thick hands of a working man.

I repeated my act with Sheryl Rose, who looked a foot shorter than her husband. After pinning on Stan's new badge, she proudly kissed him on the lips and gave me a friendly peck on the cheek. She showed the biggest smile, with the whitest teeth. I'd hire her any time to do Crest commercials. Sheryl looked a lot like Oprah Winfrey during one of her slim periods.

Stanley's two children waited patiently in the audience. I waved them over and watched a stampede resembling the Oklahoma land rush

34

at the opening gun. The boy, nine-year-old Martin, and the girl, seven-year-old Coretta, ran to their father and hugged him.

After that, we all returned to our respective seats, while Ronnie wrapped up his program.

As the crowd milled around the lobby, Tess interviewed Ronnie, and the two still- photographers took a few group shots of the happy families. By noon, the lobby of the municipal building would be back to normal with no trace of the morning's festivities.

Back in the office, PO Harlan Flatt sat at Bettye's desk, answering the phones and dispatching our cars. I sent him back to work on the road. Bitsey and I would handle the desk job until Bettye got back from the extended lunch I suggested.

Chapter Six

Tuesday October 24th

The next morning, I sat at my desk again thinking about Murray McGuire. We picked up his life when he joins the Army in, we assumed, Montana. The documentation from the Military Records Center in St. Louis didn't specify his point of enlistment. I made a note to check on that. After discharge, we found him in Knoxville and then Prospect.

All his family members were deceased, and when he moved, it wasn't just across town. I thought about his accent—only slightly southern—more Tennessee than Louisiana. But he lived here almost thirty years. After fourteen years in the Smokies, even my wife, a nice Polish girl from Long Island, started pronouncing a few words like a local. Accents are funny. I've known natives of New Orleans who sounded more like they came from Brooklyn than south Louisiana. Who can figure?

Without a crime scene to walk through, I wasn't sure we even had much of a crime. There was no place to look for physical evidence, no smoking gun hidden in the potted palm. Colonel Mustard wasn't hiding in the library with a lead pipe. I decided to take a walk north of the town center and look at Murray's house.

I told Bettye what I'd be doing and walked out through the municipal lot. Earl the mechanic waved as I passed the garage. I smelled old grease in the deep fryers at Hardee's across the street.

I traveled north on Main Street and, after half a mile, crossed the narrow stone bridge over Crystal Creek where Main Street changes its name to Prospect Road. The colorful sweet gums, oaks and maple trees growing near the banks of the creek offered a distinct contrast to each other. The sweet gums blazed with blood-red leaves, and the maples a cheerful bright yellow, while the oaks only managed a muted yellow-brown.

Autumn in the Smokies could fool you into thinking you were in New Hampshire. Spectacular colors brought visitors by the thousands to drive the scenic backcountry roads or attend the numerous festivals and fairs held in all the small communities surrounding the mountains in Tennessee and nearby North Carolina.

Some thought of autumn as a time of dying. Those with a more optimistic outlook thought of it as the beginning of a rebirth scheduled for the springtime.

After walking another two blocks, I turned right on Blackberry Road. Two more and I made a left on Old Piney Drive, a dead end street that backed up to undeveloped woodland with a small farm behind that. Traditional frame houses sat on the corners of Blackberry and Old Piney. Wooded, vacant lots separated those dwellings from Murray's home, which occupied the last lot on the left.

His house was a small one-story rectangle void of any style or niceties. I thought it might have been built in the late 1970s or early 80s. A carport abutted the left side. The lawn, such as it was, had been cut recently, and only a few stray leaves lay on the grass. Several lonely bushes stood around the foundation on both sides of the front entrance. Murray spent little on landscaping. Like the architecture, the grounds looked neat but without style or class.

I walked around the house and found no oil drips on the slab under the carport to show that Murray owned a vehicle at one time. A power push-mower, a couple of garden tools, a trash can and an old bicycle sat neatly stowed out of the direct weather. I looked through a couple of windows. The interior appeared neat and relatively clean, the furnishings inexpensive. I saw no photographs displayed or other unmistakably personal mementoes. The motif reminded me of a contemporary Motel 6.

At the end of a short driveway, I found the roadside mailbox empty, and no newspaper tube mounted on the stanchion beneath it. I guessed Murray might be one of those guys who didn't read papers and listened to the morning news only to hear if we were officially at war or if he could expect rain.

On the corner of Blackberry Road, I found a man snipping old roses off the bushes in front of his bay window. I introduced myself and told him about Murray's background investigation, strictly a formality for a long-time employee. He told me Murray kept mostly to himself, could be seen walking to and from work each day and occasionally riding his bike. They always waved to each other. He considered Murray a good neighbor. The man never heard loud parties, never saw a vehicle parked there, doubted Murray ever received visitors and only saw him picked up by a taxi a few times over the years.

The woman who lived on the opposite corner repeated almost the same story. No other people lived nearby.

I'd have Bobby call the local cab companies to see if anyone could tell us something interesting.

As I approached the municipal building, I decided to save Bobby the trouble and check with our records department myself. If no one knew anything about Murray, perhaps they knew something about his house.

I trudged upstairs to the Registrar of Deeds. Ivy Tucker, one of the clerks, buzzed me through the Dutch door to their file room. Ivy looked like a forty-year-old woman in a sixty-year-old package. I watched as she pulled out a scrolled map of the Old Piney Road vicinity. Armed with map and book numbers and the parcel location where I told her the house stood, she extracted a ledger roughly eighteen by thirty inches from a rack at the back wall and laid it on a table to thumb through the large pages.

"Chief, there's no house on that lot," she said.

"What?" I felt my eyes begin to blink uncontrollably.

"The lot is vacant—no house." She looked at me as if I was crazy.

"The last lot, northwest corner. House number 4106. It's the only house north of the corner of Blackberry Road. I stood in front of it. I looked in the windows. Can you check the map again?"

She did. The locator numbers she used were correct. No house had been recorded.

"Amazing." I said. "Is there any other place this building could be listed?"

"No, sir, this is it."

"Is anything erased, torn out, look tampered with? *Anything* look unusual?"

"Well, these are just loose-leaf pages. They could be replaced, but everythin' is handwritten, and there's nothin' written at all."

"If he's not in this book, has he ever paid property taxes?"

"Probably not. The assessor gives us the information to register when a new house is completed. Nowadays they issue a certificate of occupancy, but years ago, they didn't have any building codes and never did that. From the assessor's information, we enter the data in these here books and keep on updatin' the register in case there are additions built or old buildin's are tore down. The Tax Department works from these books to make their lists, and they send out the tax bills."

"So if someone removed a page from this book or deleted a line from the list you make annually, the tax assessment would cease or never would have started?"

"I guess so," she said.

"Incredible. The phantom strikes again. How about the county? Where do their records come in?"

"I'm not certain, but Prospect's incorporated and is responsible for every buildin' within the city proper. We tell the county what's here to be taxed on their end."

"How long have you worked here, Ivy?"

"Six years."

"Before you were promoted to head clerk, who was in charge of these books and records?"

"A woman named Beryldine Parsons worked here since before this buildin' existed, back in the old city hall on Blount Street. She's retar'd now."

"Do you know if she was especially friendly with Typewriter Murray?"

"I would guess so. Murray was always in here fixin' things, helpin' and so forth." She nodded. "I guess so."

"Where does Beryldine live now?"

"Florida, I think. She was pretty old and always complainin' about the cold winters. Payroll could tell you where they send her pension checks."

"Thanks, Ivy. You've been a big help."

After giving up a fellow employee, Ivy may have felt like Judas on the morning after.

I just witnessed how the insidious tentacles of the good ol' boy (and perhaps ol' girl) network enveloped the workings of small government. I wondered who else wasn't paying their taxes and wished one of them could be me.

Back in my office, I called the county. From them I heard the same story. An ancient-sounding clerk said, "Course there ain't no house. Hit's jest a vacant lot."

I hung up and thought she may have dropped her phone back onto the cradle and said, "Silly po-leece. Man must be crazy."

I needed a drink. Much more of Murray and I'd develop a permanent facial tick.

I settled for banging my head against the raised panel door to my office. Bettye looked at my display of emotion. New sergeants rarely question their boss's motives for odd behavior.

She just walked out toward the lady's room and said, "Oh, my poor Sammy, you havin' another hard time today, darlin'?"

Yes, Bettye, you think?

I often remember the phrase about lack of progress. "We take one step forward and two steps back." I felt close to that. Only I had yet to take that first step forward. It seemed like I was driving flat out in reverse and just realized the car needed new brakes.

Already after eleven, I had exhausted all my possibilities and began getting hungry. I told Bettye she could find me at Howell's Pub where I'd have a sandwich and talk with the manager about Murray. I assured her I'd be back before one when she went to lunch, but based on the aggravating morning, my sobriety upon return might be in question. She just smiled for me.

Howell's Pub wasn't far off. Murray may have liked to walk there, but I chose to drive. I pulled into the gravel lot as Boyce, the cook, added several pork loins to the grill of a large black iron smoker sitting at the front edge of the parking area. Fragrant hickory smoke belched from beneath the rain cap of the chimney and floated away on the October breeze, destined to mingle with the smell of burning leaves somewhere far off. Boyce closed the half-round top of the grill, looked in my

40

direction and waved. I held the door open for him on my way in.

"Hey, Boyce, how's it going?"

He was short and bald and of medium build except for his basketball-sized tummy, wore a white T-shirt, baggy jeans and a stained white apron wrapped around his hips.

"Okey dokey, Sam. You doin' aw rot today?"

I nodded.

Boyce turned left in front of the swivel-stools at the lunch counter. I followed. When he made a hard right behind the counter and walked toward his kitchen, I continued through the dining area and said hello to a waitress named Dossie who was in her late twenties. Her uniform-of-the-day consisted of a pair of washed-off jeans, pink and white Nikes, a short carpenter's apron with lumberyard advertising and a tight white T-shirt from an old concert in Nashville. Dossie wasn't particularly pretty, but she was a friendly and happy-looking, well-endowed girl who didn't trouble herself with pesky things like underwear. I assumed she usually received generous tips from the male patrons.

At the back of the dining room, a doorway led to the pub. Howell's manager, Reggie Smethurst, an ex-pat British chap and former resident of Newcastle upon Tyne in Northumbria, ran Howell's place like a neighborhood pub in the UK. Reggie looked about fifty-years-old and spoke with a distinct north-country accent. When the owner, Howell Watkins, built an extension onto his restaurant to accommodate a barroom and an outdoor patio, Reggie set up the bar to look like a typical English beer-joint. Howell's became a popular watering hole for office workers and blue-collar people alike. Everyone loved the food, me included.

I took a seat at the bar. The only other customers sat at a table, two local men I knew to be employees of the cablevision company. They munched on burgers and occasionally sipped from bottles of Bud Light.

"Hi ya, Reggie. How's it goin'?"

"Hello, Sam. You're looking chipper today. Lovely weather lately, isn't it?"

"Lovely indeed, Reginald, old stick, lovely indeed." I used a posh London accent to make him feel closer to home.

"You are a lad, Sam." He shook his head and smiled. "What can I get you?"

"A large barbecue on a wheat roll and a pint of black and tan, please."

"Ah, an excellent choice, sir. Stick your head out there and tell Dossie to get you the sandwich whilst I draw your black and tan."

Formality at Howell's Pub has always been a little lax. Dossie waved to acknowledge my order, and I sat back on my stool as Reggie added the Guinness Stout to the Bass Ale, thus making my "black and tan."

Howell used rough-sawn weathered barn boards to cover the walls of his barroom. Reggie hung old beer signs everywhere.

"In addition to feasting on your award-winning barbeque and drinking the best mixed black and tan in this county, Reggie my dear fellow, I'm here on some official business. Got a minute or two for your local constable?"

"Of course, I do, *Chief* Constable. But you must acknowledge this as the best black and tan mixed in the US *or* the UK, for that matter. Ain't easy to mix'em like that, ya know." He set the pint mug down on a clean coaster.

"I sit corrected, my dear boy." I sipped my drink "Ahhh, a splendid pint indeed," I acknowledged, again with the London accent.

He waited for my question.

"You know Murray McGuire? The guy everyone in Prospect calls Typewriter Murray?" I took another long drink from the black and tan.

"I do indeed, Sam. He comes in here a few nights a week. Thursdays especially, to throw darts. And does it quite well, I should add. Thursdays are league nights."

"Does he drink much? Ever get loud? Give you any problems?"

"Good Lord, no. He's a small man, doesn't eat much and doesn't drink much—maybe two pints over a night, always Guinness. He may drink three whilst throwing darts, but holds it well. Never gives us any trouble."

Reggie set down the glass he had been drying and reconsidered his last statement.

"Oh wait, I tell a lie. A fortnight ago, perhaps a little more, there was something, though not his fault, not his fault at all. Another chap playing darts accused him of cheating. I can't imagine how one can cheat at darts, but the man, a lad by the name of Dermott Halloran said so. Dermott did drink a bit much, wasn't throwing well himself and accused Murray of being dishonest. Howell was here, too. He and I got Dermott quiet straight away. I bought him a coffee, sat him down, and it seemed over until he left. Nothing much then, really, just a comment made toward Murray, and then out he went, old Dermott did. Murray's quite good at darts, perhaps the best here. Has his own set, good ones, too. GLDs, tungsten barrels, steel tips—professional darts. Told me he paid sixty dollars for them in Knoxville. He's quite the serious competitor."

"Has this fellow Dermott been back since?"

"He has," Reggie said.

"Has he seen Murray? He still play darts?"

"Yes, life goes on. No more problems that I've seen."

The two cable guys dropped a pair of dollar bills on the bar as Reggie's tip, waved and carried their checks out to the cash register.

"Does Murray ever talk about himself? About anything now or any past history?"

"I can't say that he does. He talks about sports, college football— American football, that is." He smiled; I suppose to indicate he thought American football wasn't as real as European football. "He sometimes speaks about baseball, seems to follow the sports. He did mention that he inherited his fondness for Guinness from his Irish father. Can't say I remember anything else. He's not much of a philosopher."

As Reggie ended his statement, Dossie brought me a platter with a barbeque sandwich the size of a small beach ball, a mound of homemade potato salad, a dish of baked beans and one quarter of a mammoth dill pickle.

"Dossie, you keep feeding me this much and I'll lose my boyish figure," I said.

"Shoot, honey, yew've got a long way ta go 'fore you git fat. Jest git out there an' chase down some bank robbers, an' yew'll burn them calories rot offa yew."

I decided to forgo a second pint of black and tan. I couldn't remember a bank robbery in Prospect's recent history.

Halfway through the sandwich, my cell phone sounded off. The

Rolling Stones played *Paint it Black* in my pocket. I answered and heard Bettye's voice.

"Sam, please git your ass back here b'fore I have ta break up a fight all by m'se'f." She sounds a little more "country" when she gets excited. I assured Bettye I was on my way.

"Reginald, wrap this up, please. There's the good lad." I said. "I'll be back later to fetch it and pay you."

He nodded and looked a little confused.

"Thanks very much," I said. "Duty calls."

A minute after switching on the Ford's ignition, I heard Bettye on the car radio.

"Prospect Headquarters to all units, unless you have an emergency, hold all your transmissions, I'm busy in the squad room. Prospect Headquarters, out."

In five minutes, I bounced through the back door and heard Bobby Crockett's voice.

"Goddamnit, ya little maggot. How long ya 'spect me ta listen ta yer lies?"

"Gee, Bobby John," Murray said, "I don't know why you're getting all mad at me. I swear I'm tellin' the truth."

"That's Officer Crockett to you, bud. And do me the courtesy, don't keep spoutin' that stuff, huh?"

"Bobby," Bettye said. "Why don't you give it a rest? Go get yourself a soda, and I'll stay here for a while."

"Yes, ma'am, Miss Bettye. I 'spect that's the best thing ta do."

I stepped into the squad room just before Crockett passed through the doorway. I turned and followed him.

"What's up, kid?" I asked.

"Sam, it's the same ol' goddamn story with that guy. One lie after another. And if I question somethin', he don't remember."

"Are you working a car today?"

"No, sir. I'm on overtime 'til four o'clock."

I looked at my watch. "Okay, it's lunchtime. Go take an extra half hour and stop at Primo's Gym. Pump some iron for a while, and get that guy out of your head."

"Lord have mercy! That man's gonna drive me ta drink."

"That's not the worst thing in the world. Go out and relax. Bettye and I'll take care of him."

Back in the squad room, I saw Bettye standing over Murray, talking to him like an unhappy mother.

"Hi, Sarge," I said. "Mind if Murray and I have a word or two?"

"Thank you for stopping in, boss." she said. "I'll just go back to my desk and see if there's an emergency I can handle."

Bettye rarely huffs. That was an exception. If their encounter lasted a few more minutes, I wouldn't have bet on Murray coming out a winner.

"Murray," I said, "I think you've gotten two of the most even-tempered people pissed off at you."

"Gee, Chief, I can't understand why everybody's mad at me."

"Can it, please. Go tell your stories to people who may believe you."

He began to speak again, but I held up a hand to stop him.

"Save it," I said. "We've given you every opportunity to tell us the truth. You chose not to. Okay, we'll leave it at that. I hope you don't think we're stupid enough to buy all your noise about not remembering things and how all the people on earth who never heard of you are fabricating stories."

"Chief, I don't…"

"Murray, we're done here. I expect you'll be hearing from the Mayor next."

The little man got up and sheepishly walked out.

Oh, well, I enjoyed a lovely, but interrupted lunch. I learned nothing extraordinary about our little Irish dart player, but a new name came into my world. So, Dermott Halloran went into my mental file for future use.

Because it proved necessary to break up an incident where my beautiful desk sergeant might have seriously injured the object of our current investigation, I felt the beginning of a world-class tension headache. My next decision of the afternoon forced me to take things to a higher level. Finding anything about Murray failed locally, so I'd see what my friendly neighborhood G-man might know.

Chapter Seven

After a quick trip back to Howell's to pick up my unfinished lunch and settle the bill, I stood in the parking lot of the municipal building, enjoying the weather and the modern magic of the cell phone.

"Yo, Ralphie, wa's goin' on?" I spoke to Special Agent Ralph Oliveri at the Knoxville FBI field office.

"Either someone is calling me from Brooklyn or I know exactly who this is."

"J. Edgar would be proud of you, Ralph. How are you?"

"Why would he be proud? You think I wear a dress when I'm off duty?"

"Hey, paisan, one of your bosses may be listening. You're speaking ill of an American icon. Anyway, how'd you like to get involved in the most interesting case of your career?"

I stuck my left index finger into my ear to blot out the noise of a police siren screaming somewhere close by.

"You're here what," he asked, "three months now? And you constantly tap me for favors. You think the Bureau is your personal information service?"

"Well, if something with interstate connections doesn't interest you, okay. This is so weird it may have intergalactic connections. Help out with this one and you could be famous."

"Oh, Jesus, what do you want? I hope you're rememberin' all the favors I'm doin' for you."

"I'm older than you, Ralphie, but I've still got a good memory. I just made a note on my mental calendar. I-owe-Ralph-another-one. Listen, here's what I've got…"

I explained the Typewriter Murray story to Ralph before dropping my small bomb. "What I need you to do, it's simple, really, check and see if McGuire is a federally protected witness."

A second siren, this one the lazy high-low of an ambulance, sounded in the distance, no doubt responding to assist the police unit I heard only moments earlier.

"Are you crazy?" His voice took on an emotional, squeaky quality. I could hear him easily above the wails of the siren. "You know I can't tell you that, assuming Justice or the Marshall's Service would tell me."

"What you can tell me, my old goombah, is that he's *not* in witness protection. If that's the case. You could also tell me to stop spinning my wheels over something that's of no concern to the likes of me, if that's more appropriate. Then those with more control over this than you or I could either leave him alone or pack him up and send him to Dubuque to work as a greeter in Wal-Mart."

"Okay, okay, I'll see what I can do. But don't forget this one, pally. This is a biggie."

"No problem, guy. Anytime I can do something for you, all you have to do is whistle."

"What the hell could a guy in a thirteen-man police department do for the FBI?" he asked.

"You never know. Got a pencil?" He grunted. "Ready?" I heard a second grunt. "Murray Neil McGuire." I spelled all three names. "DOB 1-14-55. Need anything else? Want his code name at the KGB officer's club? Citizen's ID number from the Klingon home world? DNA factors?"

Ralph didn't acknowledge my clever suggestions. But he said, "I'll call you back," and hung up before I could offer my sincere thanks.

* * * *

At two o'clock, Derek Foxwell called. He located two copies of the book I wanted and needed a decision on which to order. I left the department in Bettye's capable hands and took the short drive to the Fox and Quill Bookshop. When I arrived, Derek looked busy with two customers. Bridget sat behind the cash register reading a book about the early Scotch-Irish immigration into East Tennessee. Eleanor must have taken the day off.

"Good day, Sam. Lovely out there, isn't it? And my, don't you look handsome in that dashing tweed sports coat?"

"Thank you, miss. And how's Ireland's finest export doing today?"

"Oh, stop your noise. You're quite the cavalier, aren't you?"

"Gee, no one's called me that in over three hundred years—right before I slugged it out with Cromwell."

She laughed, used a bookmark to keep her spot and gave me her attention.

"Derek called about the book I ordered, but I see he's busy. Can you and I do business?"

"I'd love to do business with you, Mr. Jenkins, but I've no idea what *he* has for you." She gave me a look any middle-aged man would be thrilled to get.

"Well then." I cleared my throat and blinked a few times to let her know her comment wasn't lost on me. "While we're waiting for the lord of the manor, tell me how you found your way from Killarney to East Tennessee."

She shifted slightly on the stool and pushed a few strands of red hair back from her cheek. "Oh, it's quite simple really. I'm following the Irish immigrants of the eighteenth century. Lots of Irish and Scotch-Irish settled here. Your county library has a grand genealogy department, and they're helping me tremendously with my research."

"That's fascinating. Why are you doing all this research?"

"I'm studying for my master's degree in Irish History," she said. "So, I'll get all I need for my thesis and a wonderful holiday in the States, too."

"Terrific. Good luck to you. I'd like to read your paper when it's finished."

"I shall see that you get a copy, sir."

A man and woman walked out from the rear of the store, followed by Derek.

"Oh, Sam, good of you to come by," he said. "Please come over here whilst I bring these books up on the computer, and you can decide what we shall do."

Bridget smiled and wiggled her fingers to wave good-bye as I headed for Derek's computer set-up.

In a few minutes, I arranged to buy a book that cost as much as a good dinner for two. I hoped old Benedict Arnold, the subject of my book, was worth it.

* * * *

At 3:45, Stanley Rose came to work, and we spoke about the Typewriter Murray caper. I hated to admit being baffled, but I couldn't hide the truth. Stanley recited a list of things he thought of to see if Bobby or I checked them out. We had done them all and more.

"Come on, Stan, you think you're dealing with an amateur?" He shrugged. "But do me a favor. While you're working tonight, keep thinking and jot down any new ideas you get. Maybe we did miss something."

The phone on Bettye's desk rang.

She buzzed my intercom. "It's your friend, the FBI comedian."

"Thanks, Betts." The transfer clicked in.

"Ralphie, whatcha got?"

"Nothin', kiddo. Nobody knows him and never heard of him. I ran his name in all combinations. Nada, zip, nothin'. You know as much as I do."

"Wonderful. Just freakin' wonderful." I sighed before continuing. "You know anyone at NASA?"

"What?" Ralph sounded exasperated.

"Maybe we could ask a couple of the astronauts. See if they brought him back from outer space."

"You want me to try and run him down some more?"

"Ralph, I'd love the help, but honestly, I've tried every possible lead we could come up with. Me, too—nada, nyet, zip, zilch, zero. We just sent his prints and a check off to AFIS. You have a friend there who could expedite the name and print search? How about some loophole in the Patriot Act? I could say people in town call him Ali Ahmed Bin Murray if that would help."

"Let me talk to the boss. He probably knows someone with horsepower up in DC. But—and don't take offense at this, pal—he'll probably want a list of what you've already checked and done. You know us Feds. We never think the locals are as thorough as we are."

"Hey, I'll give him my secret recipe for Greek beef stew if he can find something new on this guy," I said.

"Keep the faith, bubbee. I'll get back to you."

"Thanks. I'll talk to ya."

I looked at Stanley. "Shit!"

"I hear ya," he said.

So much for my bright idea of getting Federal help. I may have hit a stonewall, but at least I stood amongst good company. For some reason, I thought about Scarlett O'Hara. Maybe it was the Irish name, or maybe I just remembered her saying, "Tomorrow is another day."

Chapter Eight

Before re-entering the ranks of the gainfully employed, I often took on the job of preparing dinner. Occasionally, Katherine got home around six o'clock after a tough day at the mahjongg tables or after working for nothing more than the grateful thanks of the Blount County Library patrons. More recently, we'd begun the routine of eating out a few nights a week.

The dog and I got home at 5:15. I popped the cap off a bottle of Black Hook porter, close to one of Reggie's black and tans, but not quite. I opened a can of Mighty Dog chicken with bacon, mixed half of it with some dry dog food designed for old hounds, and gave it to Bitsey. She looked enthused and ate it quicker than I can devour one of Howell's barbeque sandwiches. I sat down with my glass of porter and thumbed through the latest issue of Smithsonian magazine. At 6:05, Kate walked in.

"Hi ya, slinky. What's happenin'?" I asked

"Hello, Sammy." She kissed me on the forehead. "I won seven games today, seven. Are you proud of me?"

"Sure, but did anyone else win anything?"

Kate shook her head.

"You know, you're like the guy who plays golf with his boss and always wins. Maybe you should lose a few, or everyone will hate you, like the Yankees. People love underdogs, like the Cubs."

"Oh, who asked you?" she said.

She went to the fridge and poured herself a glass of Pinot Grigio from an open bottle.

"So, what did you and your canine assistant do today?" she asked.

"The CO of my K-9 Corps slept in the office. I, on the other hand,

51

worked my ass off and got frustrated doing so."

I explained the whole Murray McGuire deal.

"Can't you inject him with pentothal or some other truth serum?"

"Sure, but that's number two on my list. First, I want to try hanging him upside down over a hot campfire. If that fails, I'll take him for a shot of truth serum—at the walk-in clinic, maybe."

"No need to get testy, big feller. I just thought modern technology might have something you could use."

Kate finished her wine after my beer was long gone. That signaled the time for dinner.

We drove ten miles into Maryville to a new Italian Restaurant owned by real Italians from New Jersey, no less. The Villa Napoli looked pretty upscale and fancy for down-home Maryville. The Cutrone family, all three generations of them, renovated an old warehouse on the main street that connected Maryville with its neighbor, Alcoa, home of the Aluminum Company of America. Inside, the Villa looked like something from Manhattan's Little Italy. The walls were painted dark red, and the lighting was soft. I heard Jerry Vale singing *Non Dimenticar* in the background. The song might have been from the *Mob Hits* album. We sat at a table on the raised level, next to the sidewall. A framed poster with a harlequin Pagliachi hung over my right shoulder. Kate drank another glass of Pinot Grigio. I ordered a Chianti Rustica. As we took a leisurely look at a menu the size of the Staten Island phonebook, I began talking again about Murray.

"Did you check with the church?" she asked.

"What? The church? For what, divine inspiration?"

"About Murray, Sherlock. Murray Neil McGuire certainly isn't Jewish. A nice Irish boy just might be Catholic. Go see if the priest at St. Michael's knows anything that can help you."

"You're a real smart-ass, aren't you?" I observed.

"Yes, and I'm cute, too." She can turn on a smile that's been successful for over forty years. I agreed: cute and smart, too. I was in love. I'd buy her dinner and maybe get lucky later that night.

On the drive home, I wondered where I'd find any useful information. The law enforcement pros had little luck getting a lead on the real Murray McGuire. I liked Kate's idea of asking at the church. My mother always told me to say my prayers at night. It was probably a good time to start.

* * * *

Wednesday October 25th

My morning breezed by uneventfully and sitting at my desk, looking through my windows into the PD lobby where Bettye sat, I contemplated what I wanted for lunch. I was on my own. Bitsey had stayed home with Katherine. At eleven o'clock, my stomach growled. After lunch, I planned to drive to St. Michael's Church, only a long bicycle ride from Murray's home.

Then the phone rang, and I spoke with Ralph Oliveri.

"My boss is interested," he said. "Thanks to me selling you as a competent guy, he didn't even want to get a complete run down on your investigation. I convinced him you probably know what you're doing and might have covered all the bases."

"Thanks, I think."

"He called someone in Washington and asked them to expedite the work on those prints. He says they won't even wait for your check to clear. You should have an answer by fax before the close of business tomorrow. Then they'll send the prints back, and you'll get the usual report by mail. That work for you?"

"It sure does, Ralphie. Thanks, I owe you again. You're a fine American. Why don't you drive down here, and I'll let you buy me lunch?"

"I think that works the opposite way around, sport. Besides, it's not safe to eat where you work. Don't you mountain people eat things like possum and greasy beans?"

"That's an exaggeration. Don't believe everything you hear."

"I hear everything is deep fried and served with sausage gravy. Hey, you are sure you covered all the bases with this guy, aren't you?"

"Everything but a national agency check. Wanna do one of those for me?" I said.

"Whoa, cowboy. That's not done for just anyone. *That* would involve a really big-time favor."

"Yeah, I know. I don't see how I can justify that for an ex-typewriter repairman who's graduated to general gopher and major domo for the mayor."

"Major Domo. I met him when I was in the Marines."

"Of course you did, Ralph. What do you think? Am I spinning my wheels over nothing here? I just hate all these loose ends and need to know why he's lying."

"Stuff like that drives me crazy, too. I'd want to smack the shit out of him until he spoke with a straight tongue."

"My wife suggested truth serum."

"Good girl. We could use her at Git-Mo."

"This conversation is going downhill. I'm going to get me a 'possum' parmiagian hero for lunch and then go see a priest."

"A priest? Are things that bad?" He wasn't looking for an answer. "Hey, don't do anything I wouldn't do." He rang off without waiting for a comment.

I went to lunch, but Opossum wasn't in season. I settled for a turkey, bacon and Swiss at Quizno's.

* * * *

St. Michael's Roman Catholic Church is the Vatican's only representative in Blount County, Tennessee. The great preponderance of the population in our section of the Bible Belt is Protestant, much of that faction made up of Evangelical Christians. I remember hearing folks of that persuasion once say they didn't consider Catholics to be Christians. Go figure.

I parked my gray Crown Victoria in the blacktop lot of the small church. What St. Michael's lacked in size, it made up for in class. Designed after a Norman castle, the church's main tower extended up several stories into the wild blue yonder. Above the arched double doors, a round stained glass window faced eastward to catch the morning sun. The yellow, tan, gold and brown mountain stone used to face the exterior walls had been set by experts; the job almost looked European in quality. Around the outer walls of the church, old rhododendrons, azaleas and Leyland cypress grew, presenting a comforting and attractive landscape. Closer to the parking lot and around the perimeter of the grounds stood several varieties of maple trees now in full color. The red and yellow leaves added seasonal color and charm. There was even a vibrant red burning bush—religiously appropriate, of course.

Long ago, I learned St. Michael was the patron of policemen and paratroopers. I thought perhaps I'd have some luck with him on my side.

Like most of the Catholic churches I've been to, St. Michael's leaves its doors open all day, every day. I walked inside. I'm not a religious person, but if I were, I'd say the interior of a Catholic church did a lot to set a mood for the religious feelings many people seek to experience.

It took a few seconds for my eyes to adjust to the dim interior light and look around. The temperature of the congregational hall felt cooler than outside. The sun had yet to warm the chilly night air trapped within.

I scanned the church's interior and wondered if the seating area for the parishioners in a small church was called a nave as it is in a cathedral. Looking up at the vaulted ceiling for a long moment, I might have appeared like the tourists in Manhattan who gawk at the skyscrapers. As my eyes drifted back to ground level, a young priest walked toward me from a door to the right of the altar.

The man wore a simple black suit and shirt with a white clerical collar. He was of medium height and build, about thirty years old, with almost black curly hair. A writer might say he saw the map of Donegal printed all over his face.

"Good morning," I said, "I'm Sam Jenkins, police chief from Prospect." I showed him my badge.

"Hello, I'm Declan McGill, assistant to Father Stephen here in the parish. Nice to meet you." We shook hands, and he waited for me to speak next.

"Father, I was wondering if you could help me with an investigation. I'm taking a guess that the subject of my inquiry is a Catholic and perhaps a member of your church. This is not a criminal matter, but an important security investigation, you might say. He's not in any trouble."

"Of course, Chief, I'll certainly help if I can."

Without compromising too much confidentiality of the investigation, but giving Father Declan the gist of my problem to catch his interest, I admitted grasping for any straw that might shed some light on my problem.

"He's been a satisfactory employee for a long time," I said, "but with this new Patriot Act we're obligated to investigate any person who works in a police facility." The word *obligated* was a stretch perhaps, but not an outright lie. "I'm unable to explain much of the void in his background. So is he. I'd hate to recommend termination because his job is convenient for him. It fits his quiet lifestyle nicely."

"I understand. I've known Murray for as long as I've been here. Five years now. He doesn't come in often, but he does visit occasionally."

"Has he ever told you anything that might lead me to learn more about him?"

"Actually, yes, he has."

Aha! I felt the intervention of a patron saint. The sun must have shifted because a new ray of light appropriately illuminated one of the statues near the altar. I love omens.

"Unfortunately," he said, "you know I can't divulge something that would breach the confidentiality of the confessional or even just a simple request for spiritual guidance."

Maybe that patron saint will be more helpful the next time I jump out of a perfectly good aircraft. So much for that omen.

"I understand, Father, that you have rules to live by. But surely, there's something not so sacred you can tell me. If not something you heard, then something you observed, a conjecture, anything. We're not in court here. I'm not going to prosecute Murray for anything. I'm just looking for something that may lead me to something else."

"Well, I suppose I can tell you that each St. Patrick's Day, Murray makes a generous donation to light a candle and have a mass read."

"I'm not a Catholic. I'm not sure of the significance of that."

The young priest nodded, looking prepared to enlighten me.

"Let's say, theoretically, the candle is lit to draw attention to a person for whom you wish to bring inner peace. The mass is said like, oh...an ultimate prayer for the person for whom it's intended."

"Can you tell me who he wanted the mass said for?"

"I can because we would say so in the church bulletin. The masses were for Murray himself."

Well, hot damn, this is getting interesting, now.

"Without going into detail," I suggested, "can you tell me if Murray has confessed something to you that would constitute either a serious legal or moral transgression?"

"I'm afraid I can't even tell you that he's confessed anything. But I can give you a short lesson in Catholic history if you have another few minutes."

"I sure do. Remember Dean Wormer saying, 'Knowledge is good'?"

"Dean who?" He looked confused.

"Not important, Father. Please continue."

"Well, Chief, since we were just talking about that famous Irishman, St. Patrick, I should tell you that much of his life and deeds are enshrouded in myth and legend. None of the scholars are exactly sure what may be truly attributed to him. However, we do know with certainty that during his lifetime he wrote a paper called *Confessio*. It was an apology against his detractors." He stopped and smiled. "Maybe that small bit of information is at least interesting and perhaps useful."

Declan held out his hand again. He had a firm grip for a gentle man.

"Thank you, Father...I think."

"Well, good-bye then, Chief, and good luck." His smile looked genuine.

I've always been hopeless trying to decipher hidden meanings in literature or poetry. Father Declan's cryptic message had me wondering. I'd have to take it to the scholar in my family, the resident ex-Catholic, my wife. Or are Catholics like Marines? Once a Catholic, always a Catholic? I'd soon find out.

* * * *

The drive from Prospect to Walland offered lovely late afternoon light and colorful foliage. As I backed into the parking spot adjacent to my driveway, I looked at the dashboard clock. 5:15 and home again, home again, jiggety jig.

As I entered the laundry room through the garage, the aroma hit me like a cloud of Italian fog. Fried onions, roasted peppers and eggplant, fresh mushrooms and ripe olives bubbled in a pot of homemade tomato sauce, melding together into a Sicilian masterpiece. Katherine stood at the kitchen counter grating a chunk of Pecorino-Romano cheese. A fresh loaf of roasted garlic bread waited on a metal tray, ready to warm in the oven. I put my arm around her waist and kissed her neck.

"Mama Mia! You've been busy," I said.

"Nothing but the finest for my boy in blue."

"I don't own a blue uniform any more. I have a green uniform, but I only wear it under duress. I haven't worn PD blue since 1979."

"Oh, shut up. Figure of speech. How about: Some good grub for the man I love?"

"Much better. And it almost rhymes. This stuff smells great. I guess Villa Naploi inspired you. How long before it's ready?"

"The pasta has to cook, so you have time to make us a drink and open the wine."

I looked on the counter and saw a twenty-dollar bottle of Luna Sangiovese. I popped the cork and let it breath.

"Wine, whiskey or song, young lady?" I asked.

"Whiskey and song, sir," she said.

I poured a couple of ounces of Canadian Club Classic 12 over ice, added a splash of red vermouth to the glasses and then made a stop at the cabinet housing our CD player. I started with *Best of the Chieftains*. A hornpipe began playing *Up Against the Buachalawans*. Soon the flutes and fiddles joined in. The Irish mood-music would get me back into the case.

"You had a good idea about going to check with the priest at St. Michael's."

"Oh?"

"Spoke with a *noice* young man, so I did. *Faather* Declan, Declan McGill. Good *Oirish* lad, so he was." Barry Fitzgerald never sounded better than me.

"And?"

"And what is it with you Catholics? He about admitted that Murray divulged some dodgy conduct in the confessional, and he won't tell me about it. It's hard to solve a case when the good guys withhold information."

"Sort of traditional, you know, church doctrine and all. There's only a couple thousand years of precedence. Didn't you flash your badge?

Wasn't he impressed?"

She finished drying a saucepan and hung the dishtowel on a hook next to the sink.

"Okay, Miss Smarty Pants, he did tell me something. Very cryptic people, these Irish monks. Now I know how Kwai Chang Caine felt when Master Po told him all those confusing things."

"Oh, yes?"

"I don't know where it fits in right now, but keep this under your hat and remind me if I need it later on. You know St. Patrick?"

"Of course, patron saint of corned beef and cabbage," she said.

The Chieftains transcended into *Boil the Breakfast Early*. I tapped my foot to the music.

"Right," I said. "Well, on St. Patrick's Day each year Murray pays to light a candle and have a mass said for himself."

Kate tilted her head. "Oh, really? For himself? Interesting."

"The good Father also mentioned—and here's the cryptic part—St. Patrick was known for writing something called *Confessio*, an apology against his detractors."

Kate raised her eyebrows and looked fascinated.

"So, what does Murray have to apologize for, and who are or were his detractors?" I asked.

"Beats me, but it would be good to remember that, Grasshopper," she said.

I shook my glass. The cubes rattled. Whiskey doesn't last as long as it used to. Perhaps global warming causes premature evaporation.

I dumped six ounces of gemelli into the boiling water and made myself another drink. When the pasta finished cooking, I canned the Chieftains and recruited Andrea Bocelli to provide dinner music.

Chapter Nine

Friday October 27th

Bobby Crockett sat waiting in my office when I walked in at 8:40 a.m. Bettye stood at the cabinet pouring herself a cup of coffee.

I hung my gray Harris Tweed sport jacket behind the raised-panel oak door.

"Doughnuts." I announced, as I set down the slightly grease-stained paper bag with the dozen old-fashioned jelly donuts I picked up at Richie Creamie in Maryville.

"Good Lord, Sam," Bettye said. "You're going to have us gettin' fat with these doughnuts you bring in every Friday."

"Every pound of you is gorgeous, woman," I told her. "Besides, doughnuts are brain food for cops. They're an integral part of scientific criminal investigation."

"If you don't keep those doughnuts to your own self, Sam Jenkins, there'll be a lot more of me for y'all to look at every day."

Bettye weighs about 120 well-proportioned pounds

"If they's brain food, gimme some," Bobby said. "I feel dumb as a stump. Cain't git one thing with this Typewriter Murray investigation ta go right. It's kindly like he's got a computer program followin' after him erasin' everthin' he comes in contact with."

I helped myself at the Mr. Coffee, while Bettye and Bobby John waited. I was never a big coffee drinker back on Long Island, but I needed to silently protest how the locals in Tennessee drink sweet iced tea or soda in the mornings. Now, after my breakfast coffee at home, I started drinking a second cup at the office. Even Bettye started drinking coffee, with fat-free half-and-half and a couple of spoons of Splenda.

I watched Bobby while he ate his first doughnut, standing in the typical policeman's posture—bent forward at the waist, leaning over a trash can. The sugar conveniently fell into the can and not on his uniform shirt. You learn that technique during your first week in the academy, just before they teach you how to turn on a police car's emergency lights.

Even with his addiction to doughnuts, Bobby weighed about the same 180 pounds as I did. And I knew he wore a 42 regular because I borrowed his uniform shirts before I got around to picking up my own. He stayed in the office with me; Bettye left us to work the desk.

"I went down the list of stuff you gave me, asked Rosie if he could think of anything else to check, and we both came up with nothin'," he said.

"Rosie?"

"Yeah, Stanley."

"Hmm. You guys call him Rosie?"

"Uh-huh."

File that one away, Sammy.

"Wait till you hear this," he said. "I called St. Mary's Hospital in Knoxville. They wanted me to come in person and bring a release for information and medical records. Well, Murray's wife died there. Her death certificate said heart failure. Shoot, she was pretty young for a heart attack. Then the doctor, he was old—sixty somethin', he ended up dyin' two years later."

"Sixty-something is old?"

"Uh-huh." He paused and raised his eyebrows so I would think he found something suspicious. "And nobody else is workin' there now who'd know anythin' more about her death. And nobody in Montana knows nothin' about his parents or their deaths either. They's no information in that whole state about any of 'em. I even called the Mounties. Canada bein' right close to Montana. Cain't find nothin' on this man. I've no ideal where to look next."

"Neither have I, Bob."

"What do you want to do with this?"

"Let's wait until after dark, then take him out back and shoot him," I said with a straight face.

"Do what?"

"Personally, I'd fire his ass for lying to us. But he doesn't work for me, and I can't give him the sack. I guess we wait and see what Big Ron wants to do with him."

* * * *

"Ronnie, the man consistently lied to us," I said. "There is nothing in his background I can verify except his time in the Army and his time here in Tennessee. Before 1975, he and his family do not exist. Something is very fishy."

The mayor sat behind his mammoth desk quietly shaking his head.

"He just listens to me and smiles and can't understand why no one knows him." I said. "If he was my employee, and I couldn't get away with dropping him off a cliff, I guess I'd settle for firing him. He owes you a good deal of back taxes on his property, you know."

"Has he committed any serious crimes?" Ronnie asked.

"Just a few two-bit violations like driving without a license, making false statements on an official document and not paying his property taxes. But he claims he never received any tax bills. Not a lot to punish him for. But let me emphasize, we have no idea what he did before 1975."

"Honestly, Sam, I'm inclined to say, where are we gonna get another man like Murray to do so much work for what we pay him?"

That statement surprised me, even coming from Ronnie.

I shook my head that time. "It's your call, boss."

"I'll tell him. O' course, he's gonna have ta start payin' his taxes like ever'one else, yes indeed. And git him a license, too."

My surprise advanced to amazement.

"Oh, indeed." I tried to keep the sarcasm from my voice.

"Would ya mind callin' him in here, Sam? He should be sittin' in Trudy's office by now."

I opened the door, gave Murray a dose of evil eye and motioned for him to come in.

That morning he wore his usual white shirt with the sleeves rolled up above his skinny elbows and the pair of eyeglasses he occasionally used. Maybe he thought the glasses made him look vulnerable, and we'd feel sorry for him, but I felt no compassion for him at all. He just annoyed the hell out of me. If someone gave him a bright green suit and funny little hat, Murray could have been mistaken for a slightly larger than normal leprechaun. I should have followed him one night to see if he stashed a pot of gold in the woods.

Before Ronnie started to speak, I took my turn with Murray. "Before the mayor has his conversation with you, Murray, I have something to say. It's very simple—I don't believe ninety-nine percent of what you've told me. And I'd love to know why you're lying."

He was about to say something, but I held up my hand for him to stop. I planned on taking one last shot at him. If I couldn't get the truth, I'd at least try and scare him half to death. Then I looked at Ronnie and knew I'd be shoveling sand against the tide.

"I don't want to hear it," I said. "You don't need to say anything. At this point, I won't believe you. But your fate isn't up to me. Look, you're a friendly guy. You do a pretty fair job here. Have a good life." When I finished, I sat on the burgundy leather couch and tried not to look too sullen.

Ronnie gestured for Murray to sit in one of the green chairs in front of his desk and then assumed his seat-of-power in the big swivel chair with the bay window behind him.

The mayor read Murray a mild form of the Riot Act. In the end, he demanded that Murray pay his taxes and obtain a driver's license before he drove a city vehicle again. Murray nodded in agreement to all the stipulations the mayor thought up. If Ronnie asked, Murray would have shined our shoes and sang, *Mammy*. It was all over in less than ten minutes—then life went on. For most of us.

* * * *

Saturday October 28th

An October weekend in the Smokies can be like rush hour on the Long Island Expressway. The cool pleasant temperatures and autumn colors in and around the Great Smoky Mountains National Park draw thousands of out-of-town tourists and an equal number of local day-trippers who drive the roads between Townsend, Gatlinburg and Cherokee, on the North Carolina side. One of the really beautiful drives available within the Park is around the eleven-mile road through Cades Cove. But the rangers take pity on early morning hikers and cyclists—they ban motorized traffic in the Cove from dawn until 10 a.m. on Saturdays. Impatient motorists begin queuing up in front of the loop road entrance long before nine o'clock. At 10:00 when a ranger swings open the snow gate blocking the single-track road, the crush of traffic resembles the commuter battle to get through the Queens Mid-Town Tunnel on a Monday morning at 8:30.

The weather that Saturday was exceptionally lovely. At 7:30 when Bitsey and I climbed the small hill behind our barn, the sky was a sea of Caribbean blue, the air smelled unmistakably like autumn, and the temperature only touched thirty-nine degrees. The predicted high that afternoon might reach the mid-sixties. It rained overnight, and the brief storm left the air clear and clean. It looked like a perfect day to put the top down and take the Healey for a drive. Only a tourist on a schedule or a local flatlander with similar time restraints would dare to tempt fate and their patience with the traffic in the national park. I decided a cruise over the Chilhowee Mountains on the Foothills Parkway and then taking back roads to the Fort Loudoun State Park in adjoining Monroe County would be scenic and painless.

Kate and I were ready to hit the road at 9:30. Bitsey promised to hold down the fort, but not before suggesting that I trade in the Healey for an MG-B with a terrier-sized carpeted jump seat.

We started east on US 321. Two miles down the road, I downshifted into third, listened to the Abarth exhausts gurgle and then accelerated quickly onto the entrance ramp of the Foothills Parkway. At the Yield sign, I stepped down on the gas pedal and charged up the hill with the revs climbing and the twin pipes growling. I intended not only to blow any carbon out of my engine, but also to blow out the cobwebs Murray McGuire had created within my head.

As the tachometer needle approached the red line, I heard, "Whoa, Parnelli, you blow up your baby on this road and it's a long walk home."

I had already crested the steepest portion of the first hill. The road leveled out a little, so I shifted up to fourth. The exhausts calmed down.

"You forget, my dear," I said, "the modern technology in my jacket pocket. I now possess the wonder of a cell phone. One call from the honcho of Prospect PD and all sorts of po-leece cars would come to our rescue."

"Aren't you just so clever?" she said.

We made a few stops at the overlook parking spots to admire the views and then twisted down the incline toward the shoreline of Chilhowee Lake.

Driving a vintage British sports car on a winding road, on a beautiful day, with a good-looking woman sitting in the shotgun seat felt like one of Life's great pleasures. The diminutive Celtic weasel who invaded my thoughts all week was nowhere to be found.

After crossing the causeway over Tellico Lake, we entered the town of Vonore and at the main traffic light, turned left again onto Miloqua— the Cherokee word for Great Island. One mile down the road, we turned for the last time into the long driveway of the Fort Loudoun State Historic Area.

I parked in the small lot close to the boat dock and the visitor's center, and we walked down the narrow blacktop path to the reconstructed 18th century British fort.

In a quarter mile, we entered the fort grounds through the sally port in the stockade wall. To our right sat the King George bastion and a stone-walled powder magazine. In front of us, we saw a recreation of Britain's western-most outpost during the French and Indian War of 1754 to 1763. The grounds sloped steeply toward the lakeshore. There were other buildings: soldier's barracks, officer's quarters, storehouses, a blacksmith's shop, and even a covered beehive oven. Outside the stockade stood a small representation of the Cherokee village of Tuskegee representing the Indian village that grew up around the fort. The fort would provide those Native Americans with the European trade goods they had grown dependent upon.

The lake surface hardly rippled. The water sparkled like a blue-green gemstone in the sunlight. The opposite shores were heavily wooded, and beyond the colorful trees stood the mountains we had just crossed.

The life of a British soldier in mid-eighteenth century America barely equaled the current existence of the residents in a modern shelter for the homeless. Nonetheless, one look at the scenery and the lake made me think this wasn't a bad a place for a young Redcoat to be stationed.

We walked through the fort, out the water gate, past the glacis with its fascines and locust thorn bushes, over the field and found two seats on a large outcropping of rock at the water's edge.

A small school of gar broke water not twenty feet from where we sat. The long, skinny fish rolled and squirmed on the surface, feeding on tiny baitfish. Someone, somewhere, had a wood fire burning. The fragrance added appropriateness to the setting.

For an hour, Kate and I sat there talking about nothing of much importance. After the fish left, I picked up a handful of pebbles and threw them, one at a time, into the lake to see the circles spread out on the mirror-like surface. All was quiet. Time stood still. It could have been 1758 or 1958—until a Jet Ski rider, wearing a full wetsuit, sped by at thirty miles an hour. The noise seemed louder than the Healey climbing a steep hill in second gear. The wake he created lapped on the shore. The rider waved. We waved back. I snarled and wanted to give him the finger.

"Welcome back to the twenty-first century," I said.

"What do you say, scout?" Kate said. "Let's head back, and I'll buy you lunch."

"Sounds mighty good, ma'am. I'm a'fixin' to git me some 'possum stew and a jar o' corn likker."

"Yum. Sounds tasty," Kate said.

As we retraced our steps, I looked over at Kate. She wore a snug-fitting, gold turtleneck sweater and tight, not snug, blue jeans. I thought she looked delicious. Her hair was perfect, and her face glowed in the brightness of the noon sky. If I were a casual observer, I would never imagine her to be sixty years old. If I were a kid with no morals, I would have whistled and shouted some sexually oriented remark in her direction. But I was a public servant again and had to keep my lecherous thoughts to myself. At least until we got home when I'd take my chances and see if I could get this mature but sexy lady into a compromising position.

We left the park, drove north on US 411 into Maryville, and back toward the mountains. At twenty after twelve, I pulled into the lot of Howell's Pub.

We chose a table next to the back wall. Groups of two and four people occupied the half-dozen other tables around the dining area. Conversations buzzed while a sports commentary show played on the large screen TV. The noise of other patrons talking while country music played in the pub area behind the rough-paneled wall where we sat added to the sounds of the busy restaurant. Howell Watkins, the owner, stopped to take our order, his pad and ballpoint pen held at the ready.

"Howdy, folks. How are we doin' today?" he asked. "Can I start you off with something to drink?"

I chose a pint of black and tan, and Kate wanted a diet Pepsi. When Howell returned with our drinks, we ordered lunch. She, the fried chicken tenders with potato salad and cole slaw while I couldn't resist another king-sized barbeque sandwich, this time on a fresh onion roll with cole slaw and baked beans on the side. Not exactly things you'd find on the Weight Watcher's menu, but it was a weekend so what the hell.

In twenty minutes, Howell, who wore a black T-shirt from Smoky Mountain Harley-Davidson, served our lunch. Katherine ate slowly, opting for the Emily Post approved method for finger foods, dipping her chicken strips into honey mustard dressing. I try to slow down, but often resemble a restrained cannibal when dealing with food, which requires no cutting. A few minutes into the meal and I was caught with my mouth full.

She walked briskly out of the barroom, the outfit she wore, a gray sweatshirt, tight washed-off jeans, and an orange UT baseball cap with her red ponytail poking out above the adjustable strap, looked much different from the L.L. Bean catalog selection I last saw her wearing at the bookstore. Bridget Dwyer looked to her right and stopped.

"Hello, Sam," she said.

"Hi, Bridget. I didn't know you were one of Howell's customers."

I set my sandwich aside and stood up.

"Oh, indeed, I am. I heard about the dart league and the Guinness on tap and couldn't resist. It's an Oirish thing, boyo." Without waiting for a proper introduction, she turned her eyes to Katherine. "Hello, I'm Bridget Dwyer."

"Where are my manners?" I said. "Bridget, this is Katherine, my wife. Kats, Bridget works with Derek and Eleanor at the bookshop."

"Hello, Bridget. Nice to meet you," Kate said, while placing a piece of fried chicken back into the basket in front of her. She wiped her fingers before shaking hands with Bridget.

"I knew Sam would have himself a pretty wife."

"Oh, thanks," Kate said. "It seems my husband surrounds himself with good-looking women."

Did I detect a slightly catty comment?

They both smiled.

"Sit down, Bridget," I said. "Would you like something?"

"No. Thank you, Sam. I've just eaten lunch, and I must be going. But I'll sit for a moment."

Katherine said, "I won't be silly and pretend you might be local. What part of Ireland do you come from?"

"I'm from Killarney. I understand you two have been there."

"Yes, I love Killarney," she said.

Funny, I remember her telling me she thought the town looked dirty.

Kate continued. "We took one of those wonderful jaunting carts for a ride through the national park. That was fun. And we loved the Ring of Kerry and the Dingle Peninsula. Such pretty country and the people were so friendly." Katherine beamed; she should be an ambassador.

"Yes, it's a grand country. I miss it," Bridget said. "And what did you like best in Ireland, Sam?"

"Smithwick's ale. And the girls are kind of cute."

"Oh, you're being silly now, aren't you? If you two are planning another visit, please stop in to the shop, and we'll talk. I can tell you about all the lovely things tourists never find."

"We'll do that," Kate told her.

"That would be just grand," Bridget said as she stood. "But I'm keeping you from your lunch, so I'll be off. Lovely meeting you, Katherine, and I'll see you, Sam—when Derek receives the book you ordered. Bye for now. Bye." And off she went.

"Sure'n she's a pretty one, isn't she...boyo?" Kate said, a little sarcastically.

"Yep," I said, with half a mouth full of barbeque. "Pretty girl."

"No, Sammy, she's more than pretty. She's bloody beautiful."

"Aye, good lookin' girl, so she is. But no better lookin' than yerself, darlin', thinks I."

Was Barry Fitzgerald sitting on my shoulder ready to rescue me when I needed him or what?

"You do a pretty good Irish accent for an old Scotsman. You really think I'm just as good-looking?"

"I certainly do. Ever since I was a kid I've had the hots for older women."

"You give new meaning to the word *smooth*."

I smiled and took a gulp of black and tan.

Before leaving, I dropped a few singles onto the table as a tip. With the check in hand, I turned to follow Katherine toward the cash register and bumped into a man just leaving the barroom.

"Oh, I'm terribly sorry," he said. "I should be more careful."

I thought I heard a Boston accent.

"No, my fault, I think. You okay?" We had a fairly robust collision.

"Yes, I'm fine. Again, forgive me. I'm sorry." He straightened his jacket and left.

The man looked to be about forty, five-foot-nine and in pretty good shape. He wore an expensive-looking gray herringbone jacket, light blue shirt and pleated khaki pants, a bit more upscale than Howell's usual customer. If he worked anywhere other than Maryville College, I'd have been surprised.

"I see we're not the only classy immigrants to hang out in Howell's," I said to Kate.

"Immigrants?" She shook her head.

In short order, I'd again meet the 'immigrant' I just tripped over.

Chapter Ten

Monday, October 30th

At 9:20, Stanley Rose stuck his head in my doorway and rapped his knuckles on the jamb.

"You got a minute, boss?" he asked, standing there in a sweatshirt, jeans and a warm-up jacket.

"Sure, come on in. Get some coffee, sit down and take your shoes off. Anything for you, rookie road sergeant."

He smiled. I waited. Stan sat in one of my guest chairs, stretched out, removed his Rams ball-cap and tossed it on the second chair. He looked like a high school coach on his weekend off.

"Does Roman Gabriel still play for the Rams?" I asked.

He shook his head.

"How about Roosevelt Grier?"

"Gimme a break."

"Are they still in Los Angeles?"

"Not since '94."

"You make me feel so old. Okay, what's up?"

"Bobby told me what Shields said about Murray. Unbelievable, huh?"

"Yeah. Is this any way to run an airline?"

He shrugged. "I'd sure like to know the real story someday."

"Me too, but we may never know," I said.

He nodded. "The reason I stopped in...I got a phone call over the weekend. Seems your televised promotion ceremony got picked up by the local station's national news network and was broadcast all over the place."

"And Hollywood wants you to be the next Denzel Washington? Don't quit yet. You can never believe a talent agent."

"Not quite. I got a call from the president of the National Guardians. You know, the headquarters of the black...uh, African-American police association. He'd like to come and meet me...and, uh, see you," he said.

"You think he's impressed that I promoted you and wants to make me an honorary brother? Or does he think you're an Uncle Tom and wants to smack you around a little?"

"You're not making this any easier. I want to ask you a favor."

"Ask away. But under the circumstances, shouldn't you call me Bwana?"

"You never let up, do you?"

"Okay, no more jokes. I'll be good. Pray continue."

"He'd like to go to lunch with us."

"Who pays?"

"Him, I guess. Jeez, he wouldn't ask you to pay."

"Good. I'd love to go to lunch. Just give me a time."

"Okay, thanks. Anyway, he's from New York. He says he knows you."

"Intimately or just one of my admirers? I was a pretty famous guy."

He rolled his eyes. "He knows you. Says you're friends. His name's Alonzo Crosby. He retired from your old job."

"Lon Crosby," I sighed. "Yeah, I know him. And that makes me ask, what's he want from you? Or me? Or us?"

Stanley frowned. "He didn't say exactly. Said he was impressed seeing a black man and a woman getting the first promotions in a small Southern department like this—only black man, only woman, first people to get made sergeants. I guess he wants to talk about that. Maybe ask me how I get along with the other guys. You know?"

"Look, I don't want to rain on your parade. And maybe I spoke too soon. I'm not sure you want me to interact with Lon Crosby."

"What's the problem?"

"It's a long story. You may not want to hear it, and it would depress me to tell you. Let's just leave it as I think Alonzo turned out to be a first-class back-stabber."

"Wow. I didn't know. He sounded like you two were old friends."

"We were friendly once, but that changed—because of his conduct."

"Okay, sorry about that. I guess I'll give him a call."

He retrieved his cap and stood up, looking like a little kid whose father forced him to give away his new puppy. Being a schlep sometimes, I felt sorry for him.

"Sit down," I said. "Would this meeting be something important to you?"

Stan sat again, this time leaning forward, dangling the ball cap from his finger.

"I don't know exactly. I guess so. It just seemed like an honor. He said we'd get our pictures in the national magazine. You know, you and me together. I thought it would be a nice thing for you, too."

Alonzo Crosby was one of the last people I ever wanted to see again. But I liked Stanley. He did a great job, and I relied on him to run the department at night.

I am getting so easy in my old age!

"Okay, Stan, I'll go to lunch with you guys. Pick some place nice. Knowing Lonnie, money is no object. I'll behave myself—don't worry. I hope this is something good for you. Maybe you'll get to be their poster boy. Make us honkies think all black men are big and good-looking like you. Well, maybe not. Some of us old-timers still remember Sammy Davis Jr."

"Thank you." He showed me a huge smile. "You really think you can behave yourself?"

"Uh-huh."

"How's Tuesday? Uh, tomorrow. He'd like to meet us here at eleven, talk for a while, then go to lunch, come back here and take a few pictures. And that's it."

"You already arranged things?"

"Uh-huh."

"The people in this department take me for granted."

"No, we don't. We love you like a father."

"I don't want Bettye to think of me as a father."

"You're bad."

"You want me to tell Crosby the guys call you Rosie?"

"Who told you that?"

"I have informants everywhere. Anyway, if he's going to take pictures, I'd better tell the mayor. I guess he'd like to meet Alonzo and get his photo-op, too."

"Oh, yeah. I never thought of him."

"That's why I get the big bucks, partner."

* * * *

Tuesday, October 31st

At exactly 11 a.m., Alonzo Crosby and his assistant, Robert Brame, walked through the front door of our headquarters. Alonzo retired as a detective from the same department on Long Island where I worked for twenty years. Brame left Baltimore City PD on a disability pension.

Bettye Lambert gave them a proper greeting and ushered them into my office where Stanley and I waited. For the occasion, Stan wore a dark gray suit. I wore the only suit I owned, a tan camel hair with a two-button jacket and flat front pants. A light blue shirt and plaid Black Watch tie completed my outfit.

Alonzo sported what I guessed to be a light gray Armani suit with a subtle blue pinstripe, a pearl gray silk shirt and a blue silk tie complimenting the pinstripe. On the hoof, his clothes may have cost as much as a two-week vacation in St. Tropez. Brame looked sharp in a black suit and starched white shirt.

Lonnie Crosby was two years younger than me. He stood three inches shorter than my six-feet, but outweighed me by fifteen pounds or so. He was a solid barrel-chested man who at best was a mediocre cop. Crosby's promotion to detective came because his mother once worked as the police commissioner's secretary, and his father was a state trooper with political clout in the New York Guardians Association.

"Well, well, well, Sam the man," Lonnie said. "How're you doin', LT?"

He extended his hand. I hesitated for a second, but shook it.

"Lonnie. I'm well, thanks. You're looking prosperous. You float a municipal bond to buy that suit?"

"Same old Sam Jenkins." He laughed to give his statement an air of familiarity. "Hello, Stanley." They shook hands. "You know, there were hundreds of people named Jenkins on Long Island—Sam was the only white one." He chuckled again at his witty recollection.

"Gentlemen, this is my personal assistant, Robert Brame. Robert was on the job in Baltimore. After he went out on three-quarters, he came to work with us."

"Hello, Robert," I said.

Stan, who was standing in front of my desk, smiled and shook hands with Brame.

"Hello, sir," he said to me and took a step closer. He and I shook hands, too.

After our round of manly greetings, Alonzo spoke first.

"It's been a long time, Sam," he said. "How long? Ten, fifteen years?"

"I've been out fourteen now. So, something close to fifteen, I'd say."

"Had some good times up there, didn't we?"

"Yeah, Lonnie, there were some good times. Some shitty times, too, but that's life."

My remark seemed to go by the wayside.

"I was surprised to see you when the footage of Stan's promotion aired," Lonnie said. "You still look pretty sharp in uniform, probably haven't gained a pound. I never thought I'd see you in police work again."

"Yeah, me, too. I was sort of fed up with the job when I left. And I sure never thought I'd be back in the bag." I used a New York cop's slang for being in uniform. "Sit down, guys. Anyone want coffee?"

I saw three sitters, but no coffee drinkers.

"So what's up, Lonnie," I asked. "You went from county Guardians' president to retired cop to national president?"

"That's about it. I live in D.C. now. Do a lot of lobbying, a lot of political work."

"Uh-huh. Good for you."

"Same old Sam. A man of few words. Except when you get him talking about the Army. Man's got some war stories. Funny as hell and some of 'em probably true." More laughs.

"So, Robert," I said, "how long were you on the job in Baltimore?

What did you do?"

"Ten years, sir. I worked patrol the whole time."

"I'm sorry to hear about having to go out on three-quarters. What happened?"

"Writing a ticket one night, I got hit broadside by a DUI. Spent almost a month in the hospital before I could get around on my own. Another year of therapy and I had to fight in court to get disability. I get around okay, but every time it gets cold and damp, I feel like a hundred-year-old man."

"Sorry to hear that," I said. "I don't know how many times I've seen guys who were legitimately injured on the job get grief over line-of-duty disability." Everyone nodded. I touched a sore subject with cops. "And then some of those slick malingerers with expensive lawyers claim whiplash from a fender bender and get it approved one, two, three. It's a real shame."

"Yes, sir, I hear that," Brame said.

After a short lull in the conversation I said, "Okay, Lonnie, what's next?"

"You up for a formal interview, tape recorder and all?"

"Sure, why not? This for your national publication?"

"It is."

"You gonna send me a copy?"

"Of course. I'll even spell your name right."

"Okay, shoot—so to speak."

He took a small recorder from his breast pocket, set it on my desk and clicked the record button.

"How did Stanley come to be promoted?" he asked.

"That deserves a complicated answer, so hang in here with me."

Lonnie nodded, acting like a network reporter listening to a big story. I sat back and presented my documentary.

"I'm sure from visiting various small departments all over the country, you must know that very few places have the formal method of selection and promotion we had thanks to the New York State Civil Service Law."

He nodded again. Stan and Robert listened patiently.

"Here," I said, "we have none of that—at present. But I do have the authority to change it a bit, locally."

I got nods from my three companions.

"So, you ask, how did I choose my two new sergeants? Simple, I made a list of the twelve POs on board and threw two darts."

I got three wide-eyed stares.

"Just kidding. Actually, I took a page from the old method of selecting officers in the colonial militias. I asked everyone here who they thought would do the best job. I coupled the opinions of the other cops with what I've seen over the last few months."

I paused for a moment and sat forward.

"Look, if I'm going to be doing all the talking, I need a coffee." I stood up. "Anybody want a cup?" Again, I saw no takers.

I poured a cup, sat down, shifted to get comfortable and began again. "Let's talk about Bettye Lambert first. Not a potential Guardian member, but very important nonetheless. When I met my predecessor, not exactly a rocket scientist among policemen, he said, 'This little lady just about runs the department.' He was correct. Administratively, Bettye is a crackerjack. No one could ask for a better admin sergeant. She was number one on the list.

From the lobby, I heard the radio crackle. Car 506, Vernon Hobbs, called in a patrol pick-up of first aid case. Vern said, "Got me an idgit mowin' the lawn in shar shoes. Cut his got-damn big toe off. Git me clearance to BMH. I'll transport him an' his wife."

Bettye acknowledged the call. We all looked at each other and smiled at Vern's lack of radio diplomacy.

With their attention back on me, I continued. "Number two would be the road honcho, someone content with straight four-to-twelves, someone to act as the nighttime chief. So, potentially, this road supervisor had to either know all the answers or know where to look for them."

Lonnie nodded, making it look like he agreed with my logic.

"Stanley came here from LAPD, already a good cop. And it's not possible to work for almost four years in a place like this and not learn something about the local ways. I learned that, prior to my time here, Stan became the informal leader of the street cops. I believe the past chief offered little in the way of leadership. So, Stan filled in by necessity. His prior experience helped the other cops deal with incidents they may never have encountered before. Stan was able to assist the other men—train them, if you will—in solving their professional problems or just answering their questions. I figured if he was already doing the job, why not give him the stripes?"

Lonnie nodded again. Robert smiled, looking proud of his new friend, Stanley. Stan sat there, impassively, not even trying to look shy. Stan is a pretty straightforward guy. I do enough acting for the both of us.

"Also, why not make use of the halo effect?" I said. "He's a big, impressive-looking man. You gonna smart-mouth him, Lonnie?"

Alonzo smiled and shook his head.

"Of course not, nor would I. And none of the others will either. It's good to couple respect with an abject fear of getting your ass whipped—you can't miss. He's a natural.

"Voila, the decision came easily. Bettye's the administrative whiz. She'd be the desk sergeant. Stan's the smart, tough street-cop. He'd be the road sergeant."

"And your desk sergeant's pretty good-lookin', too." Lonnie interrupted me and snickered.

"Don't be getting fresh with her, son. Husband's a contract killer for the hillbilly mafia, and she shoots better than me," I said.

"Now I know that's a damn lie," Lonnie said. "Nobody shoots better than you." Then turning to Rose and Brame, he continued, "I shot next to him at the range one year. Easiest target I ever had to score—all in the black. Not just the big black section—all in the damn ten ring. I didn't have to count anything. And since he's so uptight and white, I knew he wouldn't lie. I just asked him if he got all his rounds off and wrote 300 on the target. Good man to be with in a firefight. Right, Sam?"

"Well, perhaps my former colleague exaggerates a little," I said. "I probably missed a few Xs." It's polite to act modest after someone tells you you're so damn good.

"Back to the two new sergeants," I said. "I'm sixty years old. I've got a five-year contract here in Prospect. At sixty-five, I may be too damn old to keep working. Who knows? Personally, I can't see any reason why either Bettye or Stan shouldn't be chosen as my successor. I intend to give a promotional test if and when I decide to pull the pin. The choice won't be mine, but I do plan on writing an evaluation of each supervisor and giving that plus the test results to the mayor."

"You could do that?" Lonnie asked.

"The mayor's always up for a good idea," I said. "So, I would say to you now, Sergeant Rose, get yourself a copy of O.W. Wilson's *Police Administration* and a good set of law books and do some light reading. Mr. Crosby here can tell you that as a former lecturer at the Police Academy, I write a mean multiple-choice test." I turned to Lonnie and asked, "Does that satisfy you, sir?"

"I guess it does. You have anything more to ask, Robert?" He looked at me and then at Brame.

"No, I sure don't. Like you said, Chief, that was a complicated answer."

"Good, glad to hear that. Now, Alonzo, shut off your tape recorder. Gentlemen, it's after noon, and another thing Mr. Crosby will tell you from our past association is that lunch is an important part of my day. Where are we eatin', Stanley?"

"I made reservations at Milton's Paradise Found for one o'clock. Okay with you, boss?"

"Terrific. Good char-broiled food with religious overtones. Fill my tummy and save my soul all at the same time. Am I correct in thinking that after the recent county referendum, Johnny now serves some sacramental wine or other spirits with his parochial grub?"

"What the hell is he talking about?" Lonnie asked.

"I'm sure he'll tell you all about it," Rose said.

* * * *

Johnny and Nyana Milton owned the Paradise Found Steak House in Prospect. I always thought they should have added "and Discount House of Worship" to the name of the business. Johnny, a personable and conscientious restaurateur, offered good food, but couldn't resist his religious upbringing by filling the dining room with old-time instrumental favorites like *Onward Christian Soldiers, The Old Rugged Cross* and *Rock of Ages*. If you were an ungodly, borderline atheist like me, you could enjoy the Musak strictly for the classical sounds. But majestic landscape posters hung on the walls, featuring quotes from the scriptures superimposed on a cloud or spot of clear blue heaven to consider, too. Fortunately, my philosophy of live and let live kept me in a good mood each time I ate there.

Bottom line—Stanley made a good choice of restaurants. And since Blount County no longer occupied a spot on the list of "dry" places in Tennessee, there would be a good choice of wine, beer and other assorted hooch to sample while we waited for a table. Even before I looked at a menu, I knew I wanted the grilled tuna steak, Nyana's spinach casserole and a rice pilaf. Police work can be good—if you eat well.

* * * *

I had just ordered my second mug of Killian's Red draught when the salads came to the table. While many modern restaurants rely on bottled dressings, that was not the case at Paradise Found. Their chef created a half-dozen homemade specials. I chose his parmagiana peppercorn.

Just before I got the first forkful of greens to my mouth, the Musak began playing *We Shall Gather by the River*, a little louder than the previous selections.

Lonnie asked, "What the hell is that?"

"What's what?" Robert said.

"The music. It sounds like we're in church."

After twenty ounces of beer, my ill feelings toward Alonzo began to fade. I thought his observation deserved a humorous comment.

I admit, over the years I've enjoyed trying to imitate famous people. Sometimes they come out pretty good—sometimes not. Lonnie's question reminded me of one of my favorite actors. I doubt there are many comedians who imitate Lawanda Page, the inimitable Aunt Esther from *Sanford and Son,* but I thought she should offer an opinion.

I looked at Lonnie and said, "F'ed Sanford, you a heathen fool! You a blasphemous old dog, destined for hell. Take him with you, Satan. He's one o' your own! Praise the Lord!" Then looking at Stanley, I said, "Lamont, take me home!"

Stanley gave me a look like I just wet my pants in public.

Lonnie looked at the others and laughed, "He used to do that all the time. He's pretty good at impressions, just like Little Richard."

I rolled my eyes. "That's Rich Little, genius."

"Oh yeah. Rich Little."

* * * *

After lunch, we stopped in the mayor's office for him to meet our visitors and get his picture taken. Twenty minutes later, we were back at the PD, again sitting in my office, each of us with a mug full of Yirgacheffe—direct from an Ethiopian coffee plantation probably in business since the British colonial days.

"You mind if I speak with your other cops about what they think of their new road sergeant?" Lonnie asked.

"I've got no problem with that. How are you going to do it?"

"I thought you could help me with that."

"Yeah, I can." I thought for a moment. "Why don't you see how they work with Stanley, instead of interviewing them? If you just ask, everyone will just tell you he's the best thing since 3-D and the hula hoop. What cop, especially in a department this size, would bad-mouth a co-worker to a stranger? So, go and take a look, see how he does on the road."

Lonnie sat there nodding. Stanley seemed to have no problem with my suggestion.

"Tennessee encourages a thing they call 'ride along'," I said. "Personally, I can't understand why. Who wants a bunch of civilians riding around in police cars? But in this situation, it makes sense. Sign a release absolving Prospect PD of any liability in case of an accident or incident, and you ride shotgun for a tour with Stan. I'll work a night shift, too, and Robert can ride with me if he wants."

"I've got to sign a release?" He sounded surprised.

"Of course you do. If you get shot, your wife will sue me for the hole in your suit jacket. If I lose in court and have to pay, that would screw up my budget for two years."

He smiled, taking my remark as a compliment.

"Okay, I like it," he said. "We've got to be in Nashville on Wednesday and part of Thursday. We'll be talking with some Guardian members there. We could be back here and work a four-to-twelve tour.

How about Friday?"

"That's fine. I'll arrange for us to chase some moonshiners and maybe even find a missing bloodhound. Sound exciting to you?"

"Okay, I'm ready," he said.

"All right. See you guys Friday. Wear four-to-twelve detective clothes."

Chapter Eleven

Wednesday, November 1st

My desk phone rang.

"Hello, Sam?"

I recognized the British accent. "Yes."

"This is Derek, Sam. I've got your book in."

"Hello, Derek. How's everything?"

"Oh, just fine, thank you. Thank you very much. Are you well?"

"As we say in the hills, I'm jest fair ta middlin'. Thanks for finding the book. I'll try to get to the shop either today or tomorrow and settle up with you. That okay?"

"Yes, of course, that shall be fine. If I'm not here, the book is in the glass case behind the cash box."

"I'll be there."

"Thanks, Sam. Bye." Then as an afterthought he added, "By the way, Sam, you really don't sound like a hillbilly."

"Gee, and I thought I was getting the local accent down pat. Good bye, Derek."

That started Wednesday morning.

The remainder of the day got a little busy. Nothing heavy, just a lot of phone calls and a few people requesting to be fingerprinted for their new concealed carry pistol permits. The state of Tennessee determined we should keep the public armed and dangerous.

* * * *

Thursday, November 2nd

On Thursday at lunchtime, I drove down Main Street to the Fox and Quill, swung the Ford into the parking lot and noticed Derek's XJS wasn't there. I chose the space next to a white Chevy Cobalt. Being a big-time investigator, always on the lookout for clues, I glanced at the rear bumper of the Cobalt and noticed a square sticker with a green lower-case "e", something used by Enterprise Rent-A-Car for rentals and lease vehicles. Actually, I bent over to tie my shoe and on the way up, looked at the bumper. Out of danger from tripping on my laces, I trudged up the three steps, opened the front door of the shop and walked in.

No Derek, no Eleanor. No anyone else as far as I could see.

"Hello? Anyone here?"

Bridget looked out from behind the last row of bookshelves.

"Oh, saints preserve us. You scared the life out of me, Sam Jenkins." She placed a stack of four books on the floor and walked the short distance to where I stood.

"I'm sorry to startle you," I said. "You must be very diligent to be so engrossed in your work."

"Actually, I was singing to myself," she said. "It helps pass the time."

"I'd like to hear you. I'll bet you sound like Enya."

"Now who's full of blarney? I think I sound rather professional though, but not like Enya, more like Joe Cocker. He's Irish, you know."

"That's hard to believe. That you sound like Joe Cocker, that is. And you even know him. I think he was before your time."

"Joe and I aren't on speaking terms, but I do remember hearing him on the oldies station from Cork."

"Now you're making me feel ancient again."

"Oh, stop, Mr. Jenkins, you're only as old as you feel. You seem pretty chipper to me. Now, sir, what can I do for you today?"

"Derek called and said my book came in."

"Oh yes, I remember seeing it. I thumbed through it, actually. It's about your Revolution, isn't it?"

"Yes, it is. It's a compilation of diaries and letters written by the soldiers who marched with Benedict Arnold from southern Maine all the way up to Canada in 1775. I think it would be a hit in Ireland. They intended to fight the British."

"Maybe so. Those Brits aren't too popular in my country."

"Their loss."

"Now what are you wanting that book for? Isn't Benedict Arnold your most famous traitor?"

"It's all interesting stuff, hearing what the actual soldiers from the period had to say. And yes, Arnold is most famous for collaborating with the British. He conspired to turn West Point over to General Clinton. And he helped them almost capture George Washington."

Bridget stood there smiling, fluttering the lashes over her shamrock-colored eyes. "Did he now?"

"Yes, but no matter how bad a decision Arnold made, he did have justification for being disgruntled. He was always at odds with the Continental Congress. I think Arnold was arguably the most capable commander in the Continental Army up to that point. Amongst a bunch of amateurs, he looked like something of a super-soldier."

Her smile got even bigger. I grinned myself and felt a little foolish.

"I guess I started giving a lecture, didn't I? Sorry. Anyway, I like the way Kenneth Roberts writes. And Arnold's life is interesting. Nobody likes a traitor, but he's a favorite character of mine, turncoat or not."

"You're right about no one liking a traitor. And Ireland has had its share. But I suppose if you admire Arnold's soldier skills..."

Bridget walked behind the cash register counter and opened a glass-fronted cabinet to get the book. She wore a purple Henley shirt with the sleeves pushed up on her forearms, snug-fitting gray slacks and a pair of penny loafers. The girl had a great figure—hard to believe she could put down many pints of Guinness and keep a shape like hers.

"You're a pretty smart guy—for a copper," she said with a little laugh. "And I like to hear you speak. No 'you alls' or 'do whats' as the local men say."

"Someday I'll do my Brooklyn accent for you. I can sound just like Tony Danza."

"Well, I don't know this Tony Danza, but if you take me for a ride in that fancy sports car of yours, you can talk to me any way you'd like, Sam."

Uh-oh!

I could almost hear my eyes click open with surprise and couldn't think of anything clever to say, so I invoked my right to remain silent and probably looked like the village idiot just standing there.

Bridget, on the other hand, never seemed at a loss for words. "You show me your sports car, and I'll show you the lovely little log cabin I'm renting. It's quite new and beautiful in a rustic sort of way. From the back porch, there's a grand view of the hills. Just like the Sperrin Mountains back home."

She stepped a little closer and stood there looking into my eyes. A faint smell of perfume drifted toward me.

"I thought you said you've never been north of Connemarra?" I knew the Sperrins were in Northern Ireland.

"Oh, shoo with you, Sam, a figure of speech, nothing more. Like you Yanks would say, 'The Rockies' when you speak of mountains out west. Forget about the mountains, Sam. I've got a brand new bottle of Jameson's and my very own hot tub. We could have a drink or two, get wet and see how passionate a handsome Scotsman and an Irish lass can get."

Quite an offer for an old man to consider.

"Bridget, you sound serious. Have you looked recently? I'm old enough to be your father."

"My father, rest his soul, would be younger I think, was he alive. Yes, boyo, I'm serious. I don't care how old you are. You're a big good-looking man who treats a lady like she's a princess. Of course I'm serious."

"That's the most flattering thing I've heard in a long time. But I have a wife, Bitsey's mother. You met her. She's a great girl—most generous, but I doubt she'd go for sharing her husband."

"I'm not asking you to marry me, Sam. I'm lonely, I like you, and I think you like me. I just want you to give me a damn good shagging, that's all."

"Wow. Three cheers for you liberated women. Bridget, I mean it, this is most flattering, but I've been married for a long time."

"No reason for her to know. Would you be telling her?"

"Probably not, but I'd know. I love her, and I like the idea of her loving me."

I felt the need to explain more.

"The older I get the more self-image means to me. Having a romantic time with another woman would be a breach of loyalty, and I'd like Kate to think I'm a loyal, trustworthy guy. I'd be upset if she didn't."

"Oh, Sam, there'd be no strings attached."

"I'll bet making love with you would be something to remember, but at my age the stress may be catastrophic. What would you do with a hundred-and-eighty-pound corpse on your hands?"

She laughed again. "No girl has ever heard a more elegant refusal. Your wife is a lucky woman, boyo." She went up on her toes and kissed my cheek.

"Yes, ma'am. Well, I guess I should take my book and go."

"If you change your mind, Sam, you know where to find me."

"Is it getting hot in here, or is it just me?" I asked.

"Oh, here's your book, and be off with you, now. You settle up with Derek when next you see him. And, Sam, you're a good man. Don't forget I said so."

"No, I certainly won't forget—any of this."

I wondered if I could make it back to my car without tripping and looking even more foolish.

"Take care, Bridget."

Jenkins, how do you get yourself into these situations?

* * * *

The damp chilly air made it a night for a wee dram of Laphroaig, my favorite peat-flavored, single-malt cool-weather Scotch. Katherine drank Shiraz from a round, footed glass. Bitsey was on the wagon.

"I picked up my new book today," I said.

"Good, reading will keep you out of trouble for awhile."

"Trouble is my middle name, sweetheart." I used my Humphrey Bogart voice.

"Your middle name is Edward, dear."

I ignored her snide remark and, for some idiotic reason, told her about my last visit to the bookshop.

"Bridget, the Irish girl at the bookshop, told me if I took her for a ride in the Healey, she'd invite me to use the hot tub at the cabin she's renting. How about that?"

"Was she serious?"

"You betcha. My boyish smile, winning personality and Gaelic ancestry made the woman fall head-over-heels in love with me. With that car, I'm cooler than Rod Stewart, and I have a better haircut."

"Uh-huh, but you're sure she was serious?"

Kate didn't seem angry, but she looked like she had something on her mind.

"She said so, but I hope not. I'll be embarrassed when I go into the store again."

"When was the last time you were embarrassed, sweetie?"

"1969. I screamed when I got two gamma globulin shots on my way overseas."

She smiled, shook her head and sipped a little of her Shiraz.

"Heaven knows, Sammy, I'd never say you're not attractive to the ladies, and I've been in love with you for years, but you may wonder if she just wanted a romantic friend, or she's looking for something from the local police chief."

* * * *

Friday, November 3rd

The day tour proved uneventful. Anticipating I'd work until at least midnight, I decided to take a long lunch. I picked Kate up at home and treated her to a meal at The Cholon Garden. I ordered a bottle of Tsing Tsao beer, while Kate drank hot tea. We both started with the Tom Yum Gai soup. I asked for the red curry shrimp, and she chose Evil Jungle Prince with chicken as our entrees. Kate's meal had a great name, but it wasn't spicy enough for me.

"I met the evil jungle prince in Bangkok years ago," I said.

"You might be mistaken, sweetie." Kate loves to rain on my parade.

"My life was like an episode of *Terry and the Pirates* back in the '60s."

"Of course it was, dear."

The staff at the restaurant liked me because I left big tips and spoke to them in pidgin Vietnamese. *I should be an ambassador.*

At 2:30, I walked back into the PD, settled into my office and read over and initialed a stack of reports. At four o'clock, I told Bettye to leave early. I'd answer the phones and dispatch the cars until 5:00 when I switched communications over to the county dispatcher.

Stan Rose, Lon Crosby and Robert Brame wandered in around 3:30 and hung around the office. Lonnie dressed in a gray turtleneck, stonewashed Levis and a black leather jacket that may have cost more than a truckload of French truffles. Robert looked more conservative in a windbreaker, plaid shirt and jeans. I sat at Bettye's desk remembering why I was pissed off at Lonnie—for the last fifteen years.

"Hey, Stan," I called out. "Robert and I will stay around here until five. Why don't you and Lonnie hit the bricks? We'll catch up with you sometime later. Figure out where Lonnie's buying dinner tonight. Tell him to pick someplace nice."

"10-4, boss," Stanley said.

"She-itt," was Lonnie's contribution to the conversation.

Between four and five on a November Friday evening doesn't qualify as Prospect's busiest time. A minor motor vehicle accident—called a wreck in Tennessee—occurred in PO Will Sparks's sector. He handled it unassisted. Everything else remained quiet.

At quarter-to-five, Robert Brame dropped into the chair next to Bettye's desk.

"Chief, mind if I ask you a personal question?"

"Sure you can, Robert. But I'm not much on formalities. Call me Sam. That's more comfortable for me."

"Okay. I've noticed…uh…" He hesitated.

"Just say it."

"Why have you been so…cool towards Lonnie? Is there a problem?"

"You're right. I am a little pissed off at Alonzo. And have been for a long time. I guess it shows, huh?"

He nodded.

"Lonnie and I used to be pretty good friends," I said. "He worked out of the office next to mine, and I knew his mom and dad before I knew him."

"When he made detective and showed up in the office next door," I said, "we got to know each other. We had a common thread as scuba divers in the military, he in the Navy and me in the Army. We used to tell each other war stories, shoot the breeze and look at old snapshots. He was great for pictures. I think he used to take a roll of film every time he and the other guys in his SEAL unit, they called them IUWGs back then...Inshore Undersea Warfare Groups, that is...went on some operation or just had a barbeque. I wasn't much of a photographer myself. We got along quite well."

"But not now?" Robert asked.

"Then a problem developed. But I'd prefer Lonnie tell you about that or at least have him present if we talked about it—give him a chance to swing back if he thinks he needs to. I will tell you this—he really disappointed me. I wish the incident never happened, but it did. And that's the end of my story, partner."

* * * *

Robert and I closed up shop and hit the road by 5:15. I gave him a grand tour of the district, and we listened to the radio calls dispatched to the cars. At 6:30, we met Stanley and Lonnie for dinner. Lonnie, the big sport with the expense account, sprung for sandwiches at Quizno's. I would have been more generous.

As we stood in the parking lot of the sandwich shop, Lonnie asked, "Hey, Loo, mind if I drive with you for a couple hours?"

"I haven't been a lieutenant for a long time, Lonnie, but sure, jump in, and I'll show you the parts of Prospect no tourist ever sees."

The dark overcast sky hid all but a sliver of moon, projecting only a faint glow from behind the low cloud cover. A blanket of dampness chilled the air and prompted me to turn on the car's heater.

"We used to be pretty good friends, Sam," Lonnie said.

"Yeah, we were."

"You seem a little stand-offish, a little cool towards me. There a problem?"

"Yes, sir, there sure is."

"You still pissed off over that complaint I made fifteen years ago?" He sounded surprised.

"Lonnie, your complaint stemmed from two of my guys doing their job, investigating a black civilian worker. The woman sold information to shitheads to support her drug use and alcoholism. She compromised numerous search warrants and who knows what else. Your complaint was unfounded and goddamned malicious."

"Sorry you feel like that, but…"

"*But* my ass. You were the new president of the county Guardians, and you chose to attack two good cops—and me—your friend, as racists."

"There was nothin' personal, Sam."

"Bullshit. If you had talked with me first, I would have explained, within the boundaries where I could go, that you would have been better off leaving it alone. I thought you would have trusted me. Instead, you chose to pick up that...bitch from Community Services you elected as a first vice president and go directly to the commissioner." I glanced over at him as I drove. He seemed content to hear me out.

"I can't answer for how the two other guys felt, Lonnie, but I got pretty damn pissed off. I still am. You knew better. Generally speaking, I don't see what color you are. I don't care who you are. I just give you a fair shake and let the chips fall where they may." A serious case of anger began taking hold of me.

"It had to be done, Sam. You got to understand. It was nothing personal. I knew Valerie could be nasty. Yeah, she was a bitch. But she was committed to our people. We had to start somewhere, protecting the black workers in the PD."

"Go, Martin Luther Crosby."

"Come on, man, I had to make the commissioner know we were a new group in the Guardians, not the same old club where we got together and ate watermelon and drank Ripple."

"And you thought throwing your buddy and two good cops to the wolves was the way to start?" I asked.

"Had to start somewhere."

"Yeah? Balls! Well, good for you. Then I'm not at all sorry we could stick the whole thing up your asses. It goes to show you keeping your ducks in a row is the only way. You remember the employee in question was convicted of several felonies, do you not?"

"Yeah, I remember."

"She went to trial and never entertained the usual plea bargain offer. She thought she'd get off by claiming prejudice. She thought the DA would just offer a dismissal because he wouldn't want any bad publicity. Well, ex-Detective Crosby, I didn't find her guilty...a jury did. And there were five black people on that jury."

"Yeah, I remember."

"Lonnie, what you did was wrong. I can get beyond that. But you did it to me. Do you think I told those detectives to focus on her because she was black?"

"No."

"They went after her because she was obviously dirty. She was the best and only suspect we had. And we proved her guilty. Do you believe I was or am now a racist?"

"No, I don't. And I didn't then either."

"Well, thank you for that. And fuck you, too."

"I guess I deserved that."

"You deserve a night stick wrapped around your ears."

A moment passed quietly.

"We still friends?" he asked.

"Shit. You're an asshole. You're incorrigible, and you dress funny. Who in their right mind would want you for a friend?"

"What the hell you mean I dress funny?"

I laughed. "Okay, you've got nice clothes. You want a beer?"

"You drink on duty?"

"Duty hours never stopped you from drinking back when you got paid to be a cop."

"No, you're right about that."

"Well then?"

"Okay."

"You want a mainstream beer or some of that malt liquor crap?"

"Ain't nobody drinks malt liquor but derelicts."

"I saw you buy a Colt .45 once."

He laughed.

"Come on then," I said. "I'll buy. There's a Git n' Go Market close by with a marvelous selection."

"Git n' Go? You really turned into a hillbilly didn't you?"

"You ain't jest whistlin' Dixie, partner."

* * * *

The tour turned out to be fairly busy. Full of typically unimportant Friday night busy-work calls. A couple of domestic disturbances, a motor vehicle accident, a bicycle stolen from a shopping area, the return of a supposedly stolen car and a group of unruly, underage drinkers parked behind a strip mall. The latter, expertly cleared up by Sergeant Rose who, to get the group's attention, grabbed the biggest and loudest offender by the throat and belt buckle, picked him up and slammed him down on the hood of his car. The cars were then locked, and those under the influence of alcohol began their long walks home. Stan resolved the situation quickly and easily. Some supervisors may have gotten nervous at his methods, but I was not like most supervisors.

When James Agee wrote *A Death in the Family* and said, 'You can never go home again,' he obviously didn't know a former street cop getting a second chance after a long absence.

* * * *

At quarter-to-twelve, Stan Rose requested car-to-car communications with me. I switched my radio to Frequency 2.

"Sam, come north on Main Street to the Crystal Creek Bridge. You gotta see this."

"You want to tell me on the radio what you've got?"

"Yeah, why not? In a while we'll have a mob of people crawling all around here—we've got a body in the creek."

"We're less than five minutes away."

With Lonnie in the car, I pulled up to the bridge and parked on the shoulder of the road, opposite Stan's white and blue marked cruiser. He and Robert Brame stood waiting on the roadside. The flashing blue and red lights of Stan's car colored them and everything else close by. I zipped my jacket to keep out the chill.

"A man walking his dog found a body," Stan said. "He was just coming up to the road from the creek bed when we drove by. The old guy saw us and started going nuts, waving his arms, shouting. He's in my car with his little dog—he's really shaken up."

92

"How old is old?" I asked.

"Early sixties, I guess. He lives on one of the side streets off Main below the bridge."

"Early sixties is old?"

Stanley grinned.

"Up yours," I said. "Is this *old* man so shaken up that he needs medical attention?"

"No, he's okay. But, Sam, the body—it's Murray."

"Murray? As in Typewriter Murray?"

"Yeah."

Lonnie ran into the darkness and along the cliff above the creek for fifty feet, a reasonable distance from the body, and scrambled down the eight-foot embankment carrying my four-cell flashlight. He carefully picked his way over the rocks back toward the bridge, knelt next to the body and felt for a pulse on the neck.

"I think Stan's already done that, Lonnie. Come on back up—don't be screwing up my crime scene."

"I know what to do at a crime scene, Sam. Come look at the body. He's not just dead. He was executed."

Chapter Twelve

I stood on the top of the embankment looking down at Lonnie. The bright beam of the flashlight illuminated a spot in front of him. Little Murray McGuire lay more than half-covered by water.

"Okay, Lonnie, but come back up here. The DA's a little funny in this county. He won't fly you back first-class to explain why you recovered something I admitted into evidence."

I half stepped and half slid down the steep creek bank and carefully walked up to where Murray McGuire's body lay face down in the shallow, babbling water. Only a few blocks from his home, the long-time city employee, who we learned to be something of a mystery, had been shot four times, once in each knee, once in the right shoulder, and once in the temple just over the right ear. I saw only one exit wound above his left knee, where the round wasn't centered, and encountered little resistance from bone. The wounds could have been made by low-velocity hollow point bullets, something efficient when fired from a short-barreled handgun. The hole, clearly visible in his temple, looked like a .38 caliber, 9MM or.380 automatic. The medical examiner would have to sort that out. Lonnie and I crawled back up the embankment.

"You call anyone yet? I asked Rose.

"No. What do you want to do?"

"I've got nothing special going on next week," I said. "How about you? Want to do this one with me? We still don't know who the hell he really is, but he's one of ours, so to speak."

"Sure, let's keep it in house," he said.

"Yeah, I'm still not sure how good these county dicks are, and I guess I've sort of got this thing under control."

"Do you really?" He grinned.

"Okay, smart-ass, I'll give the dispatcher the laundry list. Give me a minute and then call one of the cars to get coffee. We're gonna be here a while."

I keyed the mike on the portable radio I held. "Prospect One to dispatch."

"Go ahead, Prospect One."

"We've got an apparent 10-5, upper Main Street at the Crystal Creek Bridge. I need a county crime scene unit and the ME's wagon. We'll handle the rest."

"10-4, Prospect One, ETA should be directly. They got nothin' workin' at present."

"10-4, dispatch, thanks. Put Unit 535 out of service with me. We'll also utilize one or two additional units here. He or one of those officers will advise."

"10-4." The dispatcher signed off.

Fifteen minutes later, a white Ford Expedition marked with county sheriff's logos pulled up with its blue dome lights flashing. Jackie Shuman was the duty crime scene investigator.

"Hey, boss-man." He walked over to shake hands. A second deputy walked next to him. Both wore black nylon windbreakers with Blount County patches and embroidered badges, black tactical trousers, things that look like the old military jungle pants and white turtlenecks with BCSO embroidered on the rolled collars. Their pants were bloused at the cuffs, over black nylon-sided boots. All very paramilitary looking.

"Hi ya, Jackie," I said. "You've got a partner, I see."

Shuman was in his early-thirties, but looked younger.

"What I got is an apprentice, thank you. You're lookin' at the new *senior* crime scene investigator in the county, as of yesterday," he said.

"Sounds good. You get a raise?"

"Hell no, just means the last senior man got him a better payin' job with the railroad po-leece and left me his spot. This here's David Sparks."

David and I shook hands.

"Hi, I'm Sam Jenkins. You any relation to our guy, Will Sparks?"

"Yes, sir, we's kin somehow." He spoke with the soft accent of the mountain folk. "Cousins, I s'pose."

"Will's working tonight. Maybe you can catch him before he goes home and have a family reunion. Gents, you probably know Sergeant Stanley Rose."

Both deputies nodded and shook hands with Stan. I pointed to Lonnie and Robert.

"These two men are retired police officers who came for a ride-along and got more excitement than we have on a typical Friday night—Lon Crosby and Robert Brame."

They also engaged in the obligatory police greetings.

"Jack, the body's in the creek," I said. "Must have been a quick dump-job after he got killed elsewhere. There's not much blood. Could have bled out into the water, but I'm thinking the four shots weren't fired here. I guess the killer took advantage of this being a nice dark spot. We need a real good job with this one. Looks like a professional-style hit rather than just a killing, as ex-Detective Crosby so ably pointed out."

"They's all good jobs from me, Chief. One size fits all. If Jackie don't find it, it ain't a clue." He smiled and ran a hand through his short dark hair.

Modesty is good in a policeman.

"Okay, while you and David do your thing, we'll keep traffic moving. Another car's coming to handle that. Someone will be picking up coffee, too. You want anything?"

"Naw, I'm good," Jackie said.

"Yes, sir, bottle o' Dr. Pepper for me, please," David said.

Stan made the appropriate notation to our gopher list while I took a statement from the *old* man with the dog. His story was short and simple. While out on their nightly constitutional, his dog found the body.

In a few minutes, Vernon Hobbs, our senior patrolman at Prospect PD, arrived ready to assist with traffic control. We arranged the police vehicles so cars could pass freely with only minor rubbernecking.

It's difficult not to draw some interested stares at a big nighttime crime scene, but we tried to keep it to a minimum. We left four conspicuous police cars parked close together, one uniformed officer standing near the road to wave nosey drivers on, and the two evidence technicians working with three, five-million watt, or thereabouts, floodlights on tripods illuminating the area in question.

Shortly after Vern's arrival, the medical examiner's morgue wagon pulled up. Earl Ogle drove the ME's van and the pathologist on call was Dr. Morris Rappaport, a transplanted specialist, formerly from Essex County, New Jersey.

Compared to the last chief of Prospect PD, I'm a little sticky about unattended deaths in my city. If a family physician won't sign a death certificate, nothing short of a battalion from the 82nd Airborne Division will get me to release a body without a post mortem exam. I lack trust in my fellow humans. So, over the past three months, I had gotten to meet the ME's personnel on several occasions. As my own investigator, I'd also made the obligatory appearance at the autopsies, to be present and witness any evidence recovered.

"Hello, Earl. Mo, how's it goin'?" I said.

Earl said, "Howdy, Chief."

"What is it with you, Sam?" the doctor asked. "Prospect used to be a quiet place. Haven't you heard those tourist commercials? This is the peaceful side of the Smokies. You come up with more bodies in a couple of months than the rest of the county in a year."

"Good to see you, too, Morris. I've got an interesting one for you. The dead guy's one of our city employees. He's been executed, one in each kneecap, one in the shoulder and the coup de grace in the temple. You'll have to do some digging. Three have no exit wounds. Probably slow moving hollow points. They look like nine mil size or thereabouts. Jackie Shuman's down there now with a new CSI named Sparks. It's all yours, gents. We'll be over here working on our strategy."

I called Vern Hobbs over. After thirty years at Prospect PD, Vern knew just about everybody in our district.

"I guess you've heard about the troubles Bobby had doing the investigation on Murray?"

He nodded, looked at me without emotion, and moved a toothpick around in his mouth.

"We're far beyond a background investigation now with our mystery man. I need to know how he bought his home for cash back in the 70s. Having no mortgage, no loans and no credit card is just downright un-American. Dig around and see who built the house. I'll want to talk to him. Ivy Tucker's got no records showing that the place even exists. You believe that?"

He shook his head and moved the toothpick to the other side again.

"If you can't locate the builder," I said, "look for a former owner, and let me know."

Vern is the shortest cop I'd ever seen. When I first met him, I thought he was a Hobbit.

He scratched his grizzled gray hair, spat out his chewed-up toothpick, and replaced it with another from the supply in his shirt pocket. "Damn, sure is a can o' worms, ain't it? Poor little feller. Got more lead in 'im than Dillinger."

"I didn't know you were around when they shot John Dillinger."

"Do what?"

"Hang in there, partner. Coffee will be here soon."

Then I turned to Stan. He stood alongside my two visitors and Will Sparks, who finally showed up with the drinks.

I said, "Murray only lives a few blocks from here. Possibly he was killed there and dropped here." That didn't sound right to me. I shook my head. "But probably not. They would have just left him there. No sense getting seen moving a body." I started thinking out loud. Stan and Lonnie nodded in agreement. "If he was killed for something he possessed, I'd like to get into his house. He's been here awhile. If the killer did any looking, we might be too late."

"Any idea what he may have had someone would want?" Lonnie asked.

"This guy's a big mystery," I said. "You're coming in on the tail end of a real problem we've seen for more than a week."

"It would take more than a day to explain what's been going on," Stan added.

"He's probably got a locker or desk or something in the municipal building," I said "We need to see what's in there. And I'd sure like to know where he was earlier this evening."

"You think the ME can estimate the time of death yet?" Lonnie asked.

"Maybe Mo's already checked the liver and will take a guess," I said. "But the water's cold and would mess up the normal body cool down. I'll ask and see if Jackie's found anything." I sipped my black coffee and thought it should have been sold as old dishwater.

"Where'd you get this coffee, Willy?" I asked

"Git N' Go," he said. "It's the only place still open."

"I think Mr. Patel's selling the water from his mop bucket."

Will shrugged.

"This is terrible," I said. Turning to Lonnie and Robert, I asked, "Can you get good coffee in D.C.?"

"Sure," Lonnie said. "This is bad stuff. Worst we've had down here, which ain't sayin' much. Other than the coffee you made in the office, we haven't had a good cup in the whole state."

"Will," I said, "next time you see Mr. Patel, tell him we're going to boycott his store until he learns to make a better cup of coffee. What do you think of it? You're not complaining."

Sparks shrugged again.

"Don't drink it m'se'f. Haven't done fer years. Got me some hot chocolate."

"How much does this swill cost?" I asked.

"Dollar-thirty-nine."

"Jeez, we're in the wrong business."

"Yep," he said.

Will looked more like a grown-up version of Opie from *The Andy Griffith Show* than Ron Howard. He tried to push his bangs to the side, but they fell across his forehead again.

I walked over to the upper edge of the embankment. The floodlights on the creek bed reminded me of the lighting at a night baseball game. I called down to Shuman, "Hey, Jackie, you find any keys, a wallet or anything on the body?"

"I got the whole package. Nobody took nothin'. This weren't no robbery. He got a watch, a cheap one, but it's still here. Took a lickin', but kept on tickin'."

He waited for me to laugh at the joke cops have been telling for fifty years.

"Got some money, a wallet, keys and three pins, too."

"Let me look at the wallet," I said. "And I'll need the keys to get into his house. Pins, you said? What kind of pins?"

"Jest cheap ones, you know, Bics, ink-pins."

"Sure, I should have known. Hang on to those *pens*. I'm coming down. Let me see the wallet, and I'll sign your inventory sheet for the keys."

The wallet contained an old photo of a woman I guessed to be the late Mrs. McGuire, Murray's Prospect City employee's ID card, a grubby Social Security card, a few receipts from Wal-Mart, Food Lion and the Ace Hardware Store along with an old check stub and a 3x5 card with a few phone numbers. A hundred-dollar bill, placed between two layers of leather, represented Murray's 'tuck money'.

"Not a hell of a lot, is it" I said.

Jackie shook his head. "Nope."

"I'll take this card and start calling the phone numbers. Here, put this hundred-dollar bill with the rest of the cash, and I'll sign for the wallet and the contents, too."

"You got it, Sam," he said.

"You have anything yet, Doctor?" I asked.

"Sure. He's dead...and he's wet."

"Nothing gets past you, Morris. When did you develop this talent, as an intern or after years on the job?"

"Gimme a break, Sam. You know what time it is?"

"We're all sleepy, Doctor." I cocked my head and smiled.

"Yeah, yeah, yeah. Just a guess now—couple of hours at most. He's still stiff. This cool water doesn't help, you know. I'll have a TOD and all the niceties before lunch tomorrow—promise."

"You're a peach, Mo, a kosher peach, from Joisey."

"There is no such thing, you silly Goy."

"You want some help getting the body up the hill after you bag him?"

"I'm a fifty-five-year-old Jewish doctor, not a big macho guy like you. Of course, I want some help. Actually, I don't want to do this at all."

"Gotcha covered, Mo. We'll make it a group effort."

I scrambled up the little incline again.

"Will, drive over to 4106 Old Piney Drive. It's the last house on the left. That's Murray's. I know we're probably late, but if there's no break-in, sit on the place. Take my unmarked car." I handed him my key ring. "Then park somewhere unobtrusive and see if anyone shows up."

I turned to the others. "Gentlemen, I just volunteered us to help extricate the deceased from this declivity, soon as the doctor's finished and the body's bagged. After that, we search Murray's house."

"What do you mean *us*, white man?" Stanley asked.

"Interagency cooperation knows no color boundaries, Sergeant. Besides this is a piece o' cake. Little Murray's lighter than a bale o' cotton."

* * * *

Forty-five minutes later, we cleared the crime scene of all the extraneous law enforcement personnel. Typewriter Murray had been tagged, bagged and was speeding toward his final medical examination.

With Murray's keys jingling in my pocket, my three companions and I drove to his little house. Lonnie and Robert didn't look tired. The adrenalin rush, familiar to most cops, seemed to have perked them up. I asked Stanley to keep a choke chain on that pair as we searched the extended crime scene.

We found Will Sparks sitting in my Ford, still awake and enjoying his overtime near Murray's place on Old Piney Drive. The premises looked secure, and it seemed like no one tried to gain entry. Will and I swapped cars, and he headed for home.

The small house proved easy to search. With not much more than twelve hundred square feet to rummage around in, we found no basement or crawl space, not even a trap door to an attic area. Murray owned few belongings to weed through. He was not a material guy.

But we did find a few interesting items. One, the birth certificate Murray denied having. It showed a birth date of January 14, 1955 from St. Brendan's Hospital in New Orleans. The second item threw me for a loop: a British passport issued to Murray Neil McGuire on May 10, 1973 with a home address in Manchester. Several passport control stamps indicated he left England and checked in and out of France and Spain, but I saw only one *entry* stamp from US Customs and Immigration at Logan International Airport, Boston, for October 31, 1974. I saw no evidence that he entered or left the US other than his Halloween arrival.

So, where had Murray been back in those days? In England and Europe? Or pumping gas in Bozeman, Montana?

Another item of interest would make Vern Hobbs' assignment easier. The deed to Murray's house listed Delbert Collier of Prospect, Tennessee as the builder and seller. I'd have Vern track down Delbert for a statement.

Also tucked into the same accordion folder were things that would normally be uninteresting, except Murray claimed to have lost them all. I found the marriage license for Murray and Missy, her death certificate from the Knoxville hospital where she passed away, Murray's Form DD-214, separating him from active duty with the US Army and a short hand-written, notarized last will and testament leaving all his "worldly possessions" to St. Michael's Roman Catholic Church in Maryville, Tennessee.

Why did he lie about having lost those seemingly commonplace documents? And why in hell did a guy supposedly born in New Orleans have a British passport? Difficult questions to answer in the early hours of a Saturday morning.

Chapter Thirteen

If I say nothing else about Alonzo Crosby's abilities as a cop, the man really knew how to toss a house. I felt confident the documents we found in that accordion folder, along with almost eighteen-hundred-dollars in cash on a shelf in Murray's bedroom closet were the only things of interest in the entire house.

"You remember I was in Criminal Intelligence for three years?" Lonnie asked.

I nodded. "Of course." I think the statement was more for Stanley's benefit.

"Along with clipping newspaper articles for the files and taking pictures at Mafia funerals," he said, "we used to get all kinds of interesting shit from not only other US departments, but international agencies, too. I've seen quite a few pictures sent out of British Police Special Branch—the Scotland Yard guys—of IRA killings—both in Ireland and in England. I remember kneecapping being their trademark. A lot of times, they killed the victim, sometimes not. But when those Micks wanted to get their message across, they kneecapped somebody. Your guy Murray definitely got kneecapped."

"That's good to remember," I said. "I didn't think little red-headed Murray McGuire was Swedish. But I didn't figure him for an IRA connection. He's been right here in Prospect for almost thirty years. If he's a sleeper, why not Boston or New York?"

I looked at my three companions and saw blank stares.

"And a little worm like Murray didn't look like ex-British Secret Service material," I added.

"Not your usual James Bond image." Stan said.

"Anyone happen to know if a guy from Northern Ireland would get a British passport?" I asked. "The south is the Republic of Ireland, the autonomous part of the country. I'm not sure what they do up in the north."

"It's a different country, right?" Alonzo asked.

"It is. Let's hope we can dig up and confirm a definite Irish thing. This business is getting curiouser and curiouser all the time."

I saw three frowns after my statement. None of my associates knew any more about Irish administrative procedures than I did. They also didn't seem to be too familiar with either Lewis Carroll or Alice.

I always hated getting a big case on a Friday. The weekends bog down the process of getting the information you need to start the ball rolling. As any real cop or even a devotee of TV crime shows know, the first forty-eight hours are critical to an investigation. I didn't envision any great progress, but I'd do what I could over the weekend.

When we finished searching Murray's place, I secured the decedent's home, and we all headed back to headquarters. I'd call the mayor to let him know his trusted employee was no longer among the living. We'd check out Murray's stomping grounds in the basement of the municipal building and then wrap up the case for the night. I was too old to be up that late.

* * * *

Back at the office, I switched on a few lights, took off my jacket and started thinking about what we should do next.

"It's after 3 o'clock in the morning," I said. "I doubt there's a goddamn thing open in this county except Wal-Mart, and I'm not brave enough to go there at this ungodly hour. Their nighttime customers look like they come out from under a rock. I'd tell Stanley he was a wimp if he went home now, but how about you guys? You going back to your motel or going to hang out with us real cops until we lock up the shop?"

Both Lonnie and Robert nodded.

"We're in," Lonnie said. "What else we got to do 'cept sleep?"

"Okay," I said. "Make yourselves useful. There's nothing here to eat and nowhere to get something, but fix some coffee—real coffee, good coffee. You see the maker over there," I pointed to the counter top at the side of my office, "and the fixings are in the cabinet below. Milk's in the little fridge. I've got to call the mayor and disturb his beauty sleep. Stan, you know where we can find the keys to get into Murray's little corner of the world?"

"Hey, I've been here three-and-a-half years. You think you're dealing with an amateur?"

"Good. Give me ten minutes to wake up His Nibs, and then we'll creep Murray's office."

I hoped Ronnie Shields was a sound sleeper, and I'd get away with a message on his answering machine. I really didn't want our mayor in my office during the wee hours of the morning. My luck held. I left a brief message and anticipated Ronnie disturbing my sleep later in the day, but at least I could search Murray's work area unobstructed.

While Stan looked for the set of building keys, I spoke to Crosby and Brame. "One more call, guys, and we'll be ready."

"Go ahead," Lonnie said. "Do your thing."

Before moving on to our new search, I wanted to take care of an obligation. I dialed Rachel Williamson's office number, intending to repay her last favor. I assumed her husband might get a little miffed if I called his wife on her cell phone at that hour and woke them up.

Her station phone's voice mail kicked in. "Hello, this is Rachel. I'm not able to answer my phone right now, so at the tone, leave your name and number, and I'll return your call."

She sounded very professional on the recorder. In the background, something new had been added, the hokey, majestic newsroom theme music they play as an intro to her show. I didn't like that—very unfeminine.

When the beep sounded, I spoke. "Hello, news-lady. Since I owe you a favor, here's a big one. I don't want you learning about the interesting homicide we have here in beautiful downtown Prospect from the county sheriff's blotter or someone else. It's 3:35 in the morning. I don't know when I'm going home. I hope you monitor your voice mail. Call me at home tomorrow, uh … later today, and I'll give you the poop from group. If I don't hear from you, I'll call your cell when I wake up. Good night."

"Who's *news-lady*?" Lonnie asked, after he heard me on the phone.

"Local TV anchorwoman. A good girl. She got the promotion ceremony televised for us and made our man Stan a star. I owe her for that."

"Sounded kinda friendly to me. How about you, Robert? Like more than owin' an acquaintance something. You doin' that on the side?" He flashed a familiar lecherous grin.

Robert chose not to comment.

"No, Alonzo, I'm not. She's young enough to be my daughter—well, almost. I do no one on the side. Pervert."

"If you say so. But ain't nothin' perverted about it. What channel can I see this news-lady on?" The bastard grinned like a dirty old man.

Stanley appeared at my doorway. "You ready to check out Murray's cubby hole?" he asked.

"I'm right behind you, big feller," I said.

Lonnie and Robert followed in close support.

"Jesus, you two are nosey," I said and got two smiles. Ex-cops can be annoying.

We found Murray's office in the basement of the municipal building, next to the large supply room that held all the forms, ink jet cartridges, paper clips, lined pads, old swivel chairs, in and out boxes, toilet paper, floor wax and anything else that allows a small American city to function. Stanley opened the lock with the third key he tried. I switched on the light.

"Stan, you and Lonnie take a look in the desk," I said.

"What will you give me if I find the best clue?" Lonnie asked.

"My undying gratitude," I said. "Just remember if you find anything, hand it to Stanley and forget you ever saw it. Okay?"

"Man, you still so serious 'bout all dis shit." Alonzo added a touch of Ebonics to his statement.

"Yeah, I've got this terrible thing about wanting to win in court. Why find a clue if some shyster gets it tossed out during a Wade hearing because it was mishandled?"

"Yeah, yeah, I hear ya," Crosby said.

After a quick look, Murray's desk offered little of interest. Aside from the general work related documents and other simple items, they found two old copies of *Playboy* magazine—things not easy to come by in our area of the Baptist controlled Bible Belt, a current UT football schedule, a couple days worth of old Knoxville News-Sentinels, but nothing else of apparent interest to a homicide investigator.

From the apparent, they delved deeper to find the non-apparent. They began pulling out desk drawers to check the backs, bottoms and sides.

"Eureka!" Lonnie said, holding a drawer upside down. "I told you I'd find the magic clue. Look at this. Secret documents, I bet."

"Yeah, you've probably got Murray's orders from KGB Central. Who reads Russian?" I said.

"The KGB's outta business," Lonnie said.

"Who cares?"

Taped to the bottom of a lower drawer, Lonnie found a legal-sized envelope.

"Man, you sound ungrateful. Who else found anything?"

"Stan, open the envelope that Alonzo never touched."

"Be happy to."

Then he started making a production out of the simple task.

"The envelope, please."

Lonnie handed it over.

"May I have a drum roll?" Stan said.

We were all getting silly from lack of food and sleep.

"And the winner is... Shit, just a few twenties."

Alonzo's discovery gave us false hope. The envelope only contained five twenty-dollar bills.

"More of Murray's mad money?" I asked.

"I guess so. A hundred bucks is nothing compared to the cash he kept at home." Stan sounded disappointed.

"I'll run the serial numbers, but I've got no hope of learning any more than this is just more cash set aside for a rainy day."

Stan handed me the envelope. I tucked it into my back pocket.

"Let's start moving furniture." I pointed at Stan and Lonnie. "You two big manly guys drag those file cabinets away from the walls and give them a once-over. Robert, do me a favor, and go down the hall to that big closet where the janitors keep their shit and see if you can find a step ladder."

When Robert brought me a six-foot ladder, I lifted up each individual tile in the hung-ceiling. I found a lot more nothing if you don't count cobwebs. We searched every inch of the room thoroughly, but still came up empty-handed. The search reminded me of interviewing Murray himself—frustrating—elusive.

I checked my watch and saw the hands pushing 5:15. At time and a half, Stanley would go into a higher tax bracket.

I looked from face to face. "Ideas?" I asked.

Everyone shrugged.

"We're at a dead end, and no one, other than us, is awake yet to ask for help," I said.

We went back upstairs. I locked Murray's wallet, keys, the folder of documents, the cash we recovered from his house and the newly found hundred dollars in the evidence closet. Cleaning the coffee pot and a general tidy-up period took us to 5:35.

"You guys hungry?" I heard three different grumbles all conveying the same message. We were four cranked-up individuals ready for breakfast.

"At a time like this, more coffee is the last thing any of us need." Stanley said.

"Yeah, but pre-dawn in Blount County is not a good time to look for a pitcher of martinis to relax with," I said. "We'd better settle for a drive to the corner of 129 and Louisville Road and the Cracker Barrel which opens at six."

"I'm not used to all this work," Lonnie said. "It's been one hell of a night."

"You agree with that, Robert?" I asked.

"You old guys may be tired," Robert said, "but I'm havin' fun playing detective. How about you, Stanley?"

Stan looked at me. "Why don't you hire him, and I'll go and get me a nice quiet office job somewhere?"

All of us were ready for a relaxing breakfast, followed by a million hours of sleep. Instead, we found three idiots with too much attitude.

* * * *

I lead my troops into the Cracker Barrel restaurant at ten after six and found several tables already occupied in the non-smoking section. We all ordered de-caf coffee and perused the big foldout menus. When the waitress returned, I asked for something called Uncle Hershel's Breakfast—two eggs, hash brown potato casserole, grits, biscuits and gravy, and my choice of one of their meat products. I chose Virginia ham. The other guys wanted various combinations of eggs and pancakes, and the assorted breakfast side dishes. Stanley actually ate something larger than I did, he being much younger and a growing boy.

None of us were particularly in a rush to finish and get home, although we all might have fallen asleep if we closed our eyes and sat still for too long.

By the time we finished breakfast and drank second or third cups of coffee, the place had packed in quite a few early morning customers. Country music played over the speakers. Kenny Rogers just finished *Ruby, Don't Take Your Love to Town* and Johnny Cash began singing *Ghost Riders in the Sky.* Off to our left, three good ol' boys sat waiting for their food, drinking coffee and sweet tea. They sounded a bit louder than the other folks in the restaurant, and from outward appearances, they looked like a bunch of shitheads on their way to buy a timeshare in an outhouse. I never trust a group of men who eat with their hats on.

I stood up and told my three friends I was heading to the men's room while we waited for the check. As I stretched my shoulders, the grubbiest of the three morons at the other table, a slope-shouldered knuckle-dragger, laughed and said, "Nigga lover," and looked in my direction, getting chuckles from his two companions.

Considering we out-numbered them and didn't look like a table full of computer geeks, I chalked the remark up to their lack of manners and intelligence and to the early hour not allowing their brains to function at full potential. Normally, I would have overlooked such abhorrent behavior, but after the night I experienced, that mutt pissed me off royally.

I took off my jacket so the trio of skells could see the big Smith and Wesson and handcuffs on my belt. Even one of those nitwits would assume I was a cop. I excused myself and walked toward the table where the local yahoos sat.

Behind me, I heard Lonnie say, "Watch this. He's up to his old

109

tricks."

I stood by their table, next to the creep who made the remark and put my hand on his shoulder. "Hi guys, you doin' all right today?"

I got three stares, but no answers. I squeezed the idiot's shoulder and asked, "You wanted me for something?"

He shook his head and mumbled, "No, I ain't called you."

I pushed my holster a couple inches backward on my belt and continued, "Damn, I sure did hear you say something. I know you wanted to give me a message, didn't you?" I squeezed his shoulder a little harder. He flinched slightly.

"No, I said I ain't got nothin' to say."

I dug my fingers in to his trapezius muscle. He made a pained face. *Wimp.*

"Now, didn't your English teacher tell you about double negatives? When you ain't got nothin', it means you do got somethin'. Understand?"

I looked from idiot to idiot and saw three blank stares.

I sat down next to my antagonist and put my left arm around his shoulder. I smiled. No one else did.

As a waitress walked by, I waved for her to come closer. "My friend here needs more coffee."

She filled his mug with steaming hot brew.

Then I used one of the oldest cop tricks in the book. "Hey, I know you from somewhere. Where have we met before?" I asked, knowing I'd never seen him.

"I don't know you from nowhere," he said.

"What's your name?"

"Why you wanna know?"

"I'm a cop. I want to know everything. What's your name?"

I guess he realized resistance was futile.

"Dewey Cupps. And I done tol' ya, I ain't never seen ya b'fore."

"Oh, goodness me, Dewey, there you go again with the horrible grammar. No, I never forget a handsome face. I know where, the Justice Center. Court maybe? Or was it the sheriff's office? You were under arrest, weren't you? Sure, that's it. What were you in for? Possession?"

That question opened a multitude of possibilities. Possession of many things may cause a man to run afoul of the law.

"Yeah, mebbe. I been there for possession." He took the bait and confessed. "But I don't remember you."

"Possession of what? Stolen property, drugs, state secrets, illegal weapons? What?" I got a little pushy and jostled him, moving my chair closer, getting into his face.

"Pot. Jest a little. Hey, man…"

I interrupted, "Ah, marijuana." I gave it an exaggerated Spanish pronunciation. "The evil weed. That stuff's no good for you, partner. It clouds men's minds. Maybe it made you say those things this morning that pissed me off. You on the knob or what?"

"Do what?"

"You know, Dewey, guys with criminal records really should keep their big mouths shut when they don't know who they're cracking wise at. Don't you think?" We did the squeeze, flinch, ouch thing again. "Maybe you've got a probation officer who would get annoyed if he learned you're out in the world causing trouble for a bunch of cops minding their own business. Four guys who could rip your lungs out for fun if they wanted to."

"I done tol' you, I ain't said nothin'."

"Oh, I'm sorry then. I've been interrupting your breakfast. Here you don't want your coffee to cool off." I moved the cup of hot coffee a little closer to him, faked a sneeze, pushed the cup over and spilled the hot liquid into his crotch.

"Je-sus Christ!" he squawked. "You shouldn't a' done that. Got-damn!" He stood up and started wiping the coffee from his jeans.

"Oh, I am sorry." I grabbed a napkin from in front of his friend.

A few other customers began looking at the spectacle. No one seemed to be laughing.

"Here," I said, "let me help you mop this up." I set my foot behind his right leg and moved my hand like I wanted to dry his pants.

I guess the thought of me touching him made my new acquaintance take a step back, trip on my foot and topple over onto the floor, sending his chair three feet to the side.

"Poor ol' Dewey, you fell, man. I am so sorry. I better stop trying to help and let you gentlemen get back to your breakfast." I tossed the napkin at moron number two. "Y'all have a nice day, fellas."

I walked back to three grinning faces, picked up the check and left. I felt so good, I paid for everyone's breakfast.

What fun after a frustrating and tiresome night.

I walked out into the sunshine wanting a quiet undisturbed day of rest and remembered the old adage, 'There is no rest for the weary'. I believed   it.

Chapter Fourteen

Lon Crosby and Robert Brame promised to stop back at the PD after they slept for a day or three. Stanley grunted something that seemed to convey he'd see me at four on Monday afternoon if he didn't die in his sleep.

I walked into my house at 7:30 to find a wife and dog worried sick about my wellbeing. Overtired and confused, I kissed Bitsey and scratched Katherine behind the ear. Then I took a shower and fell asleep before 8 a.m. At 9:15, I felt a gentle shake.

"The mayor's on the phone, sweetie," Kate said.

I grunted and stuck my head under the pillow.

"Oh, my poor boy, I'll tell him you'll be right there."

A few minutes later, I explained the situation to Ronnie Shields, giving only generalizations, no speculations on IRA hit men or mafia vendettas or whatever else might be conjured up as a possibility. I emphasized that I'd been up for twenty-six hours, hoping I sounded eager to get back to sleep. Ronnie didn't use up much more time and promised to take care of sending out a press release some time that afternoon and arranging a press conference for late Monday morning.

November Saturdays in Tennessee are for only one thing—football. And Sundays were for church. In these parts, nothing else much mattered. Murray would have to wait. By the time the world would learn what we knew, Murray's story would be old news. After Ronnie's call I went back to sleep and at 10:30 received another not so gentle shake.

"You awake?" Kate asked, rhetorically.

I am now.

"Your TV star girlfriend is on the phone." She left the bedroom briskly.

What did I do? I'd been sleeping.

I walked into the other room where we kept the upstairs phone.

"Hello?"

"Hello, Sam? You have another murder? Do you know who the killer is?

Obviously, she thought I'd recognize her voice.

"Hi, Rachel. Yes, to the murder. That's why I called. But I have no idea who the killer is."

"Who's the victim?"

I gave her Murray's professional biography.

"You said it's an *interesting* homicide. What does that mean?"

I told her a brief story about Murray's unusual background investigation.

"You sound funny. When did this happen? Are you okay?" Rachel fired her questions at me a mile a minute.

"Rachel, whoa, slow down. I'm fine. There was no shootout. Stan Rose found a body in Crystal Creek around midnight. I've just been up all night. But even without much sleep, I'm terrific at telling a story. So, just sit back and listen to my ripping yarn."

I told her most of what I knew, leaving out our conjecture about an assassination and the nature of the wounds. I assured her no other news agency had been called and if she hurried, she'd have the first story on the air. The only way anyone else from the media might learn what happened in Prospect was from reading the county duty officer's log which would only contain our request for a crime scene unit and an ME's team. I offered to be ready and willing to do an interview at 9 a.m. Monday morning before the press conference. I also promised to catch up on my sleep and shave before going on camera.

Then the devil took hold of me, and I asked a loaded question, "Did I ever mention I dreamt about you?"

"Uh, no...what was it about?" I heard a little apprehension in her voice.

"I don't know you well enough to tell you." I grinned to myself.

"Ooooh my," she said.

"You're the only person I've ever heard make *oh* a three syllable word."

"Uh-huh."

"Okay. Good talking with you, lady. Have a nice weekend. I'm going back to sleep. See you Monday. John coming with you?"

"I guess so."

More apprehension detected.

"Good day, Mizz Williamson. Get out there, and scoop the competition."

"Bye," she said.

* * * *

At four o'clock I got another gentle shake from Katherine and a less gentle leap on the bed by Bitsey, the wonder dog. While I blinked and tried to wipe the sleep from my eyes, I received several licks on my face. Only half awake, I knew Bitsey had gotten affectionate; Kate is not into licking, no matter how amorous she gets.

"Hey," Kate said, "you might want to get up, or you won't sleep tonight. It's four o'clock. When you wake up a little, we'll figure out what I can make for you to eat. You okay?"

"Yeah, I'm fine. I feel like I've got jet lag, but I'm okay."

"Can I make you coffee?"

"I don't think so. I ingested enough caffeine last night to put me in orbit. I'm surprised I slept at all. Give me a few minutes to get cleaned up, and I'll meet you in the kitchen."

She kissed me and left, taking my canine partner with her.

Thirty minutes later, I appeared downstairs scrubbed, shaved, combed and brushed. I looked human again. With a little more time, I might have started to feel like it.

It was one of those days when I felt like moping around the kitchen and eating last night's cold pizza and the dregs of a stale beer. But I had neither, so I got innovative. I went into the basement fridge and took out a bottle of champagne and a pint of fresh orange juice. Mimosa time. I bounded up the stairs, enthused over my clever idea.

"Hey, Kats, you on some Taoist or Confucian diet this week?"

"No. Why?"

"Good. Can you drink alcohol? I'm mixing some champagne with

OJ—a little eye opener. What can I give you?"

"Champagne would be just lovely, dear. But I'll rough it. No orange juice."

Katherine had already tuned in XM Radio on the satellite TV. The 60s station was playing Manfred Mann's *Do Wah Diddy Diddy Dum* as I popped the cork. They finished, and I poured two glasses of vino as The Beach Boys began singing *The Sloop John B.* After mixing my mimosa, I took a couple of sips and then cut a slice of homemade cinnamon-raisin bread and tucked it into the toaster oven. After that, The Association started *Never My Love.* All great stuff.

Not everyone will agree with me, but I think the finest music ever written was produced between 1957 and 1972. I guess I'd throw in several favorites from the 1940s for good measure, but since then, I doubt I've really liked more than a dozen songs. After having a night like I experienced, I felt less prepared than usual to listen to any 21st century music. Without an oldies station, I feel isolated from my real world.

Sleep had done nothing to rid me of the energy I built up working the homicide. I could feel the lactic acid still flowing through my body, and I was hungry. So, by 6:30 I decided rather than sitting around trying to relax and only manage to do my impression of a jitterbug champion, I'd make dinner. Learning that neither Buddha nor the Dalai Lama would censure Katherine for the meal she'd eat, I started some linguini boiling and whipped up a pasta dish with chicken and roasted tomatoes that makes my ears wiggle. A nice bottle of Columbia Valley pinot grigio made me even happier.

* * * *

Since Saturday night is a lousy time for television, we watched a couple of episodes of *Spenser for Hire* on a DVD a friend sent me. Before I knew it, I found myself back in bed reading. Thirty minutes later, I dropped off to sleep.

Long ago, I learned that my chosen profession and a good night's sleep do not necessarily enjoy a symbiotic relationship. After drifting off around 10:30, my eyes snapped open again. On the digital alarm clock, sitting less than ten feet from our bed, I read the numbers 2:02.

Perhaps my sleep during the day actually rested me, or perhaps the wine I drank that evening changed from a depressant to the stimulant it turns into after shooting sugars through the bloodstream. I changed positions—several times, trying to get comfortable and drift back to sleep, but had no luck. I checked the clock again—3:10. I turned to face Katherine, put my arm over her waist and moved a little closer. She felt warm and inviting. I started getting interested in more than going back to sleep. So, I tried thinking of peaceful, quiet things—things that would keep the invasive thoughts of work and Murray McGuire from racing through my mind.

I've never been any good at meditation, visualization or deep breathing exercises designed to relax and clear the mind. I heard the clock chime 3:30. If more conventional methods fail, I try to focus on seeing my wife in the buff; that's always a pleasant thought. I fell asleep before the clock chimed four times.

* * * *

But sleep wasn't destined to be friendly to me. Like so many others I've experienced, my inevitable dream never in reality actually occurred. It was purely symbolic, but one of the main characters was, in fact, a previous acquaintance. I found myself back in Vietnam looking up into a dark and clear early evening sky and enjoying the pleasant air temperature. While walking around inside the compound my unit shared with other soldiers, I noticed a covered "deuce-and-a-half" parked between two supply buildings. I knew the two-and-one-half-ton truck didn't belong there. Something looked very wrong.

Taking out my personal sidearm, a stainless steel Smith & Wesson Chief's Special, the same gun I kept and carried off-duty for my twenty years as a cop in New York, I moved slowly and cautiously from the front of the unoccupied cab to check the rear cargo area. Stepping around to the back of the truck, I found the tailgate open, hanging down, and ever so slightly swaying on its hinges, as if someone just lowered it. Again, I moved cautiously and popped my head past the side of the cargo bed to take a quick glance into the truck. What I found inside surprised me. A young kid recently assigned in-country from the States knelt there. He was only eighteen or nineteen years old, short, overweight and spoke with an awkward stutter. The kid worked as one of the guards assigned to the main gate of the compound. He wanted to be called David, not Dave or Davy. I must have seen the nametape on his jungle jacket a hundred times, but couldn't remember his last name. Standing behind David, a Vietnamese man dressed in black pajamas, a man I assumed to be Viet Cong, held a Russian Tokarev pistol to the kid's head.

I stepped to the center of the truck's back end and took aim at the center of the VC's chest. The whole upper-half of his exposed body made a perfect target. "Charlie" said nothing. He just held his automatic with the muzzle against David's temple and smiled at me. A look of panic covered David's face. I didn't call out or challenge the man. I only intended to get my sight alignment, hold my breath and squeeze the trigger until the discharge of the bullet surprised me. Bang! A perfect shot in Charlie's ten-ring.

I had fired hundreds, perhaps thousands of practice rounds through that gun. I stood well within effective range; the shot should have been no problem. But I experienced a major stumbling block. I kept squeezing the trigger and only felt a little travel, but couldn't move it any further back to complete the shot. I began to panic. I pulled harder. I recognized my mistake—yank the trigger, and you throw the shot high and to the right. I tried again. The trigger moved slightly, but hung up before I got half way to where the sear would release the hammer and the firing pin would strike the primer, sending the bullet speeding toward my enemy.

The VC grinned at me. Then he began to laugh. He laughed at *me*.

David began to cry. He said, "P-p-please, p-please!"

The VC continued laughing, now louder. I released the pressure on the trigger again and started all over, trying to fire my revolver. But still, I couldn't pull the trigger. Then the Tokarev fired. David fell forward. Blood ran from the single hole in his temple. The VC cackled and casually used his pistol to point at me, not in a threatening gesture, but rather as an innocent instrument, a pointer, a way to mock me. Charlie now had Murray McGuire's face.

I sat up, wide awake once more. The clock showed 5:14 AM.

When I lay back again on my pillow, I remembered David, and how in 1969 I found him in the back of a deuce-and-a-half as I walked around an Army compound one evening. David was an unhappy boy. He didn't act like a typical MP or present the imposing image of a military policeman. David represented another example of the Army's less than efficient method of career selection.

Some of the GIs David encountered made fun of his stuttering. They bullied him because he was fat. Some made his life miserable. David's only friend was a little brown and white dog who wandered into the compound one day at a time when some of the men I worked with were short timers—soldiers getting close to returning to the US. One sergeant named the little dog FIGMO, an Army mnemonic for "fuck-you, I've got my orders." FIGMO was always nice to David.

The night I found David in the back of the truck, he hadn't been held hostage by a VC infiltrator. David became his own enemy. In reality, I found the tailgate of the truck closed. I noticed blood dripping from the flatbed onto the dirt below. When I opened the gate, I saw that David had placed the birdcage flash-hider of his M-16 rifle in his mouth and pulled the trigger. The .223 caliber copper-jacketed round took off the top of the young man's head. David ended the taunting and ridicule he received from those insensitive enlisted men. The stuttering fat kid died in Vietnam, but not in battle. I doubt the other soldiers ever skipped a beat.

It wouldn't take Freud or Jung to see that my concern lies in the present. Could I finish something I just started? Could I successfully find Murray's killer? The theme is actually a common dream for cops. Now, for any chance of finding his killer, I needed Murray's true identity. But from whom could I learn that?

Chapter Fifteen

I stared up at the ceiling in the dark bedroom, and for some reason, in the archives of my mind, I heard Brook Benton singing *A Rainy Night in Georgia*. It had a soothing effect on me. I relaxed and fell asleep again until just before 6 a.m. Those forty-five minutes seemed like the best sleep I'd gotten all night.

Kate awoke and rolled over to face me.

"You have room for me?" she asked, meaning she wanted to put her head on my shoulder and her knee over my leg.

"Sure," I said. We stayed that way for twenty minutes before getting up.

In New York, autumn is beautiful. The air is cool and clear, the leaves colorful and the days grow shorter. I remember walking to my car each night at five o'clock to see wedges of thirty, fifty or two-hundred Canada geese flying south over the orange, pink and violet evening sky of Long Island. Sunsets in Tennessee are never as spectacular as those near the salt water, but the leaves are often close to being as colorful.

I sat on the front porch with a cup of coffee and scratched Bitsey's head while looking out between the Virginia pines into Glenda Mae Waddell's pasture and toward the deciduous trees beyond it. Mae currently owned seven horses, five young chestnut mares, an older bay named Julie and Julie's black colt, Willie. They, like me, seemed to be enjoying the morning.

I heard Kate come downstairs. The dog and I joined her in the kitchen. Everything needed for breakfast had been set up the night before. The table had been set; coffee maker had been prepared and only needed water. A fry pan sat waiting on the range. I made omelets with asparagus and cheese and left out four spears, cut into short lengths for Bitsey. Katherine made sourdough toast. Breakfast tasted good, and life felt the same.

"What would you say about going to church with me this morning?" I asked.

"What?" She sounded like I just suggested mooning Congress.

"You heard me, church, St. Michael's Roman Catholic Church."

"You haven't been to church since we got married. I take that back. You've probably been to a few funerals since then. Why the sudden urge toward religion?"

"I need to see a priest about a homicide. You suggested I check with him about Murray. I want to follow up on that. At least I know where I can find him on a Sunday morning."

The Mass started before we arrived. As we entered, Katherine dipped her finger into the stoup of holy water and blessed herself. We walked to a pew at the rear of the church. She genuflected, crossed herself again and sat down on the shiny oak bench. I gestured for her to slide over a little and sat next to her on the aisle. Father Declan's boss, Father Stephen, conducted the service. Once the proceedings ended, the entire cadre of holy people, the priest, deputy priest and a squad of altar boys filed out of the church. The parishioners followed. Kate and I walked in the van of the faithful. As we exited the building, Father Stephen thanked us for attending. We found Father Declan standing on the lawn a few yards away, smiling and nodding 'hellos' to the parishioners. We walked over.

"Saints presarve us, but I've made me a convert, so I have" He spoke with a pretty fair Irish accent.

"Don't get carried away now, Faather, tis a social call we're makin' t'day." I used my really cool impression of Barry Fitzgerald. "This is me wife, Katherine. Kate, Faather Declan McGill. He's Oirish himself, so he is."

"Nice to meet you, young lady." His comment got him a million-dollar smile from my wife. "And I'm glad you came to see us—true visit or not. I assume you'd like to discuss something?"

"I would," I said. "Did you hear that our mutual acquaintance, Murray McGuire, was murdered Friday night?"

"Yes, one of the Knoxville stations offered some information on the Saturday news. Poor man, it sounded brutal." When he finished speaking, he made the sign of a cross.

"Now that Murray is no longer alive and any information at all may be important to the investigation," I said, "are you free to discuss what he told you in confidence?"

A pair of small orange and brown butterflies fluttered around near us, looking like two happy children without a care in the world.

"I'm afraid the confidentiality of our conversations and his confessions go beyond the grave. I'm sorry."

"I guess the IACP never sent a lobbyist to the Vatican," I said.

"Who?" he asked.

"IACP. International Association of Chiefs of Police. I guess they never saw a need to schmooze the Pope."

He smiled. "That might have been a waste of time. I hear he's a tough nut to crack." Then he changed the subject. "Are you a Catholic, Mrs. Jenkins?"

"Yes, Father, I am," she said.

"And you're not, Chief."

I nodded to acknowledge what I told him the other day.

"Jenkins is a common name in this area, but you're not a local," he said. "Where did your family originate?"

"Long ago they came from Scotland and settled in New York."

"Ah, Scotland. There used to be lots of Catholics there, almost as many as in Ireland." He smiled again. "Hypothetically now, let's assume that hundreds of years ago one of the Jenkins family lived in the West Highlands of Scotland and was a Catholic. And something occurred in *Scotland* which involved this ancestor, something he wasn't very proud of, something which hung heavily on his conscience."

Declan locked his eyes on mine, waiting for his inference to create a revelation. I nodded.

"So," the priest continued, "the clearances come to Scotland, and your relative must leave, say for America. Many Scots arriving here were Catholics. Now, although he's not a religious man, he still believes in God and remembers his Catholic boyhood. Perhaps one day the incident, which preys upon his mind becomes too troublesome to keep to himself and he seeks a priest, wanting to unburden his soul. The priest offers him some counsel and assures your ancestor he'll never divulge those secrets, regardless of what they are.

"So, Chief, you see that regardless of time or *miles,* we're bound by church law and tradition. I'm afraid an IACP lobbyist would at most get a guided tour of the Vatican. He'd never change anything."

The two butterflies, perhaps exhausted from their frantic exercise, landed on the bright red burning bush behind Declan.

"Thanks for another lesson in church doctrine, Father. I'll certainly think about all you've told me."

"If some time you want to just have a chat," he said, "come see me on a day other than Sunday. I tend to be less metaphoric during the week."

"I think I should say, 'Thank you, Master Po.'"

He dipped his head slightly and said, "You're most welcome, Grasshopper."

I must have given him an odd look.

"What? I watch reruns, too. They have all sixty-two episodes of *Kung Fu* on tape at the library."

* * * *

"So, now that you have another cryptic clue, will you leave the monastery and solve the murder, Kwai Chang Caine?" Katherine spoke in an affected Asian accent as we drove back home.

"You know I hate all these hidden meanings and metaphoric symbolism. But surely even I can piece together some of this and come up with a Plan B approach. I just have to think up a scam interesting enough to hook someone's imagination and get them to do most of the work. I'll go to my Shaolin retreat and meditate on that one."

"Yeah, you'd better forget the 'good cop—bad cop' act with the priest. They tend to respect the notion of martyrdom."

* * * *

Monday, November 6th

On Monday morning I gave Ralph Oliveri enough time to get into the office, have coffee and settle down. But not too much time so his boss could give him something to do before I convinced him to help solve my puzzle. At 9:15, I dialed his direct line.

"Hello, Ralph."

"I knew it. I just freakin' knew it. I saw the news this weekend. You've got a homicide that looks like a hit. I knew you'd call me. Back off, paly! Don't ask me! Don't tempt me! Leave. Me. Alone." He sounded overwrought.

"Ralph, how can you say things like that? Do I pester you? Do I ask for things and not offer favors in return?"

"What do you want? I should mobilize an FBI Evidence Response Team and send them to Prospect?"

"Of course not, Ralphie. Don't be a putz. I'm reasonable. I just thought I'd tell you what I learned and see if you'd want to get involved."

"Yeah, right."

"This has the potential of branching out into something with international ramifications. Really, it's something you Feds like—something that may allow you to flex your Patriot Act."

"Don't you Ralphie me. And I don't want to get involved. I have my own work to do. Your vic is an old man from Prospect. Patriot Act my ass... When he finished ranting, he sighed. "Wait. Alright, I'll listen. You've got two minutes."

I didn't respond, and there was a moment of silence.

"Well?" he said.

"What you didn't see on the TV news," I said, "is when we tossed the victim's home I found a few items in a very accessible spot which he said were lost. Specifically, his birth certificate, his DD-214, his marriage license and his wife's death certificate. That raises the question, why did he lie about not having them?"

"Hmm."

"Additionally," I said, "I found something that showers this whole thing with confusion—a British passport. Now, my friendly G-Man, tell me how someone who claimed to be born in Louisiana, and had a birth certificate to substantiate that, can also hold British citizenship? He served in the U.S. Army as a U.S. citizen—one who claimed he never traveled anywhere the Army didn't send him."

"That is weird."

"Yes. Indeed, it is. St. Brendan's Hospital, New Orleans, which, as you know, is in the central time zone, and whose business office opens in about a half hour, will get a call from me shortly. I have no doubt they'll tell me the birth certificate I'm holding is bogus. I'll also call the Brits up in D.C. and ask what, if anything, they can tell me about a passport issued over thirty years ago.

"'Ey, Madonna mi', some can o' worms you got there, paisan. So, what do you want from me?"

"Two things. First, do you have some kind of hook who can get an honest answer from the Brits? I don't know if some clerk at their embassy can or will give me a reasonable explanation. I simply need to know if the passport is legit or a forgery. Then, can you take the old photo of him and run it through some facial recognition database you guys have and see if there's anything on file about his former life? I need anything about the pre-1975, U.S. Army enlistment days. A guy who gets blatantly assassinated—kneecapped, mind you—in small-town America, might have all kinds of interesting things in his background."

"Jeez, I don't know," Ralph said. "We've got lots of faces on file, but I'm not sure if something over thirty-years-old will jump out. We get stuff from the Brits now, but I hear back then it was different. That's long before my time. I can try, but it would have to be official. I'd have to open a case to get access. How soon can you send me the photo?"

"If you can take an email attachment, you'll have it in fifteen minutes or less."

"Okay, send it," he said.

"And how about the straight skinny on the passport?"

"An honest answer from the Brits may not be easy. You think U.S. agencies don't talk to each other? The Brits are ten times worse. MI-5 won't talk to Special Branch. MI-6 won't talk to anyone. Their guys in Military Intelligence would rather kill you than cooperate. Who knows if they'll talk to us? This may be beyond a casual favor."

"Okay, I'll try the embassy and maybe get lucky. I doubt it, but I'll let you know. If you have equally bad luck, I know someone who may be able to help with the past history angle. He'll piss and moan until I'm seventy-years-old about the magnitude of the favor I want, but he owes me a big one."

"You're a man of many resources. Maybe I should be coming to you for exotic favors. How is it you know these heavies?"

"I wasn't a potato farmer for twenty years, partner. I took a few trips around the block—sometimes wearing a couple of different hats. Anytime you need to know who I like for the Lindberg kidnapping or who *else* shot JFK, just ask."

"Yeah, right."

"Thanks, Ralph. I'll call you later."

* * * *

A little after 10 a.m., Lon Crosby and Robert Brame walked into the office.

"Hey, you can send our paychecks to Washington. A lot of OT that night, boss," Lonnie said.

"Keep dreamin' son. Stanley was the only one to make the big bucks that day. I'm on a flat salary, and you were just a guest."

"Story of my life, Sam."

"I was glad to see you again, Lonnie, and good to meet you, Robert. Thanks for going on the ride-along. You made a good partner."

Robert extended a hand for me to shake. "Good to meet you, too, sir."

"I told you, call me Sam. And keep an eye on this guy." I jerked my thumb toward Alonzo. "He's always needed supervision."

Robert Brame nodded, showing a big grin.

"And I'm glad I came here, Sam," Lonnie said. "Good we had that talk."

"Same here, Lonnie. I never asked, but how's your mom doing?" I knew his father passed away twenty years earlier.

"She's doin' okay. Retired about ten years ago. Still living in the same place on the Island near headquarters. Still driving her Cadillac."

I remembered the old girl tooling around town in her pimp-mobile.

"Say hello for me when you can."

"I will. Damned if I know why, but she always liked you."

I chuckled. "Flying out on that noon commuter jet?"

"Yeah, 12:10. Guess we'd better get going." He offered a hand.

"See you guys again sometime," I said. "Don't forget to send me your magazine. And I want a membership card. Make me an honorary brother."

Robert smiled.

Lonnie shook his head. "You're still crazy as a shithouse rat. Tell Stan to call if he needs anything."

"Okay, guys. Have a safe trip."

Chapter Sixteen

I was just about to make the phone call to New Orleans when Trudy Connor walked into my office and reminded me the press conference would kick off in the mayor's office in five minutes. I knew my sport jacket and tie were there for a reason.

As I followed her to the second floor, she looked concerned and asked if I had forgotten my notes. She shuddered when I told her I intended to wing it.

The 10:30 get-together would only be a small one, set up in the spacious reception room outside Ronnie Shield's office. Trudy arranged for a podium and put out a dozen chairs in three rows of four. People already occupied six of the seats.

The usual four networks were represented, as were the Knoxville and Blount County newspapers. Only three TV cameramen stood in the anteroom. I assumed two stations shared footage. Since we'd be offering old news, the papers would make do without photographs, so no still photographers were present.

Ronnie had yet to take his position behind the podium. The sideshow wasn't quite ready to begin, so I walked over to shake hands with my buddy, WNXX cameraman John Leckmanski.

"How's it goin', John?"

"Hi ya, Sam. Hey, I want you to meet Shauna Reynolds from the station." He introduced me to a black woman about thirty-years-old.

"It's nice to meet you, Chief," she said. "Rachel is in a meeting with the station manager and the owner and unable to attend your conference. She asked me to cover for her and apologize to you. And, Chief, everyone at the station wants to thank you for calling us so quickly. We looked really good broadcasting the early exclusive."

"Who called?" I asked. "Did I call someone?" I winked. She smiled. "And call me Sam, like your partner here does. When people call me by fancy titles I get an inflated sense of worth."

She smiled again. Shauna was a pretty woman.

"Man, you really step in it sometimes, don't you?" John said.

"Yeah, and this one is getting stranger every minute," I said. "Oh, Shauna, all this is off the record right now. We're all just shooting the breeze here, okay?"

She nodded. "Sure. Rachel told me how you guys operate. I know you'll tell us what you can as soon as you're able. Trust me, too. I can wait."

"Thanks."

"From what you told Rachel," John said, "this one should be in Belfast or Londonderry, not Prospect."

"And what makes you so wise in these matters?"

"I may look like just another dumb Polish cameraman, but I had a little experience before Knoxville."

"Yeah, I hear you. I'm going to have to dig into my sack of favors to get a leg up on this one. Stay tuned."

Off to my right, the mayor stepped behind the dais, switched on the microphone and gave it a few taps. I tossed John and Shauna a quick wave and joined Ronnie. John hit me with a sly thumbs-up the other reporters didn't see.

"Ladies and gentlemen, thank y'all for comin' this mornin'," Ronnie began. "We're all very sad ta report the death of our own employee, Mr. Murray McGuire. As y'all may know, he's been employed by the City o' Prospect for many, many years. He will truly be missed. Now, before ya begin yer questions, I've asked Chief Jenkins to read a statement concernin' the circumstances of Murray McGuire's death. After that, y'all may question the chief, who has the most recent information on the case."

I stepped up to the podium next to Ronnie, conspicuously lacking a statement to read. He narrowed his eyes and looked a little concerned, but stepped back. Three months ago, Ronnie would have started to hyperventilate if I showed up looking unprepared. Since then, he's gained confidence.

"Good morning, people." I looked up and noticed my little audience nodding at me. A few of the attendees even smiled. "I'll start by telling you that our victim, Mr. McGuire, was a friendly, personable man—a good worker, well-liked by the personnel in this building. But he was also a very private person with no living relatives, locally or elsewhere. The latter two factors make my job a bit more difficult, but not impossible."

I smiled and paused for a couple seconds.

"A Prospect PD officer, Sergeant Stanley Rose, discovered the body just before midnight Saturday."

I continued to outline the events of the night and the players involved. Then I asked for questions.

"Chief, will you be asking county or state investigators for assistance with the case?" The question came from an attractive redhead in her forties, one of the local news anchors.

"No, ma'am. Sergeant Rose and I will be reallocating our time to investigate this ourselves." I resisted the temptation to say, 'Be a piece of cake, baby.'"

Shauna threw me an easy question, "Chief, can you describe how the victim was killed, please?"

"Sure, Ms. Reynolds. Mr. McGuire was shot four times. Once through each knee, once in the right shoulder, and killed by a shot through the temple."

My description caused a few frowns and grimaces from the assembled multitude.

A happy-looking, chubby guy with a flattop asked, "Isn't that a particularly brutal murder? Do you see any organized crime connections?"

"Yes, sir, it's obviously brutal. There's much to suggest great animus between the killer and victim. However, it's too early to associate the victim with any particular person or group who may be responsible for this. If you're talking organized crime as in Mafia—I don't know. We certainly won't overlook any possibilities. And we'll muster up the outside assistance necessary to cover all the bases. If a criminal faction generally operating outside our geographic area becomes suspect, Federal authorities are available to help."

The managing editor from the local paper asked, "Do you have *any* suspects yet?"

"As of 10:30 today, Linda—no. But since early this morning, I've been making phone calls attempting to get Mr. McGuire's background into perspective and trying to construct an overview of his life. Yesterday, Sunday, I was out interviewing someone who may have provided me with valuable information. Right now, it's too early to draw a logical conclusion. The most important thing here, or in any case, is to resist the possibility of tunnel vision. We have to be open to all avenues of exploration."

And so it went, for another twenty minutes. At times, I sounded ambiguous, or was it obtuse? They tend to morph together where I'm concerned. Before fleeing the room, I promised to make any revelations public as soon as possible. Perhaps someone in the audience even believed that.

Back in my office, I called St. Brendan's Hospital in the Irish Channel section of New Orleans. The obvious pattern was disquieting; too many Celtic connections to be a coincidence. As I suspected, they found no record of Murray Neil McGuire being born in their facility. I faxed them the document I held for a comparison. They confirmed the name of the administrator and attending physician as legitimate for the period in question, but old samples of their signatures weren't even close to those on my paperwork.

My next call went to the British Embassy in Washington D.C. After being shuffled around several times, I ended up with Passport and Consular Services. A well-spoken, young-sounding gentleman answered the phone.

"Good morning, Passport and Consular Services. This is Layton St. Clair speaking."

He went on to identify himself as a Second Assistant Deputy Under-Consul of something-or-other, and pronounced his surname Sinkler.

"Mr. St. Clair, my name is Jenkins. I'm the chief of police in Prospect, Tennessee."

"Right," he said.

"I've run into a unique investigation and have a problem I believe may be of mutual interest to the British government."

"Really? Please do explain."

I told him nothing more than a municipal employee with no living relative died and while inventorying his personal property, we found both a British passport and a U.S. birth certificate.

"Really?" he said again. "That's most singular. Why do you suppose he'd have one of Her Majesty's passports?"

"I can't imagine. That's why I've called you. I hope you can track down the origin of the passport and shed some light on the subject. Perhaps he was or is a British subject, as opposed to just another Yank."

"Ah, yes ...ha, ha, that was quite humorous, yes, quite humorous indeed. Please do give me the number on the document, and I shall see what I can do." Layton spoke with a posh London accent.

I gave him all the information available from the expired passport. He told me he needed a little time with his computer. I sat there, but since the phone line remained open, I could hear him typing away, perhaps making progress.

He came back on the line to say he needed a bit of help from a supervisor. He called to Nigel, Trevor, Giles, or whomever for assistance. I heard them mumbling. Then the sound stopped abruptly, someone switched the phone line to hold, and I could no longer hear the conversation. Several minutes later, after being subjected to a muted version of *Hail Britannia*, my bureaucrat came back on the line.

"Chief, are you there?"

"Yes, sir. Waiting patiently," I lied.

"I'm dreadfully sorry, but aside from it being an expired passport, issued to whom I assume was a British subject, I can offer no additional information. The passport had indeed never been renewed, and unfortunately, our archives from that long ago are not, as yet, computerized. And I don't know if, in my lifetime, they shall be done."

I smelled a Whitehall shuffle.

"That's too bad," I said. "I thought I could rely on your government to dispel some of the problems I'm facing. Any idea why Mr. McGuire's citizenship is so ambiguous?"

"Perhaps, for some reason I couldn't speculate on, he held dual citizenship. Perhaps one parent was British? Who can say, now that the poor chap is dead and there's no family to answer our questions."

Our questions? I knew a run-around when I heard one. I offered no answer.

"Right," he said. "So, sorry to disappoint you, but I fear we've hit a dead end, haven't we? Sorry."

Not believing a word he said, I thanked the young diplomat and hoped Ralph would have better luck. I waited.

Sometime after four, Ralph Oliveri called back. He sounded disappointed.

"I got the London razz-ma-tazz on the passport," he said. "Too old to know anything like where it was issued or what documentation was seen to verify identity—typical snow job. Might be legit, but I never trust those guys. I think they believe all that James Bond crap they read."

"Yeah, I spoke to some flunky at their embassy and got a classic run-around," I said.

"My man ran the facial recognition search twice to be sure—no hits," he said. "I didn't think our collection would go back that far and even be close to complete. All that became a big priority after the first Trade Center bombing in '93, but before that...not a great selection. Sorry."

"I guess we agree that the Brits are not on top of the table with this one?"

He grunted.

"Makes you wonder. Well, Ralphie, thanks anyway. I'll let you know how I make out."

It was time to use my big trump card.

* * * *

Tuesday, November 7th

After striking out on Monday, I decided to renew an acquaintance from long ago, another ex-New Yorker employed in public service, but in a different branch of government. I'd be calling a man who, since I'd seen him last, had done very well for himself.

At 9:15—enough time for him to be sitting at his desk with coffee and a copy of the Washington Post, I dialed a number at Fort George G.

Meade in Maryland.

"Good morning, this is Sarah Wiston speaking, may I help you?"

She never mentioned what office she worked in as most civil servants usually do.

"Good morning. May I speak with Mr. Kaufmann, please?"

"What is your call in reference to, please?"

"Tell Mr. Kaufmann it concerns something from long ago. Tell him I'd like to speak to him about our mutual interests in Tay Ninh."

"And your name, sir?"

"Sam Jenkins."

"Shall I tell him who you represent, Mr. Jenkins?"

"We haven't spoken in some time. I doubt he would recognize my current affiliation. My name should suffice."

"Thank you, sir. Hold one moment, please."

I love America. Where else can you call a super-secret facility, talk a little mumbo-jumbo and get connected with a deputy director of the CIA?

I waited.

"Hello?"

"Irv?"

"Yes."

"Sam Jenkins."

"Yes."

"Good to hear from you, too, Irving," I said sarcastically. "How many years has it been? Doesn't matter. What's the haps, Irv?"

"What do you want, Sam? Why are you calling me here?"

"What I want will require more than your current monosyllabic conversational exchange. I'm calling you at work because I'm not privy to your home number."

"Yes?"

"Irv, I wouldn't disturb your office routine unless I had something I thought you and your employers may have an interest in and may be able to assist me with."

"Yes, I'm listening."

Irving always annoyed me.

"Since retiring from my old employment and my military reserve obligations—I'm sure you remember both—I've accepted a new position where I am in need of professional assistance—interagency co-operation, so to speak." Two can play the spook-speak game.

"Oh?"

I described my new employment endeavor and the murder investigation. I specifically requested assistance with a foray into the world of British governmental intrigue and the possibility of a new biography for Murray Neil McGuire. I left my request open ended with the possibility of new ideas from him—perhaps something to pique his interest, get his creative juices flowing and get more than a one-word response.

"Sam, we're really not in the business of assisting local police agencies with rather uncertain requests. Perhaps you should try the Bureau."

"I did. Their resources seem to be limited to the present and regular channels. Those avenues have proven fruitless. I thought perhaps using the *ultimate* resource would be the quickest and best course of action." *Perhaps a little flattery would help.*

"This is very irregular. Interesting perhaps, but I don't think we can help you."

Okay, you bureaucratic bastard, time for my trump card.

I gave an exaggerated sigh before beginning my next statement. "Irv, far be it from me to mention past history." Well, maybe not if it was to my advantage, "But if you think back more than thirty-five years and ask an impartial observer, they may refresh your memory about how you should consider yourself obligated to me."

"Oh?"

"Yes—oh. I won't mention saving your ass in some hot and sticky, rotten little jungle. I would have done that regardless and probably forgotten it." Or not. "But perhaps a former career-conditional status employee of that noted three letter spook agency became a made-man because of the efforts of yours truly and his band of merry men who helped put your name on that seedy little map of Southeast Asia. Through no fault of your own, Irving, your station chief became quite proud of you. I don't think it's an exaggeration, *Irving*, that you owe *moi* your job with CIA, which led to this big assignment at NSA as chief computer geek of spooky operations. Whaddaya think, partner? Huh?"

"Yes, point taken. Look, Sam, this is a secure line, but there is no need to get so graphic and specific on the phone."

Always good to know when you touch a nerve.

"Agreed," I said. "Your point is then taken as well. I felt the need to get your attention."

"You did."

"Can you contact the Brits, George Smiley or James Bond perhaps, and find out who my mystery man is and how he got into this country with a queer British passport, in possession of a bogus birth certificate and social security card, and why he's been living in the U.S. since 1975?"

"I would imagine."

Of course you would. You're an egomaniac.

"Good," I said. "I'm glad I placed my faith in the right person. Next question. Assuming you get me the good poop on my victim, will my phone go up in smoke and will you disavow any knowledge of me and the City of Prospect?"

"You watch too much television, Sam."

"Can I mention your involvement should your information lead me to arrest a suspect?"

"Probably not."

"Hard to get a conviction that way."

"I understand. Perhaps it's a bridge to cross at a later date."

"Okay, I can live with that for the moment."

"Good," he said. "Give me your data and contact numbers. I'd rather a personal phone number. A cell phone would be best. Also, the older passport photograph you have would be essential. I'll give you a number you can use to fax the image to me. Are you ready to copy?"

I gave Irving what he required, exchanged a few additional pleasantries, and thanked him. Then I waited—again.

Chapter Seventeen

Later Tuesday morning

Just before lunch, Vern Hobbs came in to gas his car and gave me an update on his part of the investigation.

"Hey, Vern, what's up?" I asked.

"Got hold o' Delbert Collier. Done moved hisse'f an' his operation over ta Townsend. Found him on a job site halfway up this pretty ol' hill, property backin' up to the park. Shoot, ol' boy builds some nice houses, surely does."

Vern didn't have the most direct approach to oral reporting, but he was usually thorough.

"Hit's a long time ago," he said, "but Delbert, he says he r'members Murray buyin' that lil' ol' house from him. Delbert wasn't too busy back then, so he had went and built that place on spec. Lookin' back, he thinks hit wasn't his best ideal. Nobody wanted hit 'cause hit was the first house on the block. Block was unrestricted then, too—coulda had a singlewide end up next ta ya. Hell, coulda ended up with a machine shop or junk car lot next ta ya, too."

"Ummm," I said.

"So, then Murray comes along and wants the house. Says he'll pay cash-money. But with a cash deal, he wants a low price. Askin' on the place was twenny-seven-five. Delbert really woulda took twenny-five, but there was no takers. Murray, he offers twenny thousand—no more, no less. So Del, he figgers he gets his money back and jest a few bucks fer his trouble and accepts. End of story."

In spite of my directive for all patrol personnel to wear long-sleeve shirts starting on November 1st, Vern persisted in wearing short-sleeves. The weather had gotten cool enough to make the skinny little bugger shiver.

"Twenty thousand cash in 1978? Not exactly the Trump fortune," I said, "but a nice piece of change back then for an ex-G.I. with a minimum wage job. Even in those days twenty-seven-five was a decent price for a home around here, wasn't it?"

"I s'pose. Close to town an' all. Place had p'tential."

Officer Hobbs popped a toothpick back into his mouth and gave a curt nod to punctuate his final statement

"Thanks, Vern. With luck and a little help from an old friend, we may know who our friend Murray really was by later today or tomorrow."

* * * *

At a few minutes before noon, my stomach started growling, and I thought I'd better go out and feed myself so I could be back to answer the phones when Bettye took her lunch period at one. I walked across the square to Wah Lum, the Chinese restaurant in town.

A late morning breeze whispered through the trees in the town square. It felt crisp and cool and delightful to an ex-northerner who favored the autumn weather above all else. The tulip poplars in the square and around town were at peak color, a rich deep yellow-gold. Squirrels ran around in a frenzy, criss-crossing over the lawn, foraging for anything they could find.

Wah Lum is a small, New York-style Chinese kitchen with only a dozen little two-place tables, the business aimed mostly at the take-out trade. Their food was always good. They kept a large urn of hot jasmine tea available at all hours, and I considered Mr. Lum, the owner, a cool guy. He was pushing seventy-years-old and looked a lot like the Chinese actor James Hong. Lum's three daughters ran the business, while he acted as overseer and cashier. He could have retired and trusted the girls with the business, but I think he liked to harass the customers too much to stay home. When I walked in, he greeted me like an old friend.

"Oh, Chief...Mr. Sam, how are you today?" He spoke with a thick accent and gave me a big smile.

"I'm good, Mr. Lum. How are you doing?"

"I'm an old man, how can I feel? I'll be dead soon, and the restaurant will probably fail because everyone knows my daughters have no business sense."

"Don't worry. When you're gone, I'll come in more often and help keep the business going. Aside from your unfounded fears, are you doing okay?"

"Of course. As you Americans say—you can't kill an old horse, you have to shoot him." More of a philosophical offering than a straight answer.

"You're hot stuff, Mr. Lum."

"Yes, Mr. Sam, hot and spicy, like my Hunan specialties. What you want to eat today?"

After a brief moment of looking at the take-out menu on the counter, I made a choice. "How about the home-style tofu with vegetables." I said. "And steamed rice, not fried rice. But make the tofu spicy, please."

"Oh, excellent choice. Not many Americans order tofu. Probably don't know what it is, heh? You like spicy Chinese food, heh?"

I didn't get the chance to answer.

"Oh, good for you. You want hot tea to go? How about spring roll? Very good today. You like spring roll?"

"Yes, to all that. A spring roll sounds good, too," I said, envious of how the old pirate could manipulate me and drum up extra business.

"Okay, you wait here. Ten minutes, fifteen maybe. You wait, we talk."

He took a hand-written slip of paper toward the kitchen, stopped near the urn of tea, drew a cup, brought it back to me and then continued his journey back to the kitchen. When he returned, I sat patiently sipping my hot tea.

"You have another murder in town," he said. "What's happening? Two murders in only few months? Is bad business. You need luck to find killers."

"I know, big stuff in little Prospect…"

He diverted his attention to another customer.

"Ah, excuse please!" he said, as a man and woman started leaving the restaurant. "Hey, sir!" he said to the man. "You pay maybe?"

"I left the money on the table with the check," the man said.

"I bring food to your table, why you not bring my money to counter?"

I thought there was logic in that.

The man looked confused for a second, then waved his hand dismissively at old Lum, took his wife's arm and walked out. Mr. Lum went into a thousand-word tirade in Chinese and then ended with, "Customers!"

"I know. Pain in the ass, huh?" I said.

I took my home-style tofu back to the office. It tasted wonderful. Bettye told me it smelled good and asked what I'd chosen. When I told her, she made a face and refused to try any.

* * * *

I had to admit, the mundane logistics of running a police department was beginning to get in the way of my homicide investigation. I liked being a detective again. Too bad I didn't know of a place where I could just work on cases with a few assistants to help me out.

At 3:45, Irv Kaufmann called my cell phone. "This is more interesting than I gave you credit for," he said.

"Thanks, I think. It's always nice to hear an ego booster. What have you got?"

"First, your man isn't Murray Neil McGuire. His real name is Seamus Michael Darby. An Irish national—not British. And certainly not American."

I knew from experience that when Irving shared information and got on a roll, it worked best to sit back and listen. I did just that—attentively.

"Darby was born in the South of Ireland to a Catholic family, but lived in the North most of his life, to be exact. His date of birth is not January 14, 1955. Change the year to 1952. Things get interesting, very interesting, from here on."

"I'm all ears," I said.

"Our Mr. Darby served as a low-level IRA functionary for some time," he said.

I just love professional spook lingo.

"Nothing requiring much in the way of talent or bravado. No gun work, no explosives—mostly a wheelman. However, he was definitely in with the in-crowd back during the early 70s. The best I could learn was that he started his terrorist career at around sixteen years-of-age—1968ish. After a few years, he became involved with higher-level personnel—some really bad guys. Most of his criminal activity took place in Northern Ireland."

I grunted to let him know I was still awake.

"The Royal Ulster Constabulary would credit him as an accessory to several killings—two police officers, a school bus bombing in Omah and the deaths of a couple of the more vocal Protestants in his area of operation. The Ulsters thought a single cell of IRA soldiers was responsible for all this—Darby always involved."

I shifted in my chair, fascinated at the amount and quality of information Irv found in a short time. Big Brother really does have his eyes open.

"Wow. Interesting," I said.

"Yes. Right. Then, as the hunt for these individuals continued," he said, "and became more intense, it seems Mr. Darby tired of his life of running and living under pressure. Then for his own reasons, certainly not due to an infusion of altruism, he made it known to a certain operative that he wished to terminate his IRA affiliations and saw a profit in turning informant. Darby laid the groundwork with the RUC to collaborate with the Intelligence Corps for certain compensation, immunity from prosecution and a new life. Young Seamus suggested to his masters that he offer up four major players and their safe house for what seemed to all concerned like a reasonable stipend and then subsequent assistance with relocation—something similar to our Witness Protection Program. Since the deaths of two police constables were involved, the Ulsters were not inclined to be so enthusiastic. But London was, and their cards trumped the RUC objections to amnesty."

I thought the story sounded fascinating, but only grunted a few more times to let him know I was listening with enthusiasm.

"To make this story short," he said, "Darby received twenty-thousand pounds-sterling, new identity papers, a one-way ticket to Boston and the suggestion to lose himself in the U.S. All that in compensation for the bodies of those four heavies, specifically Michael

O'Shea, Tommy Sullivan, Paddy Mellon and Francis Harper.

"The betrayal went down without a hitch. Four gunmen apprehended, a safe house compromised and a large cache of weapons, ammunition, explosives and cash—lots of cash, all out of circulation. The infamous quartet was incarcerated in Maghaberry Prison, which, as you know, is in Ballinderry in County Antrim."

"Of course, I knew that, Irving. Something I think of daily."

He gave a barely audible snort and continued. "But as luck would have it, only one ever lived to go to trial and be convicted. That was Harper. The others, O'Shea, Sullivan and Mellon all died a few years later of malnutrition as a result of the hunger strikes to which they subjected themselves while behind bars."

So much for speedy trials in the Irish criminal justice system.

Irving let out another theatrical sigh and paused for affect.

"So, there you have it," he said. "Your Mr. McGuire was an informant—given a new life, thanks to the British Intelligence services. Fascinating, isn't it?"

"It is indeed. From the manner of his murder, it seems that he may have been found by his former colleagues and paid back for his betrayal. Only my conjecture at this point, but it looks like classic retribution, doesn't it?"

"Umm, perhaps."

"The IRA has been quiet lately. Would these people have memories that long? We're talking more than thirty years, Irv. Would they go to the effort and expense at this late date to hunt down and whack a traitor from that long ago?"

"So it would appear," he said. "Obviously, their statute of limitations is...limitless," he chuckled at his wit. "The message sent when the death of Seamus Darby becomes public knowledge is priceless propaganda and does wonders for IRA retention efforts. As they say, old friend, payback is a bitch."

"Sounds about right. Did your source mention any knowledge of a plan to assassinate Darby?"

"They did not."

"Did they have a case officer monitoring Darby?"

"Not actively. Darby was cut loose to fare on his own. But, I dare say, a local MI-6 agent probably knows enough about Seamus Darby to keep Whitehall informed and happy."

"There's a British agent operating in Tennessee?"

"If not there, close by. Atlanta, perhaps."

"I'd like to speak to them," I said.

He snickered. "Not possible. You have no need to know."

Arrogant schmuck.

"I need to know who killed Seamus Darby. Speaking to the agent might help me find the killer."

"I doubt the Brits regret Mr. Darby's demise."

"Maybe the killer is IRA, but we don't know that for sure."

"Do you normally have murders highlighted by kneecappings in sleepy little Prospect, Tennessee?"

"We don't usually have serial jaywalkers in beautiful downtown Prospect."

"My point exactly. As far as the Brits are concerned, it's all IRA internal strife, not their problem."

"This gives me another piece to my puzzle, Irv, but it goes nowhere, at present, toward solving the case. I have very few known IRA sympathizers listed in my intelligence files, and East Tennessee is famous for its population of Ulster-Scots and Irish folk."

"Your problem, Sam, not mine."

"Thanks a bunch. Suppose I find my IRA revenge seeker? You interested in hearing about it before you read of it in the papers?"

"Of course. The arrest of an IRA assassin on U.S. soil would be of great interest to both us and the FBI."

"Then with luck, I'll be calling you again."

"Good. And shall I call my outstanding debt to you satisfied?"

"Half satisfied. Under the nunc pro tunc provisions of professional interaction, your one good turn cancels out my prior good turn of giving you a priceless reputation. But setting aside my assistance to you in time of mutual need and the boost your floundering career received from said assistance, the fact remains that during our service in Southeast Asia I *was* your savior. What price can you place on your life? Ask yourself that while I'm slaving away at my investigation."

Irving decided it was his turn to grunt.

"By the way," I said, "if I come up with a suspect, can you assist with identification and linking them to the IRA, if I have as little as a photo or fingerprints?"

"I'd rather not. If this person is a current IRA member and operational enough to be given an assignment as we've just discussed, the FBI may well have the information you need. See them first, me only as a last resort."

* * * *

My investigation turned into an open can of worms. However, thanks to Irv Kauffmann, a lot of unanswered mysteries had been explained. The lack of background, the house for cash—I remembered the exchange rate and how it favored the British pound back in the 70s—the reclusive lifestyle, the penance through the church. But who was the killer—or killers? I really didn't have a clue.

I started to go over all the notes I had taken—things on reports, scraps of paper with little notes and like Lieutenant Colombo, a few things written on napkins. I've always saved everything.

Then one napkin with a circular stain from a beer glass jumped out at me. On it was a name I'd picked up at Howell's—Dermott Halloran, Murray's rival at the dartboard. His name certainly sounded Irish enough, and he was local enough. Perhaps not a dispatched killer from the old sod, but maybe a sympathizer with enough balls to off an old man for his past sins.

I'd known other IRA sympathizers and money raisers back in New York, plenty of them. On any given St Patrick's Day in the Big Apple, it would be difficult not to find at least a few. I'd been in many Irish bars in the city and on the Island that were meeting places for the local Hibernian Societies. Some of the members were hard-core, dyed-in-the-wool IRA supporters. So, why not find another one here in the heart of Scotch-Irish country?

Groups like the IRA are extremely well-organized and have far-reaching networks. Perhaps they put a sleeper in place, someone who fit well into the local populace and went about his daily, unrelated business until needed for a mission.

Dermott Halloran looked like the best place to start looking for my

Celtic killer. But I wished that local British agent would at least make an anonymous phone call to our police tip line.

Chapter Eighteen

Wednesday, November 8th

I needed to clean up a few things around the office and the municipal building before moving forward. I went up to Mayor Ronnie Shields' office and not only brought him up to speed on my findings, but swore him to secrecy about the IRA connection.

"Why, Sam, I feel downright foolish, me tellin' ya ta drop yer investigation inta Murray's background. I'm truly sorry." Ronnie looked like a little boy caught with his pants down.

"Forget it, boss. Events would not have been altered if we continued to peek under Murray's curtains. He was a dead man just waiting for the big day. This couldn't be helped."

He looked a little relieved after I tried to take him off the hook.

Then I broke into his rarified world by bringing him back to my own piece of reality. "But I can't impress upon you strongly enough our need to keep things confidential. What we now know *must* be kept secret until I locate the IRA gunman. These people do not fool around. They can be genuine bad guys when they want to be."

"You have my solemn promise, Sam. Before God, my lips are sealed." He sounded sincere—and more than a little scared.

"Okay, Mr. Mayor, I believe you. But remember, secret means *nobody* hears about this. Nobody."

"Sam, in all my life here in Prospect and Blount County, nothing has prepared me to deal with the likes of this. I am surely glad y'all are here to sort this out for us. I don't mind tellin' ya, I am im-pressed with your connections."

Aha, another member of my fan club. Good for me.

"Let's just hope I can locate whoever is responsible for this and get them before they get me." I said that to impress him, but hearing myself made me think this may be a bit more than I should tackle at my age.

Was I stepping too far into a young man's game again? Hell no, this stuff is like riding a bicycle. Perhaps the adrenalin-junkie side of me was taking over. I only needed to remember all the fundamentals of good sleuthing—and combat shooting—if and when the time came.

* * * *

Tangling with the IRA would require competent backup. But I was reluctant to make my new information general knowledge among the Prospect POs. I didn't distrust anyone, but I kept remembering the old "need to know" theory Irv Kauffmann was so fond of. It seemed best to keep the foreign intrigue business limited to as few people as possible.

I decided to make my loop include Bettye and Stan Rose...and Ralph Oliveri as soon as I needed another favor from him. I felt confident trusting those three.

I walked out to Bettye's desk, turned a side chair around and sat down facing her. I hoped the phone didn't ring, and we didn't have a walk-in complaint while I explained everything.

"Sam, that is amazin'," she said. "Typewriter Murray with the IRA? I can't believe it. And how did you learn this?"

"From an old acquaintance. Someone still in the business of knowing all this international stuff. It's good information, Betts—no doubts. I even know his real name, Seamus Darby. There's confirmation that the British gave him a fake passport, a U.S. birth certificate, a Social Security card, lots of money and then told him to get lost in America."

Bettye shook her head in disbelief.

"He got here and joined the Army," I said. "Not a bad idea, was it?"

Bettye shrugged and made a face indicating that she wasn't all that sure.

"Being in the military kept him out of the mainstream. The Army gave him three hots and a cot, and his uniformed brothers did a lot to protect him, especially when he served overseas. Now, we just have to identify the person or persons who found him after all this time and killed him."

"I can't believe it," she said again. "An assassin somewhere in Prospect. Lord have mercy. Sam, this is way beyond my understandin'. I don't mind sayin', I don't like this at all. You have to promise me you'll be careful while you're out there investigatin' this murder."

Bettye didn't seem terribly happy about our future involvement with terrorists. On the flip side, I was glad to hear her concern for Prospect PD's favorite boss.

"I know exactly how you feel. This is dirty business, something I would rather not see come back into my world. But I have an idea who to start looking at for this. Just a starting place for now, but stirring the pot sometimes makes things you didn't see before float to the surface."

She looked at me, waiting to hear my clever plan.

"Don't you just love how I come up with those home-spun metaphors right off the top of my head?"

She gave me a dirty look, much like the looks my wife has dished out for so many years.

"When I pick up this guy," I said. "I'll want Stan along with me. Will you call him and tell him what's going on? Just tell Stan, not his wife, and nothing about this to any of the guys—not yet, anyway. We've got to consider the shooter to be a genuine bad guy with more than the average amount of talent at killing. Mum's the word, Sarge."

"Mum it is, boss. "

From the day we first met, I've found it easy to trust Bettye.

"I'm going out for a bit and see if I can learn a little more. I'll be back before one. If you find Stan, have him call me at quarter-after. See you later, kiddo."

She gave me a nervous smile as I walked out.

* * * *

I began my journey at 11 o'clock. In another half-hour, Howell's Pub would be open for lunch. I found the front door locked and then tried the back—wide open. Howell and Reggie were working in the storeroom arranging cases of beer in an order they understood. We exchanged greetings.

"You gents have a few minutes to talk about one of your

customers?" I asked.

"Of course." Howell answered for both. "In here alright?"

I nodded my okay.

"Reggie," I said, "when you and I last spoke about Murray McGuire, you mentioned an altercation in the pub room. I guess you've heard about last Friday night when we found Murray murdered?" Both Reggie and Howell acknowledged knowing about the killing.

"You mentioned Dermott Halloran. What do you know about him?"

"Not a great lot, Sam," Reggie said. "He's in often enough to call him a regular. Works at Maryville College. Teaches there—Celtic Studies and Literature. He loves everything Irish. You know people who love England are Anglophiles. What is it you call people who love Ireland?"

"Beats me," I said, "paddyphiles, maybe?"

He and Howell laughed. "Well, then, that's Dermott."

"Was his argument with Murray an isolated one?" I asked.

"As far as an open argument, yes," Reggie said. "Dermott was feeling his Guinness that night. He drank a pint or two more than his usual. But having said that, there was no great love between them. No great animosity between them either, but what? What would you call it, Howell, a constant bit of tension perhaps?"

Howell nodded.

"Can you explain that to me?" I said.

"Well, Dermott fancies himself an expert on Ireland," Reg said. "Murray was knowledgeable about the country, too. Whilst Murray didn't speak of extensive visits there, he seemed to know the country. Dermott didn't like being corrected or bested in a discussion. A teacher thing, I suppose. Mind you, there were no other arguments. Dermott mostly sulked—remained quiet. Better for us that way, wasn't it?"

Howell nodded again.

Several flies buzzed around the storeroom in unison, acting like a small squadron of manic pilots.

"Did you ever see anything that would lead you to believe Dermott may have any vindictive or violent tendencies?" I asked.

"No, not I," Reggie said. "But that's hard to say. What do you think, Howell?"

"No, I can't say I ever saw him as other than one of the better-behaved customers. He always tried to be friendly. I think he wanted to be liked. Maybe a little more than some, but he never caused me any trouble."

"When exactly did this altercation between Dermott and Murray take place?"

Howell answered. "Oh, let's see, it was a Thursday night. Yes, they were playing darts." He thought for another moment. "How about two weeks from last Thursday? That sound right, Reg?"

The flies landed several times on a wall or a case of beer and then took off quickly for no apparent reason. They seemed tireless.

"Yes, I believe you're right," Reggie said. "Two weeks before the poor little sod was done in. Tragic end, eh?"

"Was Murray in on the Friday he was killed?" I asked.

"Yes, he was indeed," Reggie said. "He had been here for most of the night. Then he left sometime close to ten. Yes, that's right. I saw him leave just before ten."

"How about Dermott? Was he here on Friday last?"

"He was," Reggie said. "Came in a bit later than usual for a Friday. He usually stops here just after he leaves work. Has his pint of Guinness and either something to eat or he goes on his way—to eat somewhere else, I suppose.

A single fly buzzed my head, annoying the hell out of me. I waved it away.

"I'm guessing he came in near seven-ish and left a couple of hours later," Reggie said. "He threw some darts—with Murray, in fact. Just a casual practice game. Then he had a meal with us, talked with a few of the others and then off he went."

"No new arguments? Just a game of darts with little Murray?" I asked.

"No words," Reggie said. "But I thought Dermott was off his game again. He didn't like getting beaten by the little chappie. He also didn't like Murray being friendly with that lovely Irish lass, Bridget. Our Dermott rather fancies her, I'd say. Don't know if the feeling is mutual, but you can see old Dermott would like to have her as a close friend. Can't blame him there. She is a stunner, eh, Howell?"

"You bet," Howell said. "Good-looking girl, that one. Can handle her Guinness, too. Good as any man. Must be in-bred with those Irish. Throws a mean game of darts as well. She and Murray were always talking about Ireland. Murray told her, and everyone else, his father was born there."

For no apparent reason, the group of flies left us to explore the outdoor world.

"Jealousy can be a terrible thing," I said. "Did Dermott and Bridget, I assume we're talking about Bridget Dwyer, spend much time together?"

I received two nods.

"Oh, yes." Reggie said. "Bridget and our Dermott played darts all the time. Ate together sometimes. Left together on occasion. She's a lovely girl, friendly to most everyone. She seemed to like Dermott, but you'll have to ask her how much, won't you?"

"Indeed I will," I said. "Now, what does this Dermott look like?"

"Oh, a good-looking bloke," Reggie said. "Very Irish-looking. Dark curly hair, medium build, well-dressed. He affected the Gaelic public-school look. You know, tweed jackets, fisherman's jumpers, corduroy pants. He even wears a Barbour waxed jacket when it's cold or wet."

"So do I," I said.

"What?" Reggie asked.

"I have a Barbour coat. It's a Scottish thing, too, you know. Green wellies and a Barbour. A plaid wool cap as well."

"Quite the country laird, eh, Sam?"

"Aye, laddie. All goes with m' Healey drop-head and m' little terrier."

* * * *

I thanked Reg and Howell, took my leave and drove back toward the PD. From this most recent description of Dermott Halloran, I felt confident he was the fellow I bumped into at the pub on the Saturday Kate and I ate lunch there.

And now, Bridget Dwyer stepped fully into the drama. Maybe the IRA thing would fizzle out. Maybe Dermott just got pissed off at Murray for making time with his girl, and he copied the methods of his Irish brethren to eliminate a source of aggravation. Who knows how far a man will go to protect his chances with the woman he covets? That would work for me. Simple is best. Next to money, love or sex is one of the greatest motives for murder.

Back in the office, Bettye told me she had contacted Stanley Rose. He wanted to run a few errands, but would be in early wearing plain clothes. It's always good policy to do your policing at a college campus without a conspicuous uniform, and Stan knows good police work.

One of my neighbors, Dean Barrett, was the president of Maryville College. Most college administrators are apprehensive when the local gendarmes want to do some gumshoe work on their campus. I always tried to contact the campus chiefs of security at any college where I wanted to conduct an investigation. It's just good practice and shows respect for their position. Most of these chiefs were stand-up guys; a few others could be genuine pains in the ass. The annoying ones generally acted like cop buffs, but instead of wanting to hang out with the real cops, they appeared resentful and never made life easy for the detectives who needed to tread on their turf. Since I had an *in* at the highest level, I called the college president first—he could alert his campus cops.

Dean Barrett's secretary connected me with her boss.

"This is Dean Barrett. May I help you?"

"Hello, Dean, Sam Jenkins here."

"Hi, Sam. How are you?"

"I'm well, thanks. How's Mary?" I included an appropriate question about his wife.

"Doing fine, both of us. What's Kate up to these days?" He followed suit.

"I hope she's trying her best to stay out of trouble," I said. "She's always busy with something. You have a minute to discuss some police business?"

"What did I do?" he asked.

"Nothing I know of. You want to confess to something? I take requests and can really use a good arrest this week to boost my commission next payday."

He offered an obligatory laugh to my legendary humor and pressed ahead. College guys always think they're extremely busy with what they consider *important stuff*.

"What can I do for you, Sam?"

"We're doing an investigation, and the name of one of your employees came up. I need to speak with him as soon as possible. During the day, if he's got some free time, would be best for me—if that wouldn't inconvenience your routine."

"Who are we talking about?"

"Dermott Halloran. I believe he teaches for you."

"Yes, he does. He's an associate professor, an enthusiastic person and good teacher. Has he done something wrong?"

"I don't know yet. He's probably more in the witness or material witness category. He had a casual association with a crime victim. I'm just fishing for information right now. He may be helpful, or he may not. It's too early to say."

"I have no problem with you seeing him here. He has an office in Anderson Hall. Let me get in touch with him, and I'll call you back with his free time schedule."

"Thanks. That's helpful."

"One thing, Sam. Please check in with our chief of security first. I don't like to leave him out of the loop on these things. Okay?"

"Sure. You let me know when Halloran is available. I'll visit or call your chief beforehand and bring him into the picture. That work for you?"

"Sounds good to me. Where do I call you?"

I gave him my number at Prospect PD. With luck, he'd call before too long, and I could get the ball rolling with my interrogation of Dermott Halloran.

In the interim, I walked over to Quizno's for an Italian special on a wheat roll. I wanted an adequate lunch before I took over for Bettye while she went out to eat or shop or whatever she planned for her lunchtime. I make it a practice to never tackle an important interview on an empty stomach.

Chapter Nineteen

I sat in Bettye's chair minding the desk when Dean Barrett's secretary called. Dean set up a meeting with Dermott Halloran for 2:30 and requested that I meet his chief of security, Tony Dubois, at 2 p.m. She said Tony would escort Stanley and me to Halloran's office.

At 1:30, Stan Rose sat in my office.

"You know this security guy, Tony Dubois?" I asked.

"Nope."

"You know your way around Maryville College?"

"Yep."

"Have you ever had to do an investigation there before?"

"Nope."

"The name 'Dermott Halloran' mean anything to you?"

"Nope."

"Oh, great," I said. "I hit the road with the black Gary Cooper. You gonna be this talkative all day?"

"Little talk, lotsa action." He smiled like a Cheshire cat.

Sounding a lot like 'The Duke', I said, "Well, come on, Coop, we'll take my horse and go find this pilgrim. And keep yer shootin' iron ready, case we find him at the OK Corral and he starts throwin' lead at us."

Stanley scowled. "Sounds like a fun afternoon, Marshal."

* * * *

Maryville College sits along U.S. Highway 321 in the small city of...where else? Maryville. To immediately gain local acceptance, sound like a native East Tennessean, and not be thought of as a "furriner" or "imuhgrint" like Stanley or me, we don't carefully pronounce the name

Maryville. We practice a combination of mumble and slur and say something that sounds like Murr-vull.

About a year ago, the college spent damn near the gross national product of an emerging nation on redesigning and refurbishing the main entrance area. Today, your first impression of Maryville College is an institution almost as impressive and almost as Early American as the larger, older and more famous College of William and Mary in Williamsburg, Virginia.

According to lettering on a brick wall at the entrance, Maryville College was established in 1819. A Blount County Chamber of Commerce booklet stated one Isaac Anderson, a Scottish Presbyterian minister who wanted to extend enlightenment to the 'Old West' founded the college. Depending on your time in history, geography is relative. Today, Maryville is one of the fifty oldest colleges in the United States.

We turned left off 321 onto the campus. With the exception of a few flat-roofed, yellow brick dormitory buildings that reeked of the1960s, most of the architecture on campus was Federal Period red brick. If Shakespeare had been alive in the 1960s, he may well have said, "First thing we do is kill all the architects." The modern, boxlike buildings placed along the quiet tree-lined streets were as appropriate to this Ivy League-looking college as a root beer mixer is to a good single-malt whisky.

We followed the well-placed signs to the Security office, arriving five minutes early.

The receptionist, a blonde in her late-twenties, typed on her computer keyboard as we walked in. She gave us a nice smile and was almost pretty, but like many local girls her age, she looked almost twenty pounds overweight. I stated our police business, and we all smiled again. I think she liked Stanley. I'd have to remember not to bring him along when I meet girls.

"I'll tell Mr. Dubois you're here," she said.

The nameplate on her desk told me we just met Wanda Owenby. I'd file that away in case I called in the future. Girls think you're charming when you remember their names.

Wanda spent a few seconds on the phone with her leader. "Go right in, gentlemen," she said, pointing to the door behind her desk.

Tony Dubois looked to be in his late-thirties. He was short, dark and thin with an Errol Flynn mustache. The white shirt he wore with a black clip-on tie and two gold eagles pinned to the collars looked several sizes too large for his neck. If Damon Runyan ever wrote about New Orleans, Tony could have gotten the part of a Cajun bookie in the play. Along with his ill-fitting uniform shirt, he wore the navy blue trousers of the college Security Police. He neither stood when we entered nor did he offer to shake hands. *Strike one.*

"Good morning, Mr. Dubois. I'm Sam Jenkins, and this is Sergeant Stanley Rose." I showed him my badge. "We're from the Prospect Police. I believe President Barrett told you we were coming."

"It's Colonel," he said, and dropped a cheap pen onto the large paper calendar that covered his desktop.

"Excuse me?" I said.

"Colonel Tony Dubois." He flicked an index finger under the tip of his collar.

"Oh, of course—full bird. I see." I stood corrected. *Strike two.*

"What can I do for you guys?" He gave us a look of intense interest and narrowed his beady little eyes into a squint. It must have been one of his interrogation techniques. He looked fearsome.

"We have an appointment to speak with Dermott Halloran at 2:30," I said.

"About what?"

It would have been bad form to grab the little cretin by his ankles and shake the change out of his pockets. So, I resisted the overwhelming urge. At my age, patience is not only a virtue, but a precious commodity.

"Sometimes, *Colonel,* it's about confidentiality. I'm not at liberty to tell a long story here. We believe Mr. Halloran's a casual acquaintance with the victim of a crime we're investigating and may give us additional information about that person."

"Is he a murder suspect?"

"Who, Halloran or the victim?" Tony was doing a fair job of pissing me off.

"Dermott Halloran," he said, with the look of an attitude beginning to take hold.

"No, he is not," I said, and took steps to cease all the annoying banter. "Perhaps you can tell us how to find his office—and we'll let you get back to business?"

"Sure. Follow me. We'll drive there," he said, with a weird smile on his little ferret-face.

I looked at Stanley. He suppressed a grin. Later, he told me Colonel Dubois caused the tips of my ears to turn red. I believed him.

We all walked back to the small parking area outside the Security office.

"What are you drivin'?" the colonel asked.

"The gray Ford over there."

"A regular Crown Vic, huh? Not a Police Interceptor with the big engine and handling package? Too bad."

"We're on a tight budget, and I try to get good gas mileage."

Strike three, Jerk. You're out.

"I drive that baby over there." He pointed to a red, '65 Mustang GT fastback. A "gumball machine" blue police light sat affixed to his dashboard.

"Cool," I said.

Stanley stifled a laugh.

"Okay, you guys follow me," were the new instructions from our colonel.

We all enthusiastically jumped into our cars, and Tony led us about two hundred yards up the road and turned into another parking lot. The distance wasn't worth the effort. We should have walked. But the colonel got to show us his hot wheels—the car with the genuine po-leece light on the dashboard.

Stan and I found Dermott Halloran in his office on the second floor of Anderson Hall. Reggie's description of Halloran was accurate. He dressed as if he taught at the University of Dublin, and his clothes looked expensive. Filson's expensive, or Stafford's expensive, much, much more than L.L.Bean expensive. His hound's-tooth Norfolk jacket made my Eddie Bauer sport coat look like something I bought off the rack at a Salvation Army thrift shop. A spark of happiness surged within me when I saw a bag in the knees of his corduroy slacks. We all exchanged greetings, and I felt even more elated for leaving the moron, Colonel Dubois, in the car park. I'm rarely pleased when roaming the halls of ivy.

I started by saying, "Mr. Halloran, we're investigating the murder of Murray McGuire. I understand you knew him."

"Of course, I knew Murray. He was quite the dart player. I saw him at Howell's Pub at least every Thursday when we throw in league competition. I'm very sorry to hear about him getting killed."

Are you? I wondered.

"When did you see him last?" I asked.

He thought for a minute. Or at least he wanted us to believe he was thinking.

"Hmm, Thursday. Sure, it was Thursday," he said.

"How about Friday?"

We observed more of Dermott's thinking process.

"No, Thursday. Don't think I saw him on Friday."

"Perhaps I can refresh your memory, Mr. Halloran."

That's a line that generally makes a suspect a little nervous. Never ask an important question to which you don't already know the answer.

"I've learned that Murray was in Howell's on Friday," I said. "You were there, too. Did you see him? It's a small place. He played darts on Friday evening. Remember doing that? Did you play with Murray himself, perhaps?"

"Friday night? Hmm, I worked a little late on Friday." He did his pondering the universe act a third time. "Oh yes, I did stop at Howell's for a pint. But I didn't stay long."

My prompting caused him to remember a little more. In the future, I hoped he'd think before speaking.

"What was your time frame at Howell's on Friday?" Stan asked.

"I got there, oh, about seven, maybe a little after. Had a pint, and oh yes, a sandwich, too. Now I remember. I left about 9:00 or 9:30."

"And after that?" I asked.

"I went home. Watched a movie."

"Anyone with you?" Stan asked.

"No, I live alone," he said.

"What did you see?" I asked.

"How Green Was My Valley."

"An oldie."

"Yes, I have it on DVD. I like all the old films about Ireland."

"You have your passport handy?" I changed direction and threw off his train of thought.

"What? Passport? Uh, no. It's in my safe deposit box. Why?"

"When were you in Ireland last?"

"Uh...early this summer. Why? I usually travel around Ireland every year, as soon as we break for summer. What does that have to do with Murray?" He sounded a little bewildered.

"Where did you go this year?"

"Oh," he sighed and looked off into nowhere, indicating another thought process, "I landed in Dublin and then did the southeast coast. I stopped in a few small villages with B&Bs. I went to Wexford, got as far as Waterford. Then I came back north through Kilkenny and Carlow. I was there almost three weeks."

I knew the area.

"You have family in Ireland?" I asked.

"Yes and no. No one close. My family came to New York and Boston long ago. I'm fourth generation American."

"Where did your family originate from in Ireland?"

"My father's people were from Dundalk on the east coast. Mom's family came from Armagh in the north."

"You have any political leanings one way or the other concerning Ireland?"

"Political leanings?"

I just love it when a subject answers a question with a question.

"Yes," I said, "political leanings, thoughts. What would you like to see happen in Ireland—politically?"

"Oh, I'd like to see Ireland united again. I think most everyone would."

He paused for a moment and looked at me. Stan and I remained quiet, letting him feel uncomfortable with the silence.

Then he began to elaborate. "Uh, I'm not an IRA supporter if that's what you're asking. My father's family was Catholic, my mother's Protestant—one of the few Protestant families in Armagh, I think. They went back a long way in Ulster. They lived in Londonderry way back in the 18th century. Why are you asking all this?"

"Mr. Halloran, several people saw you have an altercation with

159

Murray McGuire in Howell's two weeks ago. You accused him of cheating at darts. I don't know how that's possible. What was the argument really about?"

"Oh, that. It was stupid on my part. I argued about darts, but it was really about something else. I admit I drank one or two more pints than I should have. I wish it never happened."

"Tell us about the something else," I said.

"You're making me feel really stupid," he said.

I shrugged. "It happens."

Stan just stared at him.

"It was about a girl...a woman."

"Yes?"

"Someone I met at Howell's. I see her there a lot. She's in the dart league, too."

"Just someone you play darts with?"

"We've been out a couple of times as well. To dinner. Nothing more."

"What's her name?"

"Do we have to drag her into this?"

"We do." I sounded insistent.

"Bridget Dwyer. She's a nice person. She's from Ireland. We share common interests."

"Tell us more about Ms. Dwyer."

"She's here doing independent research for her post-graduate degree on the Ulster-Scots and Irish in America. I thought Murray was trying to get too friendly with her. I got a little jealous. It was unwarranted, but it happened. What really twisted me out of shape...oh, I thought she was responding to him as well."

That last bit threw me for a loop. "Bridget Dwyer?"

"Yes."

"The Bridget Dwyer from the bookshop in Prospect?"

"Yes. You know her?"

"Bridget Dwyer is a beautiful woman. Murray is not a...beautiful guy. He's probably close to being her father's age. Are we talking about the same people?"

"Yes, we are. I was surprised, too. In the league we're all friendly with each other. Bridget and I got a little more so. Well, we never got *that* friendly."

He made a hand gesture to clarify what *that* meant. It seemed out of character.

"But it wasn't for a lack of effort on my part. I enjoyed those times we went out for a nice dinner."

"What did you and Bridget talk about during these dinners or before or after?"

"Ireland mostly. As you've probably guessed, I'm fascinated with the country. It's my work. You understand, a passion really."

Stan and I nodded. I glanced at three framed Aer Lingus posters hanging on the walls of his small office.

"She was a wealth of information about the people, the country, about everything there. A *very* nice person. And, as you mentioned, she's someone very good to look at, too."

"Let's look at your conversations. Besides answering your questions about Ireland, did she ask you anything? Please think very carefully about this."

He pulled a bottom desk drawer out and rested his foot on the side. After a moment of nodding he said, "Well, she asked what I knew about the old days locally. About the Irish and Scotch-Irish in Blount County. You know, things of interest for her studies."

"How about things more contemporary?" Stan asked.

"Yes, she asked if I knew any of her countrymen living locally."

"And?" I said.

"Well, I really didn't. I mean, there's Reggie from England at Howell's and the couple who own the bookshop. They're not Irish, but close by American standards and Murray who said his father was born in Ireland, and oh, yes, there's an Irish woman who works here at the college, but she's been in this country for more than thirty years. Her husband was born there, too. Anyone else is strictly American with various ancestries. Most of the local people consider themselves Tennesseans first and anything else very secondary."

"What have you heard Murray say about Ireland?"

"That's funny. He said he was born in Louisiana and lived most of his life here, but he did know some very particular things about Ireland.

161

Things someone wouldn't know unless they'd been there."

"How so?"

"He told me he'd never been to Ireland, but he'd read a lot about it, because his father had been born there. If that were true, he had extremely good retention, and he chose some very interesting books."

"How did Bridget get friendly with Murray? Specifically, when you got mad?"

"Like I said, I had a couple of pints of Guinness more than I should have that night. My darts were off, and I was in a bad mood. I asked her if she wanted to go somewhere else. I was thinking the Hilton at the airport. It's more...intimate and classy. She said no. She was playing darts with Murray and talking with him a lot. I guess that's it."

"Is your temper usually that short over something inconsequential?"

He actually looked sheepish before answering. "No. I was out of line." He shrugged and tucked his right hand into his sport jacket pocket. "The Guinness, I suppose."

"And what about Friday night? What was Murray doing then? And how about Bridget? Where does she fit into Friday?" I asked.

"They were playing darts with two others—a practice match, Murray and Bridget against two other men. I asked one of the men if I could have a game. He let me stand in for him once. After that, I left, and they were still throwing. You would have to ask Reggie what happened after I left. He was working that night."

"Two things, Dermott," I said. "Listen carefully now. I want you to get your passport from the bank vault. Take it to the Prospect PD. You know where that is?"

He said he did.

"Show it to Sergeant Lambert. She'll know what I want copied. You can do this when? Tomorrow? Okay?"

He agreed.

"Then you are not, I repeat not, to discuss our conversation here today with anyone. Understand?"

He frowned.

"Not the security people here at the college, not Bridget, not with your friends at Howell's—no one. If you decide you need legal representation, I can't stop you from discussing it with your lawyer."

His eyes popped open, and his Adam's apple leaped to attention.

"I need a lawyer?" It came out as almost a gasp.

"I don't know. Do you? You do anything wrong?"

"No—no, I haven't!"

"Remember, this is a murder investigation," I said. "And I'm serious about you keeping this confidential. If any of the officers who are watching the people involved in this case or those who have you under constant surveillance see you speaking with other subjects or suspects, I will personally charge you with obstruction or hindering prosecution faster than you can kiss the Blarney Stone. Are we clear on that?"

"Yes. Sure, but…"

"Thanks for your time, sir. Hope to see you tomorrow at my office."

We all shook hands. As we turned to leave, he stood with his mouth half open.

Out in the parking lot Stanley asked, "Did I miss the new people you hired to conduct these twenty-four hour surveillances?"

"You spotted my exaggeration? You gotta keep them guessing, Stanley. Gotta provide the public service that keeps the public nervous. And as you've no doubt surmised we're far from finished with Dermott."

Chapter Twenty

Thursday, November 9th

It started drizzling around 10:30 Wednesday night. By 7 a.m. Thursday, the intensity grew to a gentle soaking rain—something we'd not seen in months. The colored leaves shined and glistened. The green grass around the house looked thicker and more like a lawn than it really was. Clouds hung low around the mountains and hills, and the air took on the clean look and fresh smell you get with a steady downpour.

I felt conflicted by mixed emotions. We in Prospect got paid on Thursdays, and that was a good thing. My inability to find Murray McGuire's killer troubled me. I hate to feel inadequate. With only one more idea in mind, I again needed outside help. It would entail asking a big favor from one of the two Feds I'd already involved in the case. Choosing the more affable of the two evils, I decided to call Ralph Oliveri in Knoxville. If this paid off, Ralphie would be satisfied with a classy lunch as repayment for the favor. If I got in the hole to Irv Kaufmann, he might ask me to assassinate the President of Venezuela in return for his help. Irv belonged on the back burner.

* * * *

"Bettye," I said, "fire up your DMV computer and run Bridget Dwyer. I don't have a DOB. She's probably around thirty-five."

Less than sixty seconds later Bettye said, "No hit, darlin'. You have anything more on her for me to try?"

"No, she's probably using an Irish license. She's driving a rental or lease car from Enterprise, I think. Give the guy in Alcoa a call and see if

164

she picked up the wheels from him and what he knows."

"Okey dokey, boss."

I dialed the Blount County Sheriff's CID and asked for Jackie Shuman in Crime Scene Investigations. "Hey, Jackie, you up for doing me a favor today?"

"Mebbe. Whatcha need?"

"I need a good telephoto lens on your camera and your best impression of a portrait photographer. It'll involve a little stake out. Think you can make some time today?"

"I guess. Where's this happenin'?"

"At the bookshop—south end of Main Street, here in town. Think your boss would give you the time, or can you just steal a little for me?"

"I'll see, mebbe both. Where can I meet ya?"

"How about here at the office? If you can get into place before ten o'clock, you may be finished by five-after. Use that unmarked Explorer you guys have, okay?

"Okay, sounds good. I'll be there in fifteen, twenty minutes."

Bettye made contact with the local agent for Enterprise Rent-A-Car. She learned he did not furnish Bridget with her car, but he tracked her name through the company records and told Bettye the Chevy Cobalt Bridget Dwyer drove came from their Atlanta airport office. Bridget used an Irish driver's license, an international driver's permit issued by the Automobile Association of Ireland and a Republic of Ireland passport as identification when she leased the little car.

Aside from an address in Killarney and a date of birth for her, I learned little else. In addition to speaking with Ralph Oliveri, I planned on calling the Killarney office of the Irish Garda, the national police in that part of the world.

When Jackie Shuman walked into my office, I gave him Bridget's description, the information on her rented Cobalt and said I needed a couple of really good head-shots to use for a facial recognition match on a federal computer.

A few minutes later, Jackie called me on his cell phone while he sat parked in a spot across the road from the bookshop. He moved into position at 9:40, and I crossed my fingers.

At 10:15, Jackie walked back into Prospect PD headquarters.

"You runnin' some hoo-doo on me, Sam?" he asked.

"What are you talking about?"

"Who was that movie star you had me git a pitcher of? I ain't seen someone that good-lookin'…" he paused and turned to his right with a big grin, "since Miss Bettye started workin' here."

Bettye smiled. "Why, thank you, Jackie. That was very kind of you."

"Yes, ma'am, Miss Bettye. Always a pleasure."

"Well done, kid," I said. "Good to see a guy think on his feet and save his ass with so much savoir faire."

Bettye smiled again but ignored me. She knew her way around cops. If she laughed, she'd only encourage us.

"Why'd you need me ta make these pitchers?" he asked.

"Come on inside." I pointed to my office.

I explained my Irish connection and my shot in the dark. Jackie shrugged, not one-hundred percent convinced a beautiful woman like Bridget Dwyer looked like the killer type. I wasn't convinced myself. As far as I knew, they still had a British agent running around somewhere in the American Southeast. It could as easily be Bridget as anyone else.

Jackie pulled a long cord from his camera bag, plugged one end into his digital Nikon D-200, and the other into the USB port at the base of my computer tower. In a few clicks, he opened a series of six photos of Bridget on my computer screen. Four of them looked adequate enough to use for a face match. A few more clicks and they were stored on my hard drive.

I thanked Jackie and thought about how I could pay him back for the favor and how all things in life were relative. A payback gesture to Jackie may involve a barbecue sandwich plate at Howell's or a luncheon special at El Jibarito. Oliveri, on the other hand, fancied himself an Italian stallion and worldly gourmet. He'd expect crab cakes at Chesapeake's or some chi chi pasta at another classy joint in Knoxville. Jackie liked free refills of his sweet tea, while Ralph would want a couple of draught beers or an expensive bottle of wine. I'd have to ask Ronnie Shields for an expense account if I continued to hang out with my new FBI friends.

* * * *

My next task required me to call the Irish Consul in Washington to get a phone number for the Garda field office in Killarney. That turned out to be fairly easy.

I made the international call and spoke with a desk officer. He transferred me to a desk sergeant. Then with a little more shuffling, I got connected to their detective section.

It's a good thing we share an almost common language with those in the British Isles. I had less trouble understanding the Irish cops than I did learning to speak Tennessean. I ended up talking to a detective sergeant who sounded like Pat O'Brien acting out his role of Father Flanagan. Or was that Spencer Tracey? It didn't matter at that point.

Without getting into the specifics of my case, I asked Sergeant Jack Doyle for assistance in determining the validity of Bridget Dwyer's driver's license and the home address on it.

I felt a bit reluctant to get into the case any deeper with him, not knowing the people who would be working on the Irish end of my undeveloped lead. But I trusted the sound of the man with whom I spoke and asked him to go a little further and run the passport number through their appropriate agency.

I hoped my apprehensions were unfounded and there was no IRA mole hiding in the Killarney Garda Siochana station. I don't speak Gaelic, but I'm sharp enough to know Garda Siochana means "keepers of the peace."

Sergeant Doyle promised to call me back as soon as he could run the numbers through their computer, make a phone call to some liaison officer in their system and have one of his squad dicks take a look at the property in question. The wheels of an investigatory progress sometimes turn slowly.

I called Ralph Oliveri, told him the saga of Seamus Darby, where I stood with the investigation and what I needed to play my latest hunch. I added a second request to the facial recognition search for Bridget Dwyer or whatever her actual name might turn out to be if my suspicions proved correct.

I thought it only good police work to also run Dermott Halloran through the FBI's National Crime Information Center, and their not-open-to-the-public intelligence files. Perhaps Dermott would prove to be as innocent as the driven snow, but perhaps he was a closet IRA wannabe or worse, an actual sleeper waiting for the big chance to get his name into the history books along with Michael Collins and some other famous sons of the Emerald Isle.

The good thing intelligence files have over criminal records is that they may be totally subjective and unsubstantiated, and only look promising when you add an ingredient learned years after the raw material surfaced. After my short dissertation, Ralphie, the boy G-Man, seemed ready to jump on board with both feet.

"Hey, I'm impressed," he said. "Cool case for a little jerkwater PD. Someone might say you know your onions, kid."

"Yeah, that's me, Sam Jenkins, man of international intrigue and onion farmer. Hey, don't get smart, Ralphie. If your father didn't pay for your education and make you a CPA, you wouldn't be an agent today. You'd be working at Aqueduct as a shoeshine boy."

"Man, that hurt."

"It's the truth."

"Nuts! When can you send me the photographs?" he asked.

"Ten minutes, maybe less. Just one thing, kiddo—don't go falling in love with my suspect."

"That good, huh?"

"Better."

"Hot damn. Like a real James Bond girl?"

"You betcha."

"Hot damn! I'm on it." He sounded enthused.

"Thanks. Call me."

I went out to lunch.

* * * *

When I returned to the PD at one o'clock, Bettye told me I missed Dermott Halloran by half-an-hour. She didn't look happy.

"What's wrong?" I asked.

"First Murray creates problems, now this ol' boy. Remind me never to go to Ireland."

She handed me a passport.

"You kept Halloran's passport?"

168

"Look inside, and you'll see why."

I felt the problem before seeing it. I flipped through the pages.

"For chrissakes. Was this in his pocket when he jumped in the ocean?"

"See what I mean? He said he was hiking in Ireland and fell into a stream. Hard to read most of the entries."

"And hard to tell if it's been altered."

"That, too. He said he plans on asking for a new one before his next trip to Ireland. But that's in the summer."

"How convenient."

"That's why I kept it. He wasn't happy, but I insisted."

"You've got a gun. I'd do anything you asked."

"Really?"

I raised my eyebrows twice. "You betcha."

"Remind me of that when I get back from lunch, big fella. But while I'm gone, can I assume you'll check this out with your Federal friends?"

"As you wish, madam."

She smiled and turned to leave. "Bye, Sammy." She always makes the word 'bye' sound like something a sheep says.

Foolishly thinking I could deal with my inquiry locally, I wasted two phone calls to Knoxville before I headed for the big guns in Washington D.C.—The Department of State, Bureau of Consular Affairs. After listening to my call being transferred twice, I spoke to a woman with enough of a foreign accent to make understanding her difficult. But before I got snitty and asked why my call had been transferred to Uruguay, we came to terms, and she promised to call back and comment on the validity of Dermott's passport.

Then I called Ralph Oliveri with my new information. After getting voice mail at his desk phone, I tried his cell.

"What?" He sounded annoyed.

"I have important information regarding that matter we last spoke about. Where are you?"

"I'm having lunch."

"Where?"

"Why do you care?"

"You have good taste. I may try it someday."

"The Orangery."

"That's a nice place. But even lunch is expensive. Who are you with?"

"A friend."

"A girlfriend?"

"What makes you say that?"

"You're on a date. You snake. And on company time."

"Don't break m... You're breaking up. My battery must be weak. Tell me what you need, and I'll call you later."

I didn't believe his story about weak batteries, but relayed my new information quickly.

"Okay, got it," he said. "I'll pull his photo from Motor Vehicles."

"Thanks, serpent. Talk to you later."

He hung up. Again, I waited.

* * * *

Bettye walked in at two o'clock after her lunch. I gave her a quick version of my attempts to learn something about Dermott and his passport.

She had picked up all our checks from the payroll office and handed me mine.

"Ugh," I said. "I see these numbers, and I ask myself, 'Is it all worth it?'"

"The numbers on your check are better than mine, boss-man," she said.

"I've got to stop remembering what the current contract is like back in New York."

"If you think about New York paychecks, you better think about the Long Island property taxes you told me about."

Sometimes women are so damn practical.

"Good point," I said. "I'll try to stay happy for another two weeks."

And I suppose I should have tried to keep an open mind about Bridget Dwyer. Would the beautiful girl who made me an offer I struggled to refuse turn out to be my killer? I'd much rather lock up that Ivy League, dart playing, Irish buff Dermott Halloran.

Chapter Twenty-One

Friday, November 10th

Thursday came and went, and I heard nothing from either the Irish cops, Ralph Oliveri or Mrs. Mendez at the State Department. There's a five-hour time difference between east Tennessee and southwest Ireland. I knew I might wait a week for a reply from Washington, but what was Ralph's excuse?

On Friday, I started getting impatient. I bothered Bettye all morning. By 11:30, she knew as much as I did and probably didn't want to hear any more from me for a while. Ten minutes later Stan Rose called. He was getting antsy, too. I promised to call him as soon as I knew anything concrete.

Just before noon, Jack Doyle called from Killarney CID.

"Trust some Scottish-American bugger like you to send over a bloody kettle of bloody fish. Who is this Bridget Dwyer you're askin' about, lad?"

"Should I infer from your statement that this wasn't a couple of simple phone calls and a quick neighborhood investigation? Maybe I should tell you about the Murray McGuire case."

"And just who in bloody hell is Murray McGuire? Some other bloody Irish bastard, I guess?"

"Forget him. I'd need half a day and a case of beer to explain that one. Have you got anything for me on the lovely Bridget?" I asked.

"I can tell you, boyo, that MOT knows nothing of a Bridget Dwyer with the driving permit number and date of birth you gave me. There may well be a bloody half-million Bridget Dwyers in bloody Ireland, but

171

none of them yours. Today I sent two good boys to that address you gave me. No such place. There is a bloody Muckross Road in Killarney town, sure enough, but no Fuchsia Cottage at number 2462—nothing even close. They checked with the council office and verified that there never was such an address. So, where do we go from here?"

"I thought you'd tell me, Jack, old buddy."

"Not bloody likely, friend. I'm still waiting for word on the passport. And I don't mind telling you that I don't like the bloody delay there. It means some bloody government types have their noses up my arse. With them you never get a bloody straight story, the bastards."

"Things are the same the world over," I said. "I called our passport people in Washington about a man named Dermott Halloran, but got no answer yet."

"Oh, Christ almighty. Halloran? Another one? Good luck to ya."

"Yeah, thanks. I'm hoping to get more information on our lovely redhead sometime later today. Any chance you can get your friends in British Intelligence to tell you if any of these people draw a paycheck from them?"

"Friends in British Intelligence? Who in bloody Ireland has a friend in British Intelligence? The fuckin' Prime Minister couldn't get an answer from those bastards."

"Okay, point taken. I know you're probably ready to go home for the day, but can I call you again if I need to send copies of the documents Bridget used locally to establish her identity? If it becomes necessary, perhaps someone you know will have an idea where those papers of hers came from. I might even have to send you something about Dermott Halloran, if you're up to doing a little more work for me."

"You can do that. I'd be happy to help if I can. And even if you don't need more help, can I impose upon you to call and tell me what the fuck you learn about this girl and your friend Dermott, just to satisfy my own bloody curiosity?"

"One way or the other, Jacko, I'll ring ya. And if I ever get back to Killarney, I'll buy you a pint, so I will," I said, using my Barry Fitzgerald voice.

"That was a pretty fair Oirish accent, boyo. I'll expect you some day. And I drink Murphy's, not that bloody Guinness like every other Paddy down here." Jack pronounced his preference in stout 'Morphy's'.

"Sounds like a deal, my friend. Thanks for the help."

Things were looking dismal for Bridget. I felt conflicted again. My hunch seemed to be paying off, and I may have the satisfaction of solving the murder of old Murray McGuire, aka Seamus Darby, in a matter of hours or another day at most. But I knew Bridget personally, and I liked her, too. It would be a shame to have to arrest such a good-looking girl. Dermott, on the other hand, could be thrown into a cell without me batting an eye.

Well, I guess I'd just have to wait and hear Bridget's side of the story. It's hard to imagine how kneecapping a guy, torturing him with another shot in the shoulder and then dispatching him from this world with a round in the temple could squeak by as a justified killing. Murray was a strange guy. Maybe his death was a suicide. Maybe not. But in my old age, I'm getting liberal, especially where pretty girls are concerned. I was certainly willing to hear what she had to say for herself.

At lunchtime I wasn't even in the mood to eat. But not eating is stupid. I'd only have a headache around three o'clock if I neglected my mealtime. I walked across the square to Wah Lum and bought a quart of won ton soup. Anyone would have room for soup.

* * * *

At three o'clock Ralph called.

"Hey, Sam."

"Sam's not here, this is John Cleese. You've reached the offices of Monty Python, Limited. Leave your name and number and one of the mad-men will call you back."

"Shut up, Sam. I've got some very serious stuff for you."

I hate guys who want to spoil my fun.

"Okay, Ralph, you've got the floor—go," After he spoke, my stomach tightened a little.

"The Irish beauty you asked me to run through the system—she's a genuine bad guy. My man ran her through the computer and got a sure

173

hit. No mistakes here. We've got the current poop on her and real good photos to match her to the pictures your guy took."

Oliveri sure knew how to rain on my parade.

"As far as the other guy, Dermott," he continued. "No score on him. He's an unknown in our files. Maybe he's a solid citizen, I don't know. We've got no record, no associations and no other flags. Or maybe he's in cahoots with the girl, and he's just been able to stay below everyone's radar."

"Uh huh, I'm still listening."

"Her name's not Bridget Dwyer. It's Maureen Sullivan. We have her as thirty-eight years old. Born and raised in Northern Ireland. She's IRA all the way. I've been on the phone with our guy at the embassy in London three times today."

I remembered Bridget's frown when I likened her to the movie star Maureen O'Sullivan.

Ralph continued. "She's been IRA for a long time, almost twenty years. The Brits like her for all kinds of stuff, shootings, bombings, you name it. They put her right on the 'A' team. Nothing is confirmed or solid enough for an arrest warrant, but they think she's good for a couple of killings herself." He stopped and let all that sink in.

"Ralph, I'm shocked, but I won't ask you if you're sure. I believe you. I'll just keep listening."

"Okay, pal, I got more. Her old man, Tommy Sullivan, ex-IRA himself, died during his hunger strike after a few years in Maghaberry Prison up in Northern Ireland."

"Tommy Sullivan was one of the four IRA hoods Murray—Seamus—flipped back in '74."

"Exactly. I think you had a vendetta playing out right there in Prospect, Sam."

"Yeah, lucky me. Your guy is one-hundred-percent sure on her ID, kiddo?"

"Like I told ya, guy, one-hundred-and-ten-percent sure—no doubts. London faxed her pics to our guy in Belfast. He got together with his counterparts. The British Intelligence types all got together and agreed for once. She's confirmed. Shit, how could anyone mistake her? Not too many girls look that good. It's a match, Sam. They have her prints if we need them."

"Did these guys have any prior knowledge of her current job over here?"

"Didn't say so—if you can believe them. They denied hearing any chatter from the Provos about a sanctioned hit in the U.S. But it sounds like IRA internal affairs clean-up work to me. The Brits would have a better chance learning about some operation against their army or the Protestants."

"Yeah, I guess so," I said. "I suppose they wouldn't know if she might have a partner over here."

"Again, they didn't say so. Our counter-intel people have nothing on that either. I had a guy run her arrival date and time, a couple of weeks before and after, for other possibles who might have entered the U.S. or got here via Canada and could have met up with her. There was nothing on record that stood out to those guys. However, that doesn't preclude her from tying up with someone who's been here and in place for a long time, someone from New York, or Boston or wherever."

"Be nice to know if she's got someone watching her back."

"Yeah, but I can't help you there. As far as anyone knows, this must be her first foray into the U.S. of A. You may have to check with whatever spook got you the info on Murray-slash-Seamus for more—if you have time to watch her a little longer, that is."

I've been told there's a British agent here somewhere close by. Hear anything about that?"

"Holy shit, no."

"Okay. I guess I'm on my own here," I said. "I've got to do something today. I can't let this sit. She's a pro and probably just hung around to keep from drawing attention to herself by disappearing right after the killing. More questions may make her think something is in the wind. Especially if she saw Jackie Shuman take her picture or someone else mentioned it to her."

"Sam, you need some kind of back-up there?"

"Thanks, Ralph. I'm okay—I think. If I need you for something your boss would approve of, I'll call. One way or the other, I'll let you know how I make out."

175

"Be careful there, buddy. She may be beautiful, but she'd whack you as quick as one of those pug-ugly boyos she hangs out with."

"I know, Ralph. I know. Thanks."

"Call me, Sam. Okay?"

"Yeah, Ralphie. See ya."

I hung up, disliking any of the options I saw on the horizon.

Chapter Twenty-Two

I cradled my phone at 3:15, expecting Stan Rose in shortly to supervise the evening shift.

I walked to the outer office. "What's happening on the road, Betts?"

"Junior and Vernon are working a four-car wreck with injuries on Sevierville Road just northeast of the thirteen curves. That happened less than a half-hour ago—they've got at least an hour to go. A state trooper's assisting. Bobby's all alone with a domestic dispute in that mobile home park near the greenhouses and the junk yard. It seems under control, but he can call the county if he needs help. You got something going?"

"Yeah, I've got to arrest someone, and I'd like at least one pair of eyes at my back. I'll try to get Stan to go with us. He's probably home or on the way in. And we'll leave a note for the first four-to-twelve man that shows up, too. But I'd like you to call the county and tell them to handle calls and dispatch for a while. You and I will be at the Fox and Quill Bookshop on South Main. Tell the dispatcher so they can send the first swing-shift car that goes in service in case they don't stop here first. Or in case they have to send one of their own cars to assist in a hurry."

"Lord have mercy, Sam. What are we gonna be doin'?"

"We've got to lock up that pretty Irish girl for killing Murray."

I dialed Stan Rose's cell phone number and got no answer. When the voice mail kicked in, I left a message. I called his home number and got the same results. Things started out problematic before we even left the barn.

"Hey, Betts, do you have a vest handy?"

"A vest? As in bulletproof? Do I need one?"

"Probably not, but I want you to wear it."

She didn't seem to like that idea.

"Sam, me getting comfortable in body armor isn't as easy as it is for you or one of the guys."

I began to understand her point. Mrs. Lambert's enviable womanly endowments didn't look ergonomically compatible with a Kevlar vest and the metal shock-plate that protected her vital organs.

"I see what you mean. But I owe it to Donnie to protect you and your, uh ...assets. Put on a vest. We won't be long, and it'll make me happy. We'll take my car."

"Okay, if you insist," she said. "But how about you? You have a vest yet?"

"I'm fine." I fingered my sport jacket. "Bulletproof tweed."

"Damn it, Sam Jenkins!" She actually yelled at me.

"Don't shout, woman." I smiled to soften the comment. "Make your phone call, and get your vest."

"Yes, sir." She shook her head like my mother used to do when I behaved badly.

* * * *

The drive from the municipal building to the bookshop lasted only a few minutes. If I possessed any sense, I would have waited for Stanley and one or two of the other cops to handle this with Bettye and me. But I didn't. Someday I may admit to myself why I didn't wait. But I'll have to learn the reason first.

On the way, I explained how Bridget Dwyer most probably killed Murray McGuire and elaborated on how Ralph Oliveri learned about her long association with the IRA. I stressed the point that even though she looked as cute as a button and acted like an innocent young lady, she should be treated as the most dangerous subject we've both ever attempted to arrest.

I pulled into the lot on the north side of the building. The white Cobalt Bridget drove sat parked near the entrance. The old Jaguar sedan owned by Derek and Eleanor was nowhere to be seen.

I stepped out of the Crown Victoria and stood on the gravel looking up. A flock of six turkey buzzards soared over the woodlands hundreds of yards away, hundreds of feet above the earth, floating in the air currents. It reminded me of the old western movies filmed in the parched Arizona desert. An odd thought to have in the heavily foliated Tennessee foothills on a cool day in November.

The crisp autumn air felt good against my face. The smell of the season blanketed the air. Leaves burned somewhere far off, and the decaying foliage yet to be burned or bagged gave the day that particular aroma I associate with my favorite time of year.

Long ago, I would have been chomping at the bit to get an arrest like this going and under my belt. I would have already been mentally composing a supplementary report I'd casually slip onto my boss's blotter, an unspoken gesture cops make when they think the collar they just made could be written up to sound extraordinary and worthy of a commendation. On that day, I would rather have taken Bettye to lunch somewhere nice, downed a bottle of appropriate wine and felt sleepy for the rest of the day.

Times and interests surely change.

Bettye stepped up beside me. She wore her Kevlar vest over her uniform shirt and a light civilian windbreaker over that.

"I guess she must be alone in there," I said. "No other cars here. That's good. But if a customer or either of the Foxwells is in there, we have to get them out quickly. Take out your gun now, but keep it out of sight until we know the situation. If she's alone, I'll take the lead. If I stop talking and you think I should still be speaking, say something—it doesn't matter what. Just start making conversation. It means I can't talk and shoot at the same time. Okay?"

"You think it may come to that?"

"Gotta plan for the worst and take what we get."

"Uh-huh."

Bettye looked like I felt. I think we both would have preferred being anywhere other than where we currently stood.

"Everything okay with you?" I asked.

"Yes, Sam, I'm okay. I'm with you." She gave me a reluctant smile and nodded.

"You're sure?"

"Yeah. Let's do this."

I shrugged and drew my revolver, working my hand around the

checkered wooden grip.

"Okay, doll face, in we go." Sometimes I sound more like Humphrey Bogart than the old boy himself.

"You think Lauren Bacall would be standing next to you wearing a vest?" Bettye asked.

"You catch on quick, sweetheart, but don't be a sap. You're more the Betty Grable type."

She growled and punched my arm.

In we went.

Luckily, the shop was empty. I didn't even see Bridget...or Maureen...or whomever.

I held the Model 15 alongside my leg and stepped into the store a few more feet, still unable to see anyone. Bettye stood on my right, far enough away from the bookshelves not to be seen from the main part of the store. She held her Glock in a two-hand grip pointing downward. I walked quietly past the register desk and toward the stacks.

"Hello?" I said.

Bridget stepped out from between the bookshelves, much closer to the rear of the shop.

"Oh!" She acted surprised. "Sam. Hello. You startled me."

"Hello, Bridget. We need to talk."

She could not have seen Bettye.

"What's wrong?" she asked. "You seem so serious."

I tightened my grip on the Smith and Wesson.

"I need to speak to you about Maureen Sullivan."

"Oh, really?" She set two hardbacks atop a row of mysteries.

"Some people tell me she's a genuine tough-guy."

"Yes, well, some people might," she said. "Do you believe them then?"

"Right now I believe you killed Seamus Darby."

She raised her eyebrows and cracked a faint smile.

"And I'm not sure I blame you," I said, "considering what he did to your father. But a revenge-homicide is not socially acceptable down here in the Bible Belt."

"You seem to know a lot, don't you, Sam?"

"I do now."

"So, what do you want?" She sounded casual, as if asking about my choice from a menu.

"I want you to come with me. I'll get you a good lawyer. You make whatever deals you can. There's nothing else to do."

It all sounded simple and reasonable to me.

"I don't think so."

Obviously, our opinions differed.

I'm not a professional negotiator. I attended a few schools addressing the topic and learned the basics. However, a regular in that line of work might think I knew just enough to get myself into trouble.

Over the years on the street, either in uniform or as a detective, I'd been confronted often enough by surprised criminals, barricaded subjects, suicidal folks or other desperate people. All that took place far enough away from the services of a professional negotiator to make taking action on my own a necessity. I was never one to wait for reinforcements.

The one thing anyone trying to gain a person's compliance will agree on is, these strung-out individuals must be kept talking to keep their minds off other potential mischief. Not being one socially adept at small talk, I always felt more prone to tackle the subject and wrestle some sense into him. While that may have been the simple solution, it rarely represented the correct one. I needed to keep Bridget's mind occupied with some devilishly clever conversation.

"Don't play hardcore with me, Bridget. We're friends. You know I can't let you walk out of here. But I want to help you get through this. I can't just look the other way."

"You can if you want to, boyo." She smiled and leaned against the wall across from the bookshelves. A row of pegs, a simple coat rack, was attached to the wall only a foot away from her. Her shoulder bag and jacket hung on two of the pegs.

"No, love, I'm sorry," I said casually. "Let's make this easy for both of us. Please. I promise to make this as painless as possible."

I wondered if she compared me to some of the tough Ulster cops or British agents she knew. Those guys would have just thrown her up against the wall and cuffed her. Maybe she considered me a first-class pussycat.

"Oh, Sam, just let me drive away. Give me a few minutes, and then make your calls and print up your wanted posters."

She made it sound like an episode of *Gunsmoke*.

"I can't do that, Maureen."

"But you can still call me Bridget, can't you, Sam?"

I listened to her voice and thought she could charm the gold from a leprechaun's kettle.

"Sure I can. That seemed to work fine for us before, didn't it?"

Was I seeing some light at the end of the tunnel?

She nodded and looked comfortable where she stood.

"Are you alone in this?" I asked. "Or do I need to look for your partner, too?"

"Since you know what I am, Mr. Jenkins, you probably know I wouldn't answer that if I could."

"Okay. I thought I'd get lucky." I smiled to take the edge off my question.

She returned a smile that lit up the room. "You could have gotten lucky, Sam, but you said no."

The woman had the face of an angel.

"Funny how things play out, isn't it?" I said. "One day we're talking about Irish whisky and hot tubs and the next we're doing this. Hell of a shame."

She nodded and then finally said, "Yes, it is."

"If this was just revenge for your father's death, it would make a big difference in court. Revenge and built-up emotions make us do things we normally wouldn't think about. There's a big difference between murder and manslaughter. A sharp lawyer could make that work." I hinted again at a deal to keep her interested.

I glanced to my right without moving my eyes too much and saw Bettye standing out of Bridget's line of sight, but without adequate cover. That bothered me. A line of prickles ran up my spine.

"I'd rather not talk about that, Sam." She didn't look any more troubled than a girl trying to choose a new pair of shoes. "But I guess I should have left Prospect days ago. I didn't play that right."

"Too suspicious," I said. "I would have closed the airports and borders. You're too beautiful not to be recognized."

"You're such a grand man. I wish things could have been different."

"They can't be different, but they can be better."

"I wish that were true. But you know Darby had to be killed, don't you?"

"Do your bosses' memories go back more than thirty years? Darby left Ireland and disappeared. This sounds like something you did on your own. Remember what I said about court. Don't tell me the wrong thing."

"Our memories go back a long way. We have to let the next guy know betrayal can't be allowed. And as you know, I have a personal interest here. It wasn't something I could ever forget."

I couldn't disagree with her logic. And in her place, I may have acted the same.

"As I've said before, I really can't argue with your reasoning."

"There's no time limit on retribution," she said.

I nodded and felt like my negotiations were going nowhere. "I understand."

I heard a car door slam outside the shop and hoped it was Stan Rose or any one of the Prospect cops. With another person present, I would stop talking and wrap up the arrest. Bettye moved up closer toward me and made a little noise.

Bridget turned toward the sound. "Ah, I see we're not alone," She saw Bettye.

"Are you ready to go now?" I asked.

Quickly, she took her purse off the peg and hung it on her shoulder.

"Leave that!" I spoke louder than necessary.

"Easy now, boyo, easy." Bridget extended her left hand in what she must have thought was a calming gesture.

Bettye raised her Glock, pointing it directly at Bridget.

The back door to the shop opened. All three of us looked. Eleanor stepped in carrying two shopping bags full of groceries. Bridget moved quickly again. She stepped behind Ellie and put her left arm around the old woman's waist. The shopping bags fell to the floor. Bridget's right hand came out of her purse with a gun and raised it, pointing it at Eleanor's head.

She held an old Beretta Model 1934, a flat .380 caliber semi-automatic. Murray—Seamus—whomever, all those names were getting to bug me, had been killed with a .380.

"Whoa, lady!" I said. "No need for this. Ellie, I know you're frightened, but don't fight. Stay as calm as you can. We're still okay here. Everything's okay. Right, Bridget?"

"Might you reconsider my request now, boyo?" Her voice sounded harder, the lovely lilt all gone.

"You know I can't do that. Come on now. We've been through this. And you can't hurt Ellie. Jesus, Bridget, she and Derek have been good to you. She's not part of this. Just let her go. Bettye can take Ellie outside. Then you and I can keep talking and reach an agreement you can live with. That work for you?"

"Oh, oi'm not stupid, bucko. Oi'm not spending the rest of my life in a bloody Tennessee prison—not for you or her or anyone."

Perhaps time for a little more soothing dialog?

"Okay, okay, just calm down. Look, just for my information, when you offered me, ah...that glass of Jameson, did you intend for me to help you find Seamus? Did you anticipate this day and figure your lover would let you go? I'd like to know for personal reasons, sort of an ego thing, I guess."

"Oh, Sam, you would have to ask, wouldn't you?"

Her voice softened again to that beautiful Irish music, not the harsh accent of a tough street kid from Belfast.

"I came here with a name," she said, "and I was able to learn for myself that the little man I played darts with betrayed my father. I just figured there was no harm getting close with the local copper. If it's any consolation to you, Sam, my love, I would have wanted you anyway. What I told you was true."

"Thanks. That helps an old man feel better about himself."

"Oh, Sam, you're such a dear."

Bridget smiled again. Ellie looked terrified.

"How old were you when Seamus informed on your father and his partners?"

"Just a wee girl of five or six. I remember going to visit m' da' in that God-awful jail for what seemed like an eternity. Then, God love him, he took his own life. They tried to keep him alive with tubes and things. Do you know what it was like for a child to see her father like that? Do you, Sam?"

"No, of course not."

"I didn't think so."

A tension pain crept up my neck and lodged in my head. My lack of patience was catching up with me. I felt like I was wasting too much time.

"This has to end well, Bridget. I can't let you go. You know that. I told you, I sympathize with you. Your father and his friends were betrayed by one of their own. What daughter could live with that memory? I promise I'll get you the best criminal lawyer in the county. This is less of a problem than you think. But if you harm Ellie—you know what happens. None of us want that, believe me. You don't want to hurt her, and I hope to hell you don't want to shoot me."

"No, Sam, and you're right. I don't want to harm this dear old girl. And I don't want to shoot you. But you can't shoot me either. I know you're not the type to kill a woman. Now just you let me drive away from here...because I will kill her!"

She quickly turned her pistol toward Bettye. I watched her thumb cock the hammer.

As we talked, I held my gun pointing in Bridget's general direction. But when her thumb snapped the hammer back into the full-cock position, I raised the Smith to shoulder height, held my breath, let out a little air and lined up my sights. And just as I'd done thousands of times on the range, my index finger snapped the trigger back to lock up the hammer, something a competitive shooter does all the time, but nothing anyone would recommend to a street cop in a gun confrontation.

At that point, my world switched to slow motion. I couldn't see Bettye; my peripheral vision narrowed down to a tunnel. Bridget looked to my right, straight at my partner. Eleanor closed her eyes and pulled her head as close to her shoulders as possible. My finger tightened, squeezing the trigger...closer to where the sear would release the hammer. Then...Bang!

The shot surprised me, just as it's supposed to do. Bridget's gun fell harmlessly to the floor. My ears rang. I squeezed my eyes shut. Eleanor screamed, bent over with both hands clutching her ears and screamed again. Bridget slumped to the floor. I stepped closer. I had been only fourteen or fifteen feet away from her when I fired. Everything happened in no more than three seconds.

I let out a long breath and looked down at her body. A hole, a little more than one third of an inch, scarred her right temple. Her eyes remained open. But none of the horror and pain of death marred her lovely face. Bridget died instantly.

Bettye holstered her Glock and wrapped her arms around Eleanor. I bent down and looked closer at Bridget. I violated police protocol and closed her eyes so she'd appear to be sleeping. Don't let anyone tell you closing a dead person's eyes is as easy as it looks in the movies.

The first phase of my intended arrest ended like a horror show. The real hassle was about to begin.

Chapter Twenty-Three

Eleanor cried softly while Bettye held her in a gentle bear hug. They swayed back and forth like a mother and child. The contact with another person seemed as important to Bettye as it was for Ellie. When Bettye looked at me, I put my hand on her shoulder and squeezed lightly.

"You okay?" I asked.

She nodded.

"I'm going to the radio. I'll get some help and an ambulance for Ellie. I know she's not physically injured, but it's best to have a doctor see her. I'll be back as soon as I can. Sure you're okay?"

She nodded again but didn't look convincing.

"Talk to me."

In a few seconds she said, "Why did she do that, Sam? There was nowhere to go."

"I know, kiddo. Sometimes you just can't figure. Maybe she thought a shot at you would buy her time to escape. Maybe she knew it was all over, and she opted for suicide by cop. We'll never know."

"I guess."

"I'll be right back. You hang in there, and keep an eye on that gun." I pointed at the Beretta lying on the floor three feet from Bridget.

I stepped outside the shop's doorway and stood for a moment on the second step. I felt genuinely lousy and remembered those same feelings, under similar circumstances, years ago. Taking a deep breath, I realized I still held the revolver at my side and holstered the gun and snapped the thumb-break safety.

Only occasionally do cops have to shoot people. More often soldiers do. And for them the deed receives less criticism. I would have been more content to jump off the skids of a UH-1D chopper after returning to base camp for a shower and a half dozen bottles of 'Bamiba' beer than go through the post-shooting ordeal cops face. But helicopters and army compounds were part of another world. In Prospect, I needed to get the ball rolling on a lengthy process.

Oddly, as I stood there, I recalled a quote by Arthur Wellesley, Britain's famous Duke of Wellington.

"Nothing except a battle lost can be half as melancholy as a battle won."

I knew what the 'Iron Duke' meant. Perhaps he felt that way at Waterloo after kicking Napoleon's ass.

I walked to my car, switched on the ignition and keyed the microphone.

"Prospect-one to dispatch."

"Go ahead, Prospect-one."

Off to my left, Stan Rose pulled into the parking lot driving his white and blue Prospect PD cruiser.

"This is Prospect-one. We attempted to go 10-32 with one subject at the Fox and Quill Bookshop, South Main Street in Prospect. We had a brief hostage situation and a gun altercation."

Stan exited his police car and walked toward me. I motioned him into the shop. He'd be a welcome face for Bettye and could start securing the scene.

"One subject is DOA," I said, focusing back on the dispatcher. "The officers involved are both unhurt. I need Rural Metro ASAP for the hostage. Sixty-five-year-old female, no physical injury, but she's suffering from trauma and shock. Get her clearance to Blount Memorial. Also give me an ME's wagon and a couple of county cars to help secure an outside perimeter around the shop."

Moments later, she spoke again. "10-4, Prospect-one. Paramedics are notified. I'll call the ME. You want TBI or county detectives as your shooting team?"

I hesitated. "This is Prospect-one. Negative on the local shooting team. Because of the nature of the incident and the subject involved, I'll request FBI Knoxville as my shooting team."

There was a long pause.

"Uh...10-4, Prospect-one. You want me to call them?" she asked.

"Negative, dispatch. I'll call. You have a county road supervisor who can spare a couple of bodies to assist here?"

"Stand-by, Prospect-one."

Ninety seconds passed.

"Prospect-one, this is dispatch. I have one patrol unit, 330, responding and one crime scene unit with two officers leaving the Justice Center now. Will crime scene be handling the forensics?"

"Unknown at this time. I'm requesting an FBI ERT."

"10-4, Prospect-one. Advise the crime scene people when they arrive."

"10-4, dispatch. Thank you."

I almost had the microphone hooked back on the dashboard when the dispatcher spoke again.

"Dispatch to Prospect-one. Duty officer requests you 10-13 his extension ASAP."

"This is Prospect-one. Advise the duty officer I'll do that, but it will be a while. I've got several phone calls to make first. Prospect-one, out."

Keep it in your pants, duty officer. You're mighty low on my priority list right now.

I looked across the street at the Smoky Mountain Butcher Shop and Sausage Company. A portable sign at the roadside advertised the seasonal specials: LET US BUTCHER YOUR DEAR. And: FRESH KILL HOG MEAT.

A 1970, 396 Chevelle Super Sport, black with two white racing stripes, ambled down the road, its twin exhaust pipes rumbling. The driver looked too young to have been born in 1970.

I tapped in Ralph Oliveri's number on my cell phone.

"Ralph?"

"Yes? Sam?"

"Yeah, it's me. You know the favor you offered?"

"Yes? You okay?"

"Yeah, I'm fine. But you could mobilize a guy or two from your office and act as my shooting team. I had to kill Maureen Sullivan."

I didn't hear a comment.

Then, "Jesus Sam. Where are you? You sure you're okay?"

"Yes, Ralph, I'm fine. We're at the bookshop in Prospect—South Main Street. This arrest sort of went south on me."

"You want us to investigate the shoot?"

"If you can. I want a good job. I don't know if I can trust the TBI or the county dicks. If you remember back to that Cecil Lovejoy case, I may not be one of their favorite people right now. I don't want the reporters here yet either or...or I don't know what, Ralph." I started getting a little impatient. "Shit, if someone complained to you about me, you'd come and investigate. Tell your boss—you helped on the case. I couldn't have closed this one without Bureau assistance."

Ralph interrupted. "Was it a clean shoot?"

"Yeah, good as gold."

"Thank God for that."

"Harmon can be at the press conference and get all the ink he wants. Ralph, I need someone who can take a good statement and make an objective call here. I don't want to go to the Grand Jury without someone at my back."

"Okay, okay, take it easy. I'll ask Carl. I'll call you right back. One way or another, I'll be there."

I hung up and then called my home.

"Hi ya, Kats."

"Hello, sweetie. What's up?"

"Nothing good. I just needed to call you. I don't want you hearing something on TV or the radio before you hear it from me."

"What's wrong?" She sounded more than a little apprehensive.

"Bettye and I went out to make an arrest. It ended up in a shooting. We're both okay. The bad guy's not. I have to wait for a shooting team to process the scene. I'm going to be late—don't know when I'll get home. I'll call you again just to let you know what's going on. Okay?"

"Are you sure you're all right?" she asked.

"Yeah, I'm fine. No kidding." Kate possessed the good sense not to press me for more details. "I'll call you again—soon, I promise."

"Sam? Is there anything I can do?"

"No, thanks. All the cops would get distracted. You're too good-lookin'."

"Oh, pooh. Hey, Sammy, I love you. Please call if you need

anything."

"I love you, too, kiddo. Thanks. I'll probably want something to eat later and a big drink or two. I'll talk to you in a while."

I dialed Ronnie Shields at his office. My watch told me it was only a little after four. Ms. Connor put me right through to the mayor. I explained what happened and told him I requested FBI assistance. He didn't know exactly what to make of that, and then I suggested he remain clear of the scene unless he wanted to get called to court and testify to why he had been there. Reluctantly, he agreed to stay away. I said I'd call him again when the process was over and give him an update. He liked that.

It might have been another five or ten minutes before Ralph called back.

"The boss likes the idea that we keep the whole investigation package between us," he said. "I won't work the scene because I've been involved elsewhere. He's sending Marty Saunders and an Evidence Response Team. Marty's a good guy, very thorough, low key, been around. You'll like him. You got an ME coming?"

"Blount County was called. They'll ship this one to UT Forensics," I said.

"Good. Who else is on the way? Who else you call?"

"Rural Metro has a bus coming for the hostage—the shop owner, a sixty-five-year- old woman. This shocked the shit out of her. I want her checked out at BMH. I've got Stan Rose securing the scene in the shop. He'll get one of my road cops to help if he needs it. The county is sending a uniform and two crime scene guys to secure the outside. I called the mayor and told him to stay away, but he'll probably call the news. If your boss wants his fifteen minutes of fame, I suggest he call Mayor Shields to coordinate."

I didn't feel any resentment toward Ralph for checking up on me.

"Sounds good," he said. "You do good work for an old guy...Sorry. I guess that wasn't appropriate right now. I just meant... You know what I meant. Mind if I show up?"

"Not at all. The more the merrier. Just sign in at the door. Tell Stanley you're my mystery guest."

"Okay, guy. I'll be down in a half-hour or so. Hang in there," he said.

"Yeah, Ralphie, I'm hangin'."

I leaned against the fender of my Ford and looked up into the sky. The buzzards were still floating, circling and riding the air currents like a merry-go-round. It didn't look like a bad life. Maybe I'd put that on my list of things I'd like to be when I grow up. I had already written down cowboy, soldier and cop, and accomplished two of the three. Riding a horse for any length of time hurts my lower back, so *cowboy* no longer seemed an option. In a few years, someone would probably look at me and call me an old buzzard anyway. It sounded like a plan.

An ambulance pulled into the parking lot, red lights flashing. Two paramedics jumped out of the cab, one male and one female, both a little overweight. They wore the white shirts and blue trousers of the Rural Metro Company. The male opened a door on the side of the truck and took out a large first aid kit. The female began trotting toward the front door. I moved closer to her. She focused on the badge hanging from the breast pocket of my sport jacket.

"You can slow down," I said. "The victim's okay. She's just shaken. Needs a check-up and probably a tune-up. An officer is looking after her. The female cop inside was involved in this, too. She might want a couple o' aspirin while you're here. See if she needs anything else, if you don't mind. And this is the scene of a shooting. Log in with the uniform sergeant inside, and don't touch anything."

She nodded. "How about you? Everything okay?"

"Yeah, I'm good. Thanks."

"You do the shooting?"

"Yeah."

"Want a couple o' aspirin yourself?" she asked, all business.

I shook my head. "Got any scotch in your truck?"

"Not hardly." She smiled for the first time.

"Thanks anyway."

She nodded again and placed a hand on my arm. Her partner caught up and followed her inside. I picked up the rear.

I wanted Ellie's home number to call Derek. He needed to know the score. Sometime later that night he'd have to secure the shop.

Both medics and I went into Stan's log of incident scene visitors.

I got the phone number and called Derek.

More sirens sounded in the distance. I looked outside again. A county deputy I didn't know parked his car and started toward the steps. Standing in the shop's doorway, I stopped him before he entered.

"Hi, I'm Chief Jenkins. Thanks for coming," I said. We shook hands. "I'm going to need you out here to keep anyone not essential to the investigation from going inside the building."

"Okay," he said.

"If any unnecessary officials—from Prospect, the sheriff's office, the county, anybody, show up, tell them nicely we can't use them here. Get the names and plate numbers of anyone who does show up, even if they just pull into the lot and start to leave because of the crowd. I'm looking for my subject's accomplice. They may stop by to see what's happening."

"Will do."

"If any press people arrive, keep them outside at a distance," I said. "If they're the normal pains in the ass they love to be, call me. I'll see what I can do."

The deputy looked like he'd been around and understood what I needed.

"The FBI is on the way to act as the shooting team. Let them in. They're supposed to be the good guys. Don't break their balls."

He smiled.

"Maybe you can help your crime scene people tape off the outside area if they need an extra pair of hands. Use plenty of cones. If you need horses, have the dispatcher send a Prospect car to our garage to pick them up. The important thing is for you to record anyone and everyone who shows up. Okay?"

"You said FBI. You mean TBI's comin' to act as the shootin' team?"

"No, FBI from Knoxville. Feds. They have a vested interest in this."

"Okay," he said, not hiding his surprise.

A white Ford Expedition, marked as a sheriff's Crime Scene unit pulled into the parking lot near the other county car. I told Stanley I was leaving again so his log would stay up to date. I didn't know the two cops who just arrived either. I had hoped Jackie Schumann would show

193

up, but he was working days that week and already left for home.

I met the two crime scene investigators, explained what I needed and then requested they help the FBI if they were asked to do so. Both men agreed and went about the business of cordons, yellow tape and cones.

I looked up again. The buzzards were still there. Unlike me, they seemed tireless. I assumed that in the next few minutes, as the sun went down, they'd pack it in for the night. Unfortunately, I wouldn't have that luxury.

I started to think how good a strong drink would taste and thought about those big locking call boxes we used to have in New York where aging foot patrolmen hid 'flutes' of Scotch for the cold midnight tours. There are no call boxes in the 21st century, so, I'd have to wait for my cocktail.

My mind began racing through the list of things I needed to remember. I wanted to search Bridget's car for a trace of Murray's body in the trunk, find her rented cabin and search it, try to find where she killed Murray, call my wife again, call the mayor again, check on Ellie and make sure Stanley was doing okay. I wanted to make nice for Bettye periodically, send one of the road cops for coffee, get something to eat and probably do a few more things that weren't on the tip of my tongue at the moment. Thirty years ago, I could keep all that crap and even more in my head. I never forgot anything; my brain functioned like a little computer. But ever since I joined AARP, I've needed to write everything down so I wouldn't forget. Loss of short-term memory was one part of membership I really dislike. I made another note to call AARP customer service and make them deactivate that feature. I walked back inside and signed myself in on Stanley's clipboard.

The medics put Ellie in a folding wheelchair and looked ready to take her to the emergency room. I stepped over to where Bettye sat and knelt down next to her.

"You want to take a ride to BMH?" I asked.

"No, I'm fine...thanks." She gave me a weak smile.

"You want or need anything?" I asked.

She shook her head.

"Have you called Donnie yet?"

"No, but I could use a little help getting out of this vest." I assisted by holding the vest after she unfastened the Velcro straps. With difficulty, I resisted the urge to make a juvenile remark about helping her undress. Once she looked more comfortable, she said, "I'll make the call now. What should I tell him?"

"Just the basics. Make sure you say you're unhurt and doing fine. Get that into the conversation quickly. They like to hear it. If he doesn't believe you or he wants to hear it from someone else, Stan or I will talk with him."

She nodded and took her cell phone from the holder on her gun belt.

"Sure you don't want something to drink? Coffee? Tea? Some other cold regional beverage?" I smiled at her.

She smiled back, one a little bigger than the last. "Actually, I could use a big stiff drink of something."

"That's my girl. I could, too," I put my hand over hers. "You're starting to act like a real sergeant already. I'll tell you when someone's going out for grub. Think of an alternative to a stiff drink. The Feds will be watching."

She gave me another smile and seemed to be doing better.

As Bettye called her husband, I looked at my watch and saw the afternoon marching on. I remembered to call Rachel Williamson at the TV station and start getting some favorable news coverage before Ronnie Shields made a blanket press release.

I owed Rachel for the televised promotion ceremony and hated not to repay my casual debts. With an early call, she might be able to scoop the other networks and get a brief story out with her news preview featured on 5 O'clock Magazine. If she hustled a crew to the scene, she could even get some top-shelf footage for her six o'clock half hour newscast.

She answered on the second ring.

"Hello, this is Rachel. May I help you?"

"Only if you have a cold pitcher of vodka martinis and are willing to deliver," I said.

"Sam? Is that you?"

"Yes, ma'am, it is. Since you're my best buddy in the news world and I have a brief break in the action, I thought I'd let you know about the shooting incident here in Prospect before anyone else."

"What shooting incident? Are you all right? What happened?"

"I'm fine. Thanks for asking. This gets complicated, and I can't stay on the phone too long. Would you like to record this, or do you take short hand?"

"Wait, I'll turn on the recorder." A few seconds passed. "Okay, ready."

One more time, I told my story to another interested party.

"Are you sure you're okay? Is Bettye okay?"

"Yes and yes. Thanks again. As far as I know, you're the first newsperson to learn about this. But I've no doubt the mayor will be making a press release as soon as he writes one. So, do whatever you want with this information. If you send a crew out now, you can get some coverage for your six o'clock show."

"We'll do something on 5 O'clock Magazine, but right now I don't know what. Maybe I can break in with an early bulletin. The bulk of the story will be on the show at six. I don't know if I'll come. I'll try. But someone will be there soon. Is that okay?"

"Okay with me. You'll only get outside footage, but if you or they see me, I'll give a quick statement. But you've got to promise to photograph my best side. That work for you?"

"Yes, sure—whatever. Your best side? Shouldn't you be serious right now?" She sounded a little surprised. Rachel wasn't familiar with my famous black humor.

"I am being serious. I'm terribly cute from my left side. Maybe it's just me, but I'm not sure I look as good from the right."

"Sam! You're terrible. You had to shoot someone. Are you sure you're okay? Did you hurt your head?"

"What a disparaging statement. Gosh, let me see if I can remember the answers. Yes and no. See, my head is fine."

I went on to explain more about Bettye, Ellie, Bridget, how hungry I felt and how I was gasping for a drink. She interjected short acknowledgements as she listened.

"I see FBI people showing up—gotta go," I said.

"Thank you, Sam," she said. "Take care of yourself. Okay?"

"Okay, lady. And I'll see you when I see you. If you don't get here tonight, track me down and call tomorrow."

I remembered that was the second time I called Rachel to repay her for arranging our televised promotion ceremony. I might have to examine my motives. Before I got too involved in that issue, I took a look back at the parking lot.

Two more vehicles had pulled onto the gravel, a brown Crown Victoria that looked similar to mine and a black Chevy Suburban. My shooting scene was starting to get crowded. Special Agent Marty Saunders and three evidence technicians had arrived.

Chapter Twenty-Four

They all stopped at the base of the steps. Saunders held out his credentials. Stan walked up behind me to log everyone in.

"Chief Jenkins?" he said.

I dipped my head. "I am he."

"I'm Martin Saunders, FBI Knoxville. You requested us as a shooting incident investigation team?"

"Yes, I did. Thanks for coming. How would you like to start?"

Saunders looked to be in his early- or mid-fifties, with mostly white hair, cut short. He was five-nine or -ten and stocky, but not overweight. His face showed those telltale signs saying he'd been around the block a few times. His dark gray suit, crisp white shirt and striped tie looked professional. Shiny black wingtips rounded out his standard FBI uniform. Martin Saunders would have made J. Edgar Hoover proud. If he only wore a fedora, he might have been a special agent in charge

I moved out of the way, and the agents entered the store.

"Let's start with a basic account of the events," Saunders said. "Mind if I use a recorder? I'd hate taking notes while you're talking?"

"I have no objection," I said, and we moved to the cash register counter.

He set up the small recorder and pushed a button. The evidence technicians efficiently started their business.

I saw Stanley hand Bridget's Beretta to one of the ERT men and then watched him check on Bettye. She looked weary, but still okay. Stan then went outside to see that the exterior troops were squared away. I thought a dozen Stanleys would make a great small department.

I told Marty Saunders the basic story. He questioned me at all the appropriate spots for any clarification he needed. Ralph hit the nail on the head—Saunders was thorough. As he sat on a stool at the counter, I thought he looked more like a lawyer than a cop. I later learned he was an attorney, but he acted all cop. I liked him.

"That sounds good for now," he said. "I'll need a written statement, but later is soon enough for that."

"Sure, we can go back to my office when you're finished here and get what you need. If you're ready to move on, the hostage is at the hospital, and Sergeant Lambert is right there." I gestured toward Bettye. "Before I start writing, let me know how far back you want me to go in the case."

"What you told me will be fine," he said. "At the end I'll ask questions and put your responses in writing. I like to do it that way."

"I agree. That's a good way. I do it myself."

"I'll need your gun now," he said.

"Want it unloaded?" I asked, but already knew the answer.

"Just the way it is, please," he said.

I turned away, unholstered my revolver and handed it to him butt first. He opened the cylinder, noted the position of the one spent cartridge under the firing pin and ejected the five live rounds and one empty into his palm.

"Bill," he called to one of the ETs "I need two bags and a tag for the Chief's pistol." He looked back at me, "Did Sergeant Lambert fire at the subject?"

"No. One shot—mine only," I said.

"I'll need her gun anyway. Excuse me." He moved over to speak with Bettye.

Saunders made a few notes, asked Bettye questions, listened to her story and went about his business with no wasted effort. It's good to watch an efficient cop work a scene. I thought things would be wrapped up quicker than I anticipated.

For lack of anything more to do, I looked out of the front door once again. The sun had almost disappeared below the horizon, and the buzzards had gone off duty. A third Crown Victoria pulled into the lot, this one silver-gray. Ralph Oliveri showed his credentials and gave his name to the county deputy before walking over.

"Howdy, mister," he said.

"Hi ya, Ralphie. Welcome to the party. You coming in to join us, or would you rather remain anonymous to history and the local court system?"

"The latter. Come outside."

I called to Stan, made a gesture to him like writing on my palm and watched him note the time I left the shop.

"I see Marty and the techs are here. Everything going okay?" Ralph asked.

"Sure. Looks like he'll be finished sooner than I thought."

"Marty's a good man. I like working with him. Mind telling me how this went down?"

"You worried about me? Think I didn't make a clean shooting?" Immediately, I realized how defensive I sounded.

"No, I didn't say that. I'm just being nosey." He seemed to take no offense at my statement.

I told him the story.

After listening, Ralph said, "Sounds like you did the right thing," nodding in affirmation. "I would have done it, too. Or at least I hope I could."

"Nice of you to say so."

He shrugged.

All my recollections were clear. I remembered Maureen's exact words, 'I *will* kill her'. And I watched the gun turned on Bettye with a snap of the hammer to full cock.

I wanted everyone to know I faced a confirmed terrorist, someone suspected of having killed or maimed numerous persons in the past. The law said I'd be justified in using deadly force to effect an arrest or to prevent the use of deadly force against me or a third person if it became necessary. In the split second I had to think, I reasonably believed shooting was necessary to prevent Bettye from taking a round. Bridget diverted our attention by holding a hostage. She was a smart and experienced IRA soldier. Shooting a cop would have been a fine second diversion to give her enough time to run out the back door. I couldn't let Bettye get shot, protective vest or not. My judgment told me to stop our suspect—the beautiful redhead—before something horrific happened. I mentioned all that to convince Ralph and myself.

"I want to toss her cabin before too long," I said. "I still don't know if she had back-up on this, and I don't have an exact location where she killed Murray—Seamus—whomever. I've got to check her car, too. I assume she carried Murray's body in the trunk. Want to tag along?"

"I guess. Yeah, sure. Let's check with Marty first, make sure he's okay with that."

"Absolutely. Marty's got a good bedside manner. I like the way he's treating Bettye, and I owe him for that. Of course, if he says the shooting was no good, he'll piss me off to no end."

Ralph shook his head, "You're a piece of work, Jenkins."

Behind us, a navy blue Chrysler mini-van drove into the crowded parking lot. Bettye's husband Donnie Lambert and their three children all stepped out. The county cop walked over to them immediately. Donnie started speaking. The deputy shook his head—international sign language for no dice. Donnie didn't look like he wanted to hear that.

"Hang on a minute, Ralphie, I've got to go play Mighty Mouse and save the day." I walked over to the crowd.

"Chief," the deputy said, "I've told this gentleman he can't go into the shop but…"

"It's okay, officer, I'll give you a hand here. You're doing a fine job, thanks. Can you give us just a minute, please?"

"Yes, sir, sure can. Thank ya." He walked over and stood with his two crime scene buddies.

"Hello, Donnie. Hi ya, kids." I tousled the little boy's hair and smiled at the two girls.

"Sam, I need to see Bettye." Donnie showed more than his share of concern.

"Sure you do. But you can't go into the shop. The FBI is processing the evidence. I'll go in and get her. She's okay—one-hundred-percent. She's just giving her statement now, but I wouldn't be surprised if she hasn't finished. You guys hang out here, and we'll be right back. Okay?"

"Sam," he asked, "did Bettye have to shoot someone?"

"No, Donnie. Bettye didn't shoot anyone. She was just here with me. This one is all mine. She didn't do anything that can get her in trouble, and she's physically okay. She's a good girl, Donnie, a real good girl." I looked from Donnie to each of the kids, Little Donnie, Missy, the oldest and Clarry, the middle child. "You all be nice to your mom tonight. She'll just want a little space and a little TLC from you guys. Don't ask too many questions. She'll tell you everything in her own time."

Everyone nodded, but no one spoke.

"Let me go in now, and I'll get her for you."

As I turned to re-enter the shop, I watched a white van from Rachel's TV station pull into the lot. My on-loan policeman jumped into motion, ready to be on the news team like white on rice. I squinted to see who sat in the van. I didn't recognize the driver, who I assumed to be the cameraman. When the light inside the van came on, I saw a cute blonde I recognized from TV. I left them to fend for themselves for the time being.

I walked inside the shop and logged in yet another time.

"Marty, can we have a word?" I asked.

Saunders and I stood near the bookcases. The ME's people had arrived and were working with the FBI technicians. Doctor Mo Rappaport and his assistant, Earl Ogle, worked efficiently at their routine chores.

"Bettye Lambert's family just showed up," I said. "Could you live with her leaving for a while to get something to eat? She could be back here in less than an hour."

"No problem with that," he said. "Matter of fact, her preliminary statement is good enough for me. Let's forget about written statements tonight. If you two can come into our office Monday morning, you can dictate a statement to one of our stenographers. That'll save you writing it out."

"Sure, sounds good to me. Next question—I really need to search the young lady's rented cabin and her car. I still want to find out if she had any partners working with her and where she may have killed my victim. You have any objections to me doing that tonight?"

"No, not at all. We should be finished here shortly. Then I'll see Mrs. Foxwell at the hospital. This thing promises to be pretty interesting. You want some company?"

"Your man Ralphie just stopped by. I was going to take him, but you're welcome to come along, too. Her place is way back in the boonies. The darker it gets, the harder the job will be."

"Hang on a minute," he said. "Hey, Bill."

One of the evidence technicians turned in our direction.

"You guys want to help us search a cabin before we go back to Knoxville?"

"Sure. What are you looking for?" he asked.

"Clues." Saunders and I spoke in unison. We both smiled.

"It's the place rented by the deceased," I said. "I need to find a location where she killed a local man last week"

The agent named Bill spoke, "See that big black van outside, Chief?"

I nodded.

"State-of-the-art portable lighting inside. I can light up your world. Don't worry about the darkness. "

"I leave myself in the hands of an expert."

I turned back to Saunders, "If you're going to be here a little longer, anyone want coffee, soda...cigars, cigarettes, Tiparillos?"

"Yeah," Saunders said, "Coffee sounds good. Who's going?"

"I think the county ETs have done a good job taping off the perimeter. If you want anything else from them, let's tell them. Otherwise, they look like good candidates to make the coffee run. After that, I'm going to cut them loose unless you need more help."

"No, we're good here," Saunders said.

"Stan," I said, "when we're finished here and Derek comes back to lock up, will you take that white Cobalt back to the lot and give it a thorough once-over then lock it in the garage for at least overnight? The keys should be in her purse or jacket if you don't already have a collection of her personal effects."

"Sure," Stan said. "I'll call you if I find anything exciting. And I'll see you tomorrow. If you need me in early for anything, give a shout."

"Good, thanks. I'll need the house keys. We're going to her rental cabin and see what's there," I said. "And, Stan, would you call the county duty officer? He wanted to know the score here. Just give him a brief sketch of what happened. They don't need all the gory details. Let them watch the news."

Stanley smiled and nodded.

I walked over to where Bettye sat and spoke quietly. "Donnie's outside with the kids. Saunders doesn't need either of us any longer tonight. We'll go into Knoxville Monday morning and sign statements for him. I'm guessing that Ronnie made arrangements for a press conference tomorrow morning. I'll call you later on. If you don't feel like answering the phone, that's okay. I'll leave a message and let you know what's happening. Now go see your sweetie and the kids. Get something to eat. And have that stiff drink you mentioned. My advice—make it at least a double."

"At least," she said. "I think I'm gettin' bad habits from you."

"You're not the first to say that. Besides being led astray, you doing all right?"

"Yes, darlin', I just need a break."

"You're sure?"

She nodded and squeezed my forearm. "Yeah, Sammy, I'm fine."

"Before too long, you and I have to have a little talk. Okay?"

"About what?" she asked.

"About you. About how you're making out. About if this business is giving you any trouble. About if you want to go and talk with someone about it."

"Like a shrink?"

"Like a shrink. I know someone good. She's a friend. I'll get Ronnie to approve payment for as many visits as you want. But if he's not able or willing, I'll take care of it myself. I'd like you to go at least once."

"How about you? You goin'?"

"Maybe. If I need to."

"Okay, Sammy, thank you. Thanks a lot."

"For what?"

"For not letting her shoot me. I was scared there for a minute."

"No big thing, lady. I can't have one of my new sergeants sitting around the office with holes in her. Not good for our image."

"See you, boss." She smiled, touched my arm again and walked outside.

"Okay, gentlemen," I said. "Start a list of wants, needs and desires. I'll get us a gopher to make the coffee run."

Waiting for the goodies list to be finalized, I walked outside, too.

"Hang in there, Ralph," I said. "Seems the whole damn crowd wants to search the cabin with us. You want coffee or something?"

He asked for a cup of regular.

I turned toward the county crime scene vehicle and stopped. Bettye stood next to her mini-van. Donnie and the kids were all hugging her. The streetlights were on, and I thought I saw a few tears shining on the cheeks of the Lambert family members. I continued walking. The three deputies stood together talking; two leaned against the side of the crime scene vehicle.

Three news vans from the TV stations had taken up spots in the parking lot. I made a quick assumption that Fox was the network who bought footage from one of the other stations. No one represented them. Cameramen and reporters hung around recording what they saw. The three uniformed cops were doing a good job of keeping the press from getting too pushy.

"Chief Jenkins." The blonde Rachel sent called to me. "Would you care to make a statement?"

I changed direction and walked toward her. "Sure, but wait just a minute, and let me give these officers an assignment. As soon as I finish with them, I'll get back to you and give you an update on the incident." I stepped away before anyone could comment.

To the deputies I said, "Gentlemen, I need a volunteer to go on a mission of mercy."

"Whatcha need, Chief?" one of the crime scene investigators asked.

"Nothing dangerous, just a coffee run." They all grinned.

"You guys figure out what you want. I'll get a list from the people inside. What's your name?" I asked my volunteer.

"Hugh Bledsoe, sir."

I handed Hugh a couple of twenties. "These FBI types sounded hungry, but if there's any change let me know."

"Sure thing, Chief," he said.

I made a quick trip back into the shop, grabbed the goodies list Stanley put together and walked it out to Hugh Bledsoe.

The time had come to meet the press. When I stepped over, all the reporters began talking at once. I held up two hands to quiet the little crowd.

"Folks, hang on just a minute. I'm on a tight time constraint here. I've got to be several other places tonight, so let me give you all a quick account of what happened.

"First, I can't identify the person who's been shot because it may have some ramifications which would be detrimental to this case."

That statement got a few frowns, but I then outlined everything I'd told Rachel and almost as much as I told Marty Saunders. All the reporters seemed satisfied with my story. They stood there listening, trying not to interrupt.

"Because of their help with this case beforehand, which has international connections, and their interest in the suspect, I called in the FBI to investigate the shooting. They're finishing up in the shop now, and I am assuming that Mayor Shields will have already scheduled a press conference for tomorrow. So, thanks for coming out tonight, but I really have to get on to other business." I walked away as reporters hurled questions at my back.

Later on, we all stood in the bookshop drinking our coffee, soda or spring water, eating our donuts, Otis Spunkmeyer muffins, Moon Pies, Fritos or corn dogs—the best junk food Git N' Go could offer. It made the not-so-perfect interlude in a truly lousy day.

I dispatched the two county crime scene cops back to the Justice Center with my thanks. Marty Saunders, Ralph and I piled into my car and drove to Blount Memorial Hospital so Marty could interview Ellie Foxwell. The three FBI evidence technicians needed more time to finish up. The ME's people transported Maureen Sullivan's body to the University of Tennessee Hospital's Forensics Laboratory for a post mortem examination.

Stan Rose would wait for Derek Foxwell to come and secure his bookshop. Our on-loan deputy, I still didn't know his name, would soon go back on patrol.

Some time ago, Bettye drove away with her family and with any luck ate a nice meal somewhere and became pleasantly anesthetized by a double martini or one of its cousins.

The logistics of a major case can always be mind-boggling. If Prospect planned on continuing to have them, I'd want to hire a half-dozen squad dicks to help me out. I could easily begin running around like a decapitated chicken, but instead, I followed Saunders and Oliveri to the hospital and hoped that Eleanor told a good story…and that hers matched mine.

Chapter Twenty-Five

Driving to the hospital, I thought about how much work still remained unfinished. After Marty took Eleanor's statement, when the FBI completed the shooting scene, after I called my wife again, after I spoke to Ronnie Shields—we'd all begin our search of Maureen Sullivan's rented log cabin, the one with the hot tub.

I sat in the hospital hallway while Marty and Ralph interviewed Eleanor. Derek had arrived earlier and stood at her bedside. I dialed my home number.

"Hello, Sambo. How're you doing?" Katherine asked.

"I'm trying to run in six different directions at once. I need more help with these things."

"No, I mean how are *you* doing? Not how is the case coming. How are you feeling?"

"So far I've only eaten garbage. I'm gasping for a whisky. I'd rather be home sitting with you and the mutt...and I've just shot someone."

"It's that last one that concerns me, Sammy. How are you doing with that?"

"I'm okay. It's so busy here, there's no time to sit back and feel sorry for myself. Anyway, that last business would be out of character for a tough-guy like me. I'm okay, really."

"As long as you're sure. Think you'll want to eat when you get in?"

"I don't know what, but I could eat the entire kitchen table right now and wash it down with a case of beer. Ralph and the other guys are probably hungry. I guess we'll stop for a snack before too long."

"I'll be sure to have something tasty when you get here."

"Okay, kiddo. I shouldn't be too much longer. See you later."

208

"Oh, Sammy. I do love you."

"You too, Kats—bye."

I hung up, called Ronnie Shields and learned that he scheduled a press conference for 11:30 the next morning. His quick press release accounted for all the reporters hanging around the bookshop parking lot. Along with my brief statement, his release must have been complete enough to temporarily satisfy the vultures.

I got up from the bench where I sat and walked to a snack machine. I looked both ways down the hall and jingled the change in my pocket, feeling like a junkie looking to score. I checked the menu, didn't like anything I saw and made a face. Cold turkey was the only way to go.

Ralph stepped into the hall, looked for me and waved me over. Eleanor and Derek wanted to see me. Derek shook my hand and thanked me. Ellie kissed my cheek. She even shed a tear or two.

I gave Derek a phone number for Stanley Rose. Stan would send a car to transport Derek to the shop where he could lock up for the night, pick up the old Jag so he could drive Ellie home from the hospital, and then Stan would wrap up his part of the job.

Marty Saunders thanked the Foxwells and left. Ralph and I followed. In the parking lot, he called his forensics crew. They had finished packing up all the evidence and their gear and were ready to travel. We all agreed that dinner before the big search sounded appropriate. The lab boys wanted burgers and would head for Hardee's next to Prospect PD. Stan Rose would show them the way.

I needed something gentler for my stomach and suggested a little Chinese restaurant near the hospital. Marty said he liked Moo Goo Gai Pan. The two couples who owned the place were ex-Brooklynites. It would be like old home week for Ralph and me. The food there was usually good, and I needed a satisfying meal. During our stay in the restaurant, Ralph wouldn't leave the two girls alone. I'm surprised one of the husbands didn't throw a cleaver at him.

* * * *

Because of total cloud cover and lack of any street lighting in the area, the sky over northeast Prospect appeared unnaturally black. More rain was predicted for that night and the following day. Finding

Maureen's rental cabin would have been a difficult job for the likes of
Daniel Boone or some other old-time long-hunter on a sunny morning. In
the pitch-like darkness, it presented me with a real pain in the ass. But
the Prospect city council spared no expense in providing its police chief
with an impressive motor vehicle. The GPS satellite system in my car
helped me navigate through a maze of country lanes laid out in the
foothills leading to the Smoky Mountains.

I drove while Ralph and Marty rode along as passengers. The big
black Suburban with three FBI evidence technicians followed closely. I
traveled on winding roads mostly named for the hearty souls who settled
the area one or two hundred years earlier: Bayless, Munsey, Hatcher,
Oliver and others.

"You ever been here before?" Marty asked.

"Not that I can remember." I wondered if he was just making
conversation or did he want to know if I had paid Maureen a personal
visit at her cabin. Factors like that tend to influence a shooting
investigator.

"I drive around and act like lord of the manor just to survey my
domain, but hell, who could remember these roads? I'm a city-boy at
heart."

"You think we'll ever find our way out of here?" he asked. "If your
GPS goes on the blink we're screwed."

"Probably a fair chance. If we get totally lost, we can always trade
Ralph to the Cherokees for a guide to get us back home."

"Hey guys," Ralph said, "it's impolite to talk about someone like
he's not here."

"You know, Marty," I said, ignoring Oliveri, "I hear being an Indian
slave isn't too bad. After you run the gauntlet and get beat up a few
times, they may adopt you into the tribe and treat you half-way
decently."

"Yeah?" Ralph said, with more New York accent than usual. "I'd do
just fine. They'd love me. I could teach 'em all about casinos."

A short distance down the road on our right, we found Paradise
View Road. I turned onto it and about a quarter-of-a-mile more brought
us to a rural mailbox, number 2207, where I turned into the driveway.
We were in lonely country. During the day, you could see beautiful

mountain views, thick forests and plenty of wildlife, but the loneliness was apparent. Many of the people who bought the large tracts of land out there ran into problems finding potable water and by necessity abandoned their ideas of building. The owner of Maureen's cabin turned out to be one of the lucky few.

After parking, we all pulled latex gloves from a cardboard box in the Suburban. I thought we looked like a team of armed proctologists walking toward the entrance. The cabin stood in total darkness. Everyone doubted an accomplice or roommate would be present, but we approached carefully. I carried the keys, so I opened the door. Marty and Ralph entered first with their guns ready. The ETs walked around back to cover the rear door. My gun still lay in a plastic bag locked in the ET's van. I felt rather unprepared. But as I expected, we found the place empty.

The forensics team did the searching while Ralph, Marty and I loitered about, staying out of their way. To kill time, I looked closely at the details of the cabin, trying to get a handle on Bridget and her personal habits.

On the refrigerator, under a magnet shaped like a black bear, hung a five-by-seven-inch slip of paper. In a neat and feminine hand, someone had written part of a William Butler Yeats poem called *Easter 1916*. The poem referred to the unrest in Ireland at that time. Yeats said, in part:

> *He might have won fame in the end,*
> *So sensitive his nature seemed,*
> *So daring and sweet his thought.*
> *This other man I had dreamed*
> *A drunken, vainglorious lout.*
> *He had done most bitter wrong*
> *To some who are near my chest.*

I've never been too good at sussing out hidden meanings in poetry, but even I could see the analogy to the story of Tommy Sullivan and his comrades betrayed by young Seamus Michael Darby. Maureen may have been as much a romantic as a soldier; the two were never mutually exclusive.

I looked further in the kitchen and on the counter next to a toaster; I saw an unopened one-liter bottle of Jameson's Irish whisky. I would have preferred not finding that, but a policeman's lot is rarely an easy one.

On a gate-leg table next to four cookbooks lay a small plastic case about three inches by six inches. Embossed on the lid, I read GLD Quasar. I opened the top and found three very professional-looking darts. Murray's—just as Reggie described.

"Bill, will you bag these darts?" I asked the lead ET. "I have a witness who can confirm Murray owned a set like this."

He agreed. I turned again and noticed the back door leading from the breakfast nook to the rear deck stood open. Ralph had stepped out onto the deck. I joined him.

"You can't see much now," he said, "but you must get one hell of a view from here."

"So she told me."

"She told you? What else did she tell you?" he asked. "How well did you know her? You two weren't...?"

"No, Ralph, we weren't. Calm down. I spoke with her in the bookshop a couple of times, nothing more."

He must have sensed a little irritation in my voice. "Okay, okay, I believe you."

"Good." The irritation lingered on. "You know I appreciate all you're doing for me, but don't break my ass."

"Sorry."

We stood on the edge of the deck looking toward the hills. The clouds traveled at a brisk pace, and the sky to the southwest cleared enough for us to see some definition in the mountain ridges. At sunset, the view would have been beautiful. I turned to my right and saw the hot tub Bridget mentioned. I switched on my four-cell flashlight and scanned the deck area.

"Hello!" I said. "What have we here, Watson? A most singular stain, I think."

A large, three or four-foot round and overly clean area on the wooden decking stood out like Warren Buffet walking down a street in East New York. The weathered gray color had been replaced by an almost new-looking, blond-wood spot. It seemed like someone used straight bleach to scrub the wood. A further scan of the light showed more scrubbing on the upright cedar siding of the hot tub cabinet.

"Looks like somebody wanted to clean up pretty bad, doesn't it?" Ralph said.

I dropped down on my hands and knees to look closer and found a long elliptical scrape on the tub cabinet. I looked along the angle of the gouge and the direction of the splinters and used my light beam to follow the path. Low on the cabin wall, under the bay window of the breakfast nook, just above the decking, I spotted a neat little hole—probably .380 of an inch.

"Ah, Watson, I fear we've found the murder scene. Yonder hole seals it!"

"Yeah, Sherlock, I think you're right. Let's get a black light out here and check for trace blood."

"There was an exit wound on the victim's left knee. Wanna bet that bullet in the wall has some Irish blood on it?" I switched back to my good old Long Island accent.

"No bet, Holmes. I think you just wrapped up your homicide."

It took the evidence technicians another couple of hours to thoroughly go over the cabin and the surrounding grounds. They found enough physical evidence to establish that Bridget probably lured the unsuspecting Murray to the cabin. We all guessed she made promises or inferences causing his middle-aged heart to pound at double-time. The poor bastard never had a chance against a well-seasoned pro with a personal interest in completing her mission.

One of the ETs found her passport in a dresser drawer. Bill, who claimed to be pretty good with document identification, said the Republic of Ireland passport looked like a fair, but not quite excellent forgery. They found no other hard evidence linking her to the IRA. I hoped for a proper ID card signed by some IRA grand wizard, but had no such luck.

I wondered how she got the Beretta. It could have come from a local accomplice or simply as a casual, undocumented sale at a good-sized gun show. A few days later, a check through NCIC by serial number provided negative results—it came back a "no hit." The Feds never heard of the gun.

That made me think the neat little Beretta had been a war souvenir, brought back to the US by a World War II GI who lived in a state not requiring handgun registration. I wondered if, during the intervening years after the war, it either stayed with the original owner or made the rounds, being sold or traded one or more times until it ended up in the handbag of Maureen Sullivan. Oh well, guns don't kill people. IRA assassins kill people.

None of us doubted that the bullets extracted from the body of Murray McGuire would match those test fired from the Beretta Bridget Dwyer possessed.

* * * *

Later, back at the bookshop parking lot, I dropped off Marty and Ralph at their cars.

"Guys," I said, "I want to thank you for your time and help with this. I appreciate what you did."

Ralph nodded. I wondered if Saunders would offer an opinion of the shooting or just let me hang suspended for a few days—over my bottle of scotch.

Marty said, "Your welcome. And sleep easy tonight—you look good with this one. There was nothing else you could have done."

"Thanks." One more potential headache averted.

They left heading toward Knoxville. The moonless sky had darkened again, but a brisk breeze from the southwest blew away most of the clouds, and millions of stars twinkled in the blackness. The buzzards slept—all the buzzards except me. That feeling similar to jet lag left me, too. My stomach felt better after a generous portion of mu shu chicken, and my legs felt strong again. I flexed my back, twisted my neck and heard a few cracks. I felt as tight as an Army snare drum. I'd go home and work on that, because as I remembered Scarlett O'Hara saying not too long ago, "Tomorrow is another day"

Chapter Twenty-Six

Saturday November 11th, Veteran's Day, 2006.

I walked into headquarters at 9:30 the next morning, the first one to arrive in the building. Ronnie arranged for the custodial staff to set up a conference area with chairs and a dais out on the lobby main floor—something similar to the arrangement we used for the promotion ceremony. Old George Files and his assistant, Spurgie Dent, waxed the floors to a high gloss and polished the golden oak woodwork to a mellow shine. The United States and Tennessee flags again stood tall, to the right and left of the speaker's podium. A large amplifier would allow the speakers to project their messages without shouting.

Stanley left a note on my desk, suggesting I go out to our bay at the garage and check the trunk of Bridget's Cobalt. I fetched the keys from the evidence locker and walked across the parking lot to open up.

A clear autumn day with the remnants of the colorful foliage made Prospect appear like the ideal American community. I looked to my left as I walked toward the garage and noticed the cars in Hardee's drive-through lane wrapped around the building. The citizens had come for their weekend cholesterol replenishment treatments.

I unlocked the overhead door to the garage bay reserved for PD cars and impounds and pushed it upward. The white Cobalt sat on an oil-stained floor surrounded by tools and other things only an auto mechanic would recognize.

The gray carpet in the trunk looked relatively clean, except for three small spots that suffered from the same bleach effect we saw on the cabin deck. I guessed again and came up with a possible scenario. After

Murray bled out, Bridget wrapped him up in a shower curtain, they seemed to be the wrapper of choice in many killings, and hauled him far from the cabin, but to a spot she was familiar with—a dark spot on a narrow road with a convenient bridge, from which to drop the little troll.

I wanted to find the wrapper, but thought perhaps we never would. Time acted against me, but I could have the troops check dumpsters and even the landfill. I'd have a crime scene investigator give the whole car a good look-over on Monday.

I locked up the car and the garage and trudged back to my office under a brilliant blue sky.

I didn't want any, but I made a pot of coffee; someone might need a cup.

Earlier that morning, I chose to wear a brown and tan Harris Tweed sport jacket, a brown sweater-vest, pale yellow shirt and a rust-colored wool tie. Kate said I looked like a model in the 1985 Sears catalog. My Glock 19 rested comfortably in a belt holster over my tan slacks, replacing my Smith & Wesson revolver, which currently resided in the FBI evidence room.

At quarter-to-eleven, Stanley Rose came in dressed in a medium gray suit, his badge hanging on a leather fob from his jacket pocket. He looked sharp and professional. Then Bettye showed up. Dressed in a simple navy blue suit, she could have passed for anything from an attorney to a very classy executive secretary.

Ralph Oliveri and his boss, SAC Carl Harmon, walked in a few minutes later dressed in FBI uniform—gray suits and white shirts.

Maybe *Gentleman's Quarterly* would send reporters to the news conference and we'd get an honorable mention for being the best-dressed cops in the South.

Ten minutes more and Ronnie Shields and Ms. Connor descended the staircase, once again like El Presidente and his Secretary of State. A few newspaper reporters already strolled around in the lobby.

By quarter-after-eleven, the TV crews began walking in with all four major networks represented. I said hello to Rachel Williamson. She asked how I felt and offered a dazzling smile to cheer me up. I appreciated her concern, grinned and pointed my right index finger at her cameraman, John Leckmanski. I almost let my thumb fall like the hammer of a revolver, what Phillip Marlowe called the gunman's salute, but decided, under the circumstances, it would be inappropriate. Surely, one of the other reporters would get the wrong idea. Image really is important if you want to look like a hero and not a psycho gunslinger.

It looked like Rachel and three other network reporters would ask questions and introduce their footage, all to be aired later. One station sent a man I hadn't seen in years, a guy who used to work with Rachel on her old morning show, prior to his defecting to the competition.

Shortly after 11:30, Trudy Connor herded Ronnie's team to the chairs adjacent to the podium.

The reporters took their seats. The cameramen and still photographers stood behind the chairs, poised and ready.

Ronnie began his statement with regrets for the necessity of the conference and sorrow for the two tragic deaths occurring in his otherwise peaceful city. He spoke of police professionalism and inter-agency cooperation with the FBI and 'other' governmental agencies. Then he turned the podium over to me.

I recapped the slaying of the man we knew as Murray McGuire, his subsequent identification as Seamus Darby, describing him in Irv Kaufmann's words as a one-time low-level IRA functionary turned informant and betrayer of four major IRA soldiers. I spoke of those four men, their years of incarceration, the long hunger strikes and their deaths.

I told them how young Maureen Sullivan visited her father in prison and how she witnessed his slow death by starvation. I quoted from British Intelligence reports of Maureen's recruitment into the IRA and the operations they suspected her to have carried out. I detailed our confrontation, the hostage situation and how she threatened to shoot Bettye Lambert—the action that prompted me to use deadly force.

Then the questions came at me. I must have been getting too old to deal with pushy reporters because I felt a world-class tension headache envelope me before too long.

Rachel started me off with an easy grounder. "Chief, how did you link the homicide victim with the woman from the IRA?"

"With the help of a federal officer, we established that the victim emigrated from Ireland to this country after being a member of the IRA,"

I said. "Later Sergeant Rose and I interviewed a mutual acquaintance of both the victim and Maureen Sullivan, who was then known as Bridget Dwyer. That person led us to believe Ms. Dwyer had been taking steps to become overly friendly with Mr. Darby. That seemed like an unlikely pair to become involved, so I requested help from the Irish National Police to investigate several angles in that country. Later, the FBI used recent photographs of Ms. Dwyer to search their database for a facial recognition and determine that she had an IRA connection. FBI personnel in the UK worked with British Intelligence and the Royal Ulster Constabulary and confirmed her real identity. Then we linked her to Darby, the man who informed on her father and three other members of the Provisional IRA."

When Rachel sat down, a big, sandy-haired guy in a light gray suit renewed my faith in the old maxim that there certainly was such a thing as a stupid question. He asked something I'd heard fifty thousand times before...Well, maybe less, but every time a cop shoots someone, the same inane question gets asked. No cop should ever be put in a position of facing reporters without being told the correct way to respond.

"Chief, did you shoot to kill or shoot to wound?" he asked.

You stupid bastard, I thought. "Neither one, sir." I offered a smirk designed to make him and everyone else present think I considered the question foolish. "We're not trained to shoot the gun out of a suspect's hand as they do in Hollywood. I shot to stop her illegal actions."

I exaggerated a sigh as I began telling the story again. "As I've already mentioned, the suspect had taken a hostage at gunpoint. There came a time when she threatened to shoot Sergeant Lambert. She turned her handgun in the Sergeant's direction and cocked the hammer—only one step away from firing. I was convinced she would use shooting as a diversion for escape. I had only a very short amount of time to react and a very small target to acquire. I fired my revolver to prevent the imminent use of deadly force against my partner."

I thought a brief lecture on the laws of justification in the use of deadly force might silence the big oaf.

After my dissertation, I heard other questions asked in unison, but my friend in the gray suit wouldn't quit, and his voice boomed above the others.

218

"Do you think you could have subdued the subject without shooting her? It was two to one, and you *were* much bigger than this woman."

Experience has taught me you rarely, if ever, look professional when you leave the podium and smack a reporter in the head with a microphone because they ask inane questions. So I opted to grit my teeth and answer like an officer and a gentleman.

"Sir, no one in the Prospect Police Department, or any other law enforcement agency for that matter, is enjoined to watch their partner take a round in the X-ring before returning fire on an armed subject. So, in answer to your question, no. In my extensive experience, getting up close and personal with a desperate, armed felon is not advisable, regardless of their size or gender. Ms. Sullivan gave up her right to gentle treatment when she told me, and I quote, 'but I will kill her', and she pointed her gun at Sergeant Lambert, the young lady sitting to my left. Next question, please." I looked toward Rachel and the other news people for their input.

A few more questions came in, mostly easy ones. The big guy chose to say no more. I traded places with Carl Harmon, who also spoke of inter-agency cooperation, bringing the case to a tragic, but successful conclusion. He told them about the FBI's independent investigation of the shooting and how Special Agent Saunders concluded I had been one-hundred-percent justified in my actions.

Good to have that on the public record.

After Carl finished, Ronnie Shields thanked everyone for coming and closed the meeting. I knew the reporters would take the next few minutes to interview anyone who stayed in the lobby, so I retreated to my office. If nothing else, I'd wash Mr. Coffee.

Ten minutes later Rachel Williamson knocked on the jamb of my office door.

"You have a minute for me?" she asked.

"Of course I do. Come on in."

I placed the clean coffee pot and basket on the counter. Rachel stood in front of my desk, wearing a shocking-pink suit with a fitted jacket and a moderately short skirt. She looks great in pink, and her legs always look good. I took a seat in one of the chairs I keep for visitors. She took the other, facing me and sitting close.

"Thanks for the friendly and easy questions out there," I said.

"You're welcome. You did very well with the hard ones, too."

"It's not the first time I've had to face off against you guys. But that big guy is a numbskull."

"He's a real go-getter, isn't he?"

"He'll learn if he comes here often enough."

"I know," she said. "I think most of us feel collectively outnumbered by you. You do seem to have your ducks in a row when you stand up there." She used one of those smiles I have a problem resisting.

"It pays to do that."

"You're already the talk of the Knoxville News Corps. Everyone says, 'Look out for Jenkins.' We think you don't just allow us to ask questions, you dare us to ask questions—at our own peril."

"Yeah, well…"

She was kind and let me off the hook by asking, "So, how are you? Are you doing okay?"

"Sure, I'm fine."

"I spoke to Bettye outside. She told me you wanted her to go and see a counselor."

"Yeah, I suggested that."

"She said that if the city wouldn't pay for her visits, you offered to pay. That's very generous."

"She suffered a serious trauma and might need someone to help her get her thoughts straight—learn how she can help herself through the problems she may experience. Bettye's got three kids. I'll help if necessary."

"You're a good guy, Sam."

I almost forgot what we were talking about as I stared at the cute little dimple in her chin. Then I came back to life and added my two cents.

"I'm also the one who asked her to tag along to the bookshop."

"It's her job," she said.

"Uh-huh. But watching someone get shot to death isn't a daily occurrence."

Rachel crossed her legs. Her skirt rode up a couple inches, and my attention began to wander.

"How about you? Are you going to talk to someone?" she asked.

I looked back into her incredibly dark eyes.

"Maybe. If I need to, I will. I have no manly opposition to that. I satisfy all my macho needs by never asking directions when I'm driving."

She gave me a little laugh, and her eyes took on a lovely almond shape.

"Have you ever had to see a therapist before?" she asked.

"Do you think I've lived a tough life?"

"That's no answer."

I shrugged. "No, I guess it's not."

She waited and then gave up. I didn't relinquish my right to remain silent.

"You said you knew the woman you shot. How well did you know her?"

"Everybody asks me that. I knew her from the bookshop. I'm a regular customer. We were friendly, we just talked—about Ireland some, about books. That's all."

"So you two weren't, ah...You know?"

I took no offence to the question and tried my best to sound like I hadn't.

"Everybody asks me that, too. No, we just talked. She was a very good-looking girl—almost as pretty as you."

Rachel smiled again, even blushed a little. "You're sweet."

"She did make an invitation once," I said, "but trusty husband that I am, I declined."

Rachel paused for a moment. "I think that's very sexy."

"A beautiful, thirty-eight-year-old woman coming on to an old guy like me. You bet that's sexy."

"No, I mean declining the offer and being faithful to your wife. That's sexy."

"Oh, yeah, that's me, trustworthy, loyal, and kind."

"That sounds a lot like a Boy Scout. I'll bet you were a Boy Scout, weren't you?"

"No. In my younger days, I was a Cub Scout. The most decorated kid in Pack 268. I had all kinds of badges and awards. But I wasn't invited to join the Boy Scouts like the other kids my age. It's a long story. Actually, I'm sort of proud of it."

"Maybe you'll tell me some day."

"Okay, some day."

"When you take me for a ride in your sports car?"

"Sure. The car's an Austin-Healey."

"I know. You told me, an old one."

We looked at each other for a long moment. Neither of us said anything. I felt a little awkward for a few seconds.

Rachel said, "I guess I'd better get back to the station and let them have all this news."

"Yeah, you don't want to get scooped. Tell John I appreciated him shooting my best side."

"I will. Your right side really looks fine, too, you know." She stood up and shouldered her black purse. "Take care of yourself, Sam."

I think she was almost about to kiss me good-bye. She didn't, but she reached out to squeeze my hand.

"You, too, kiddo. I'll see you again."

"Yes, you will. Bye."

Rachel left. I walked back out to the lobby. Stan and Bettye stood near the doors to our offices. I locked up, and we left, too.

I needed to make one additional stop before going home, so I drove to St. Michael's Church. Father Declan owed me a few minutes of his time.

* * * *

I told the young priest that the man he knew as Murray McGuire left all his worldly possessions and his cash to St. Michael's Church. I assumed he already knew about Seamus Darby's life in the IRA.

I explained about Bridget Dwyer and outlined the role of the county's Public Administrator who, if no one in Ireland claimed Bridget's body, would arrange for her burial. I thought she would have wanted a Catholic ceremony and asked if Declan would handle it.

"The church sometimes balks at allowing killers to be buried in consecrated ground, Chief."

"I know that, Father. I'm barely a step above a heathen when it

222

comes to religion, but I once heard things are different if, at the last moment, these people who commit terrible crimes repent and ask to be saved."

"The young lady didn't have the last rites administered, did she?"

"There wasn't a priest handy before she died."

I stuck my left hand in my pocket and crossed my fingers. I figured stretching the truth for a good cause might be allowable with the proper precautions.

"But prior to her dying," I continued, "I heard her say, 'God forgive me.' I had no doubt what she meant. Regardless of her criminal activities, she was a good Catholic girl."

Declan squinted at me. We were standing inside one of the church offices. I didn't think the sun was causing his eye problem.

So, I offered him my most innocent smile. "Kinda sounds like she wanted to repent, didn't it?"

"Well, my friend," Declan said skeptically, "a man in your position certainly wouldn't lie, would he?"

"Who? Me?"

Declan agreed to preside at the graveside service and find room in the cemetery for Bridget.

I left St. Michael's and drove home to be with my wife and dog. On the way, I thought about the poem Bridget kept with her for, I suppose, inspiration and motivation in her quest. I'm not familiar with much of what W.B.Yeats wrote, but I did remember something else of his.

> *The best lack all conviction,*
> *while the worst are full of*
> *passionate intensity.*

I always thought that sentiment provided a lesson we should have learned from Vietnam. Yeats wrote his statement almost six decades before Saigon fell in April of 1975. But people tend to forget, and visions of the world's players are at best subjective. Those who some see as the worst are heroes to their families and the people they represent. Those seen as the best by others are monsters to the people they oppose.

Someone, not long ago, said, "One man's terrorist is another man's freedom fighter."

Life's rarely easy to understand.

Chapter Twenty-Seven

Monday, November 13th

Early Monday morning, Bettye and I drove to Knoxville and gave formal statements to Marty Saunders. The whole experience took us a little over two hours.

Ronnie Shields started acting extremely solicitous after the shooting. I thought it might be a good time to capitalize on my status as a suffering hero and ask for favors before the adoration cooled off.

Back at the office, I called the Public Administrator. He sounded busy and overworked, but turned out to be cooperative. Bridget would get her Catholic funeral. He promised to coordinate everything with Father Declan.

I made a few other calls. One to the owner of the rental cabin that five FBI Agents and I searched the other night, one to the Enterprise car rental company, telling them we had only started pawing over their Chevy Cobalt for traces of Seamus Darby's corpse and would probably continue to do so for at least another day, and one to Dermott Halloran to briefly give him an account of where his information led us and that he could pick up his passport only after the State Department confirmed its validity. And specifically, I told Dermott if I ever learned he had any ties to the Irish Republican Army or any of its subsidiaries, I would personally hunt him down like a dog and kill him without hesitation. I think he believed me.

Having finished all that local business, I called the British Embassy, asked to speak to one of their security personnel, assumed he'd be a member of MI-6 and explained our situation. A gentleman named

Rodger Barrington-Smythe assured me either he or another representative of Her Majesty's government would visit us and take possession of the Murray McGuire and Bridget Dwyer passports.

I told Barrington-Smythe (He pronounced the last name Smith) that if he rated double-O numbers, I'd take him to Howell's for a pint of Bass Ale. I decided to wait until we met before trying out my Sean Connery accent on him. But I did tell him to give my regards to Miss Moneypenny. He gave me a chuckle after that.

Trying to contact Irv Kaufmann proved fruitless. Several times, his assistant Ms. Wiston, told me Irving was in a meeting and unavailable. I gave her a synopsis of the occurrence using my best rendition of "spook-speak" and asked her to relay the information to Kaufmann. I suggested that if Irving needed additional information, he call me. He never did.

My last courtesy call went to Jack Doyle at Killarney CID. We chatted for a few minutes and promised to keep in touch. Perhaps we will.

I'd been putting off my obligatory call to the local District Attorney General's Office. Protocol demanded I submit information to them after I caused the death of another person. All police officers who terminate a life in the line of duty have their cases submitted to the DA for presentation to a Grand Jury. If the evidence shows the officer acted justifiably under the law, the Grand Jury returns a "No Bill," and the cop is off the hook. If there's a problem, the case goes further.

The Assistant DA I spoke to, a woman in her early fifties named Moira Menzies was someone I'd met before and remembered as blonde, well-dressed and not at all bad-looking. Everyone I knew in the Blount County criminal justice system said she seemed competent and behaved like quite the professional. But the lady with the very Scottish-sounding name began giving me a hard time over having FBI agents act as my shooting team rather than the more conventional course of using TBI investigators or county detectives.

I impressed upon her that under the circumstances, my best judgment dictated I could do any damn thing I wanted—all options being legal. She informed me that things like that wouldn't cause me to make many friends in local law enforcement. I thought I could live with that and relayed those sentiments to her.

Just in case I really pissed Moira off and she turned out to be the vindictive type, I called attorney Joe Costello in Maryville.

"Good mornin'. Mr. Costello's office. May I he'p you?" A bubbly southern woman's voice asked.

"Hi, this is Sam Jenkins at Prospect PD. Is Mr. Costello in the office today?"

"Oh, hi, Chief. This is Stephanie. You remember me?"

"How could I forget the prettiest legal secretary in the county? How are you?"

"I'm fine thanks, and aren't yew just so nice? Yew doin' aw rot t'day?"

"Yes, ma'am, I surely am. The next time I'm in Maryville, I'll stop by to see you. I'll bet you'd like a nice bouquet of flowers for your desk."

Why do I say things like that?

"Oh, that would be just fine, but y'all don't have to do that."

"I know, but I'll bet I can find something nice for you. Good talking with you again, Stephanie. May I speak with your fearless leader?"

She giggled. "Yew surely may. Hang on, I'll connect ya. See-ya-bye." She, too, like Bettye, made the last word sound like something a sheep says.

I explained my situation to Joe Costello, clearly the best criminal attorney in the area. I wanted to discuss the case with him and get him on the hook, should I need representation at the Grand Jury or thereafter. He told me he'd be available if I needed him.

On Wednesday, Rodger Barrington-Smythe called me from the arrivals area of McGhee-Tyson Airport in close-by Alcoa, announcing his visit. Rather than subject the British civil servant to driving on the wrong side of Tennessee roads, I picked him up. He took possession of the two passports, copies of reports relative to the deaths of both Seamus Darby and Maureen Sullivan and listened to my oral account of the saga.

He told me his man in Northern Ireland found no family members wishing to incur the expense of Maureen Sullivan's repatriation and funeral. I assured him she would be well cared for locally.

When I broached a certain subject, I made him blink.

"A reliable source told me a British agent had knowledge of Darby's whereabouts," I said. "You wouldn't happen to know if that agent made personal contact with Darby, would you?"

I must hand it to young Rodger. After only a few seconds of mentally regrouping, he bobbed and weaved and dodged like a professional heavyweight.

"An agent of ours? Really?" He made my statement sound incredulous. "My dear fellow, I doubt seriously that we have an agent in Prospect, Tennessee. No offense, old chap, but your quaint little town isn't known as a hot-bed of activity for Her Majesty's enemies."

I took him to Howell's Pub for lunch, where he and Reggie got along famously. After spending a morning with Rodger, I decided that for the remainder of my life I would try to use words like *splendid*, *brilliant* and *dreadful* as often as humanly possible.

* * * *

Usually after all these logistical necessities are dispensed with, I put a case to rest. However, this one was a bit different. I had a hard time believing Bridget operated independently. Few agents enter a foreign country on assignment without local assistance. It's possible, but with an organization as large and professional as the IRA, it didn't seem probable.

I kept asking myself, how did she get so close to Murray? Why pick Prospect out of all the towns in the United States? Who may have been her helper—or her handler? I thought I might never know. I wondered if some IRA member living in Boston or New York or Chicago assisted her, called her in or orchestrated this whole thing. Did that IRA member hand this off to someone in my neighborhood to provide logistical support?

Or did that elusive British agent provide Bridget with the information for a future favor. Had Bridget been a double agent? In the spook business, there are usually too many possibilities for the layman to understand.

Assuming Her Majesty's Secret Intelligence Service hadn't been involved, was the IRA member now back at his or her job? Back running their bar and grill, back teaching school, back preaching in a church or were they back working in their bookshop? Does the IRA only hold a grudge against those who betray them from within? Or might they hold a grudge against someone who shoots and kills one of their own? It seemed like something for me to think about.

* * * *

On the next Monday morning at 11:00, Maureen Sullivan was buried at St. Michael's Church cemetery during an appropriate Irish-like mist. Father Declan presided. His graveside service sounded appropriate, neither too saccharine nor too critical of her chosen occupation. It seemed as if he never intended to make anyone attending the service cry with emotion.

I'm not a fan of poetry. Usually I can remember a dirty joke or famous quotation more easily than a poem. But this incident had me feeling more poetic than usual. As we stood there, under our umbrellas, in front of the open grave, I remembered a short verse of uncertain origin—it being attributed to several—from the days of the Black Hole of Calcutta in 1758, to the British and American pilots of World War One.

Stand to your glasses steady,
and drink to your comrades eyes;
here's a cup to the dead already,
and hurrah for the next that dies.

I couldn't get angry at Bridget for what she did to Murray or what she made me do. I didn't look at her as a criminal. She was a soldier for a cause. I may not have agreed with her cause, her politics or her methods, but I admired her tenacity and loyalty—loyalty to her father and her comrades. Long ago, I decided I wouldn't hate opposing soldiers. They were only doing the same job as me, but for a different audience.

Kate and I stood next to the grave, Father Declan stood to my right at the head. Derek and Eleanor stood opposite us. Shortly after Declan began his reading, Bettye and Donnie Lambert pulled up and stood off several yards from the gravesite. Then a silver Crown Victoria arrived, and Ralph Oliveri joined Bettye. When Father Declan finished the service, Eleanor dropped a small bouquet of flowers on top of the casket. After that, we all left.

I envisioned photos of Maureen's pretty face hanging in pubs in Ireland and Hibernian bars in America—a heroine of the IRA, and the one who avenged a wrong done to four of their own years ago. Many a pint of Guinness would be tipped in her honor.

Ralph invited us all to lunch. Bettye and Donnie declined, as did Derek and Ellie. Ralph, Kate and I drove to Maryville and ate at Cutrone's Villa Napoli.

Ralph wanted a bottle of Dago red to take away the damp chill of the morning, so we all chose entrees with a red sauce. The food was excellent. Ralph said the place impressed him, and he enjoyed meeting Nick, the patriarch of the Cutrone family.

Earlier that morning, I watched Bridget Dwyer lowered into the ground by four men who assisted Father Declan with the funeral. Her involvement in my life was over, but I still had a feisty ADA and the Grand Jury to contend with.

Epilogue

The Grand Jury returned a No Bill on my case after only six minutes of deliberation. With that over, I really could put the incident to rest.

Bettye agreed to see a friend of mine for a few discussions and counseling. Ronnie Shields gladly accepted the bills.

For weeks after the incident, a few new and invasive dreams were added to my playlist of nocturnal entertainment. They featured a familiar-looking leprechaun or a gorgeous Irish redhead, both dying tragically. During the days, I often felt lethargic or world-weary, and occasionally I'd feel a cold shiver run down my spine for no apparent reason. I found myself looking over my shoulder, waiting for something, but never sure of exactly what.

About the Author

Wayne Zurl grew up on Long Island and retired after twenty years with the Suffolk County Police Department, one of the largest municipal law enforcement agencies in New York and the nation. For thirteen of those years he served as a section commander supervising investigators. He is a graduate of SUNY, Empire State College and served on active duty in the US Army during the Vietnam War and later in the reserves. Zurl left New York to live in the foothills of the Great Smoky Mountains of Tennessee with his wife, Barbara.

Zurl has won Eric Hoffer and Indie Book Awards, and was named a finalist for a Montaigne Medal and First Horizon Book Award. He has written four novels and more than twenty novelettes in the Sam Jenkins mystery series.

Author Links:

Author website: http://www.waynezurlbooks.net
Twitter: http://www.twitter.com/#!/waynezurl
Facebook: http://www.facebook.com/waynezurl

Other books by the author at Melange

From New York to the Smokies